Artists Town

Friendship, first love and the secrets we keep

EMMA BAIRD

PINK GLITTER PUBLISHING

First published 2018
ISBN: 978-1-9997738-2-3
Copyright © Emma Baird 2018

Cover design by Jennifer Woodhead,
at gaiadesignstudio.co.uk

Published by PINK GLITTER PUBLISHING.
https://emmabaird.com

To Brenda — thanks for everything.

Part One

ARE YOU THE COOL GIRL HERE?

The A75, August 1990

"When I'm eighteen and a proper, proper grown-up, the world will be at my feet; I won't need to go anywhere I don't want to. I'll do what I wish all the time."

The thought must have flitted across her mind a hundred or so times in the last few hours. It began urgently, belligerently and then segued into what the eighteen-year-old Daisy would do with her freedom.

She would not, no way in the whole wide world, sit in the back of a car heading for Nowheresville. This, she promised herself. The would not's were easier to think up than the would's. Her imagination found the alternatives trickier to flesh out.

Maybe she and a mystery friend closed the front door behind them and darted off, parent-free, to seek out adventures.

Perhaps they were parties. There might even be…boys.

"Years ago, a lot of artists lived in this town."

Oh, God. Incoming, incoming dull info alert. Her father used his special voice, the 'family, listen carefully; I'm going to tell you something interesting' tone.

Daisy wondered how her mother put up with it. Daisy had only endured it for the last ten years if you didn't count ages 0 – 5 when presumably she hadn't taken account of such things. Her mum, on the other hand, must have listened to him drone on for the last seventeen years.

Urgh.

She glanced out of the car window. The scenery hadn't improved. Trees, fields, grass, water. Times twenty. It had looked the same for the last two hours.

They had turned off the main road, the fields giving way to houses that gradually got closer together. A sign welcomed them to the town, her father informing them that the man pictured there was a saint, Cuthbert, and he carried the decapitated head of an olden-days king.

Matthew, luckily for him, had fallen asleep at Carlisle. His head lolled, sometimes to the side, sometimes falling onto her shoulder. When it did, she shrugged it off as quickly as possible.

Her mum turned in her seat now, her expression anxious and concerned. Daisy hated that.

"Daisy, do you want to do a blood test, love? We haven't done one since this morning."

We? What's this 'we' thing? I don't see you stabbing your finger to get it to bleed.

"I'm all right." She did her best to make her voice sound neutral. Too aggressive, and her mum would insist she does the test, convinced she knew better than her daughter. Too flat, the same thing.

You couldn't bloody win when it came to sodding blood tests.

The car had stopped outside a terraced house, its exterior displaying a sign: 'Vacancies. Enquire within'.

"Inquire."

"What's that, love?"

They had all exited the car, Matthew having been shaken grumpily awake. The four of them stood in the street, looking up at the sign, Braemar Quality B&B.

Vacancies. Enquire within.

Quality was an optimistic description, Daisy reckoned. The place was tiny—the windows meanly small and draped with dirty-looking lace curtains. One curtain twitched, and the front door (red paint flaking) swung open.

"Aye?"

The woman crossed her arms.

"Mrs Burnett?" Her dad embarrassed her all the time. Now he was doing it again. He said Mrs Burnett like, Ooh, Missis Burrrnettt. The woman looked at him scornfully throughout.

"That's me." She stamped her feet on the mat, wiping them back and forth several times.

"We're the Walkers. We're booked in for ten days?"

"C'mon in. You're early."

Daisy's dad turned to face them and smiled widely, encouragingly. He followed Mrs Burnett into her B&B, making sure to wipe his feet as vigorously as she had. He, Daisy's mum and Matthew traipsed upstairs, Mrs Burnett telling them when they could expect breakfast and what it included.

"I will do you a Scottish cooked breakfast. But you need to ask the night before. One sausage, one rasher of bacon, one egg, beans and toast. Otherwise, cereal and fruit."

About to follow them, Daisy grimaced and then turned

her head. A teenage girl lounged against the wall in the hall-way, her expression louche.

"Enquire/inquire?" She grinned. "You snotty wee cow."

Daisy, insulated from her own rudeness most of the time because she was too scared to say it out loud, grinned back.

"Are you the cool girl here?"

The cool girl smirked, her mouth moving up, stopping and then tilting upwards once more. It was almost a smile.

"No."

She leant forward, the movement enabling her to whisper in Daisy's ear. "You cannae be cool here. This place is a dump."

Daisy wondered if she meant Braemar Quality B&B or the town itself. 'Dump' could apply equally to both. The Quality B&B was no more impressive inside than it was out. It smelled of burnt toast, and the hall carpet had dirty foot-marks on it. There were also lots of pictures of Scottie dogs, their cheeriness in complete contrast to their host.

And the town? Well, she'd only seen a bit of it so far, and none of it included a cinema, clothes shops or a McDonald's.

The cool girl said she wasn't cool. Daisy, however, had an instinct for cool girls: mainly because she wasn't one. How could she be, her mother hovering anxiously over her all the time? And being dragged along on family holidays at her age. Daisy wasn't one of her school's in-crowd.

She longed to be.

"What's your name?"

Cool girl was back leaning against the wall, arms folded.

"What's it tae you, posh girl?"

See, this is what cool girls did. Daisy answered questions straight, imbuing a questioner with automatic authority. As for being called posh; that was the worst insult, wasn't it? Cool was never, ever posh.

Greatly daring, she gave the cool girl the bird, pushing down on her forefinger hard to emphasise the gesture.

Cool girl grinned again.

"Katrina. Ma friends call me Kit-Kat. You can call me Katrina. And you? Lady something? Bo-peep?"

"Daisy. My friends call me Daisy. You can call me Your Royal Highness."

Katrina laughed—the noise, a dark, dirty cackle that sounded weird coming from a teenage girl.

Mrs Burnett had reappeared at the top of the landing, her three guests joining her to peer over the railing at Katrina and Daisy.

"Kitty," she said sharply. "You've no' finished tidying up the back bedroom."

The girl looked up and then back at Daisy, who raised her eyebrows.

"Lovely to meet you, Kitty," emphasis on the word 'Kitty', the person in question responding with something only Daisy could see, a flip of the bird back at her.

She started up the stairs, taking them two at a time. Watching her go, Daisy admired her thin legs. She wore a printed dress, much shorter than Daisy would ever dare.

As Katrina/Kitty reached the landing, the old woman startled Daisy by ruffling the girl's hair. "Hurry up, aye? And then you can go out."

"Alright, Gran," she replied.

Daisy liked building up stocks of information on people. To date: rude teenage girl; knows about inquire/enquire; name Katrina (likely); known as Kit-Kat (in her dreams); called Kitty by everyone (yup); helps at the B&B, the B&B owner is her granny.

"Come on up, Daisy!" Daisy's mum did her best not to

make it sound like an order. "We'd better get all your stuff unpacked."

Mrs Burnett looked at her first and then back at her mum. Daisy read her mind. What stuff? She's only got a backpack on.

She thought about flinging the rucksack up with the instruction: You unpack it then.

Best not to.

Upstairs, the décor was terrible. There were yet more Scottie dog pictures on the walls of the room she was in and several creepy china dogs on the mantelpiece above the fireplace and lots of china ladies in long dresses.

Daisy felt like pushing them as far back on their shelves as possible. They seemed to teeter perilously close to the edge where small boys might knock into them and send them catapulting skywards and then downwards. The wallpaper print was enough to give her a headache. It clashed with the curtains and the carpet.

And she was sharing with Matthew, who'd already bagged the bed next to the window.

On the other hand, it was bigger than her room back home, and it was right next to the B&B's bathroom. Daisy usually needed to get up once or twice during the night to go to the loo. At home, this meant traipsing all the way downstairs.

Her mum opened the door now. "Right, we'd better ask Mrs Burnett to store your medication in the fridge. And get lunch. We're a bit later than usual. Are you okay?"

Daisy gave her the same "I'm fine" reply she'd delivered earlier, careful to avoid aggression or lethargy in her tone.

Downstairs, Dad was already telling Mrs Burnett how much he liked what he'd seen of the town so far. She looked bored. Presumably, as a native, she knew the town's charms.

"Mrs Burnett?" Her mum sounded anxious. "Is there somewhere near here we can get something to eat?"

Mrs Burnett glanced at the watch on her wrist and sighed, shaking her head regretfully.

"Aye, well you're a wee bit late for most places. They stop serving at two o'clock. Try the Gordon Arms and if no', the chippie might still be open."

She looked offended when Daisy's mum grimaced at the mention of the chippie.

"Well," Daisy's dad clapped his hands together decisively. "I'm sure we'll find something. Thanks so much for all your help, Mrs Burnett."

Mrs Burnett was back to staring at him scornfully. Maybe even she knew the help she had offered so far had been shit.

"Well, see you later," she opened the front door wide and shooed them out.

As they spilt out on the street, Daisy's dad remembered to shout back, "Where is the Gordon Arms, Mrs Burnett?"

But the door had closed. The Walkers were expected to find their own way there.

CLOSED FOR LUNCH

They were meant to go to France on holiday—or at least Spain, which was Daisy's preference. For as far back as she could remember, she and her family had holidayed in France or Spain.

Tony, Daisy's dad, loved France and always used the holidays to practice his French. He insisted the children spoke it too. Daisy hated that part. She could sense the French wincing as she mangled their language. On the other hand, she spoke French much better than most of her schoolmates.

This year, though, a foreign holiday was out of the question. "I just couldn't, Tony," her mum had said. "I'd be so worried. I mean, what if…" She looked at Daisy.

Debbie meant what if something happened to Daisy. Nine months ago, Daisy's life turned upside down. She had lost a stone in weeks, which was fantastic, but she'd felt tired and thirsty all the time. Not so fantastic.

Her mum attributed it to anorexia initially—rife among Daisy's school friends, competitive under-eaters all—and began closely watching her daughter as she ate. Satisfied that Daisy was eating enough and not throwing it up or shitting it out afterwards, she took her to their GP.

He made her pee on a stick, announced she had type 1 diabetes and needed to be admitted to the hospital as soon as possible.

Her mum started to cry. Daisy was none the wiser. "What is that?" she asked. Didn't her nanna sometimes talk about her friend, Dot, who had diabetes and ate cakes even though her doctor told her not to?

"It's a chronic health condition," the doctor replied. "Your pancreas has stopped working. It's not producing insulin. You need insulin to break down carbohydrates in food."

Daisy still didn't feel enlightened. "What's the cure for it?"

The doctor sat back in his seat. The look he gave her was one of pity. "There's no cure, I'm afraid."

She spent a week in the hospital, a week where doctors, nurses and dieticians bombarded her with information. These are carbohydrates; this is an exchange. One exchange is an apple, one slice of bread or one scoop of mashed potatoes. These are syringes. This is insulin. You need to give yourself injections in the morning and at night.

One very scary doctor told her in detail what would happen if she didn't take care of herself.

"You will lose your eyesight. Your kidneys will pack up, and you will need dialysis. You will get liver disease. Your nerves will stop working properly, and you will live with pain. Your blood pressure will increase too much, and you will be at risk of a stroke or a heart attack."

Eventually, Debbie told him to stop. Daisy was white-faced, recovering from the shock of yet another blood sample taken from her arm.

Life became a constant round of injections, measuring out food and always carrying glucose tablets with her. All the activities she'd previously taken for granted—going to school, walking there and back, meeting up with friends, going to McDonald's with those friends, hanging out in other people's houses, doing PE—they weren't the same anymore.

Anything that involved being away from the house was now fraught with danger, as far as her mum was concerned. In Debbie's ideal world, Daisy reckoned she'd make sure her daughter never left the house, schooling and Vitamin D exposure be damned.

Hence, the holiday in Kirkinwall. Tony chose the place at the last minute. Years ago, before his children had been born, he and Debbie had visited the area and loved its peace and quiet. It was the opposite of London, he said, and after the year they'd had, a marvellous place for the annual Walker holiday.

Marvellous, it was not, Daisy reflected. As they'd booked so late, places to stay were limited. Their only option had been the grotty and grim Braemar B&B instead of the bijou cottage with its open-plan rooms and garden backdropped by valley views and blue skies they usually stayed in when they went to France.

In the hotel Mrs Burnett had mentioned, the Gordon Arms, the lounge bar was deserted, but the public bar was open. It seemed to have no windows, and smoke swirled around, obscuring the view.

A voice boomed, "We're closed for food." Somehow, the brassy blonde barmaid who materialised out of the gloom had worked out that two middle-aged people with a teenager and a pre-pubescent boy entering a pub just after two, wanted lunch.

Who knew?

Dad started his charm thing. "We're so sorry we got here late–"

The barmaid looked unsympathetic.

"—and we haven't had lunch! Sandwiches will do us just fine. We could have ham or cheese. Whatever is easiest?"

He rubbed his hands together. The woman glared at him. She unpeeled herself from her position behind the bar, her conversation with two young men who sat on high stools drinking pints, so rudely interrupted.

"We're closed for–"

Debbie cut her off. "For food, yes. Come on, Tony. Let's see what the chippie can do."

"If it's still open."

The brassy blonde exchanged a sly grin with the two pint-drinkers; no doubt anticipating the Walkers' trudge to the fish and chip shop only to find a closed sign swinging from its door.

They left the Gordon Arms. No-one had dared ask the barmaid how to get to the chippie.

"Harbour direction, surely!" Tony made strides that way. The rest of them followed. He was right. Five minutes later they discovered a fish and chip shop, 'open' sign reassuringly hanging from its eaves. The smell was incredible, hot batter and malt vinegar that created a welcoming cloud around the doorway and the few tables and chairs placed on the pavement.

Her dad stood outside the door. "Right, orders then! Tell me what you want I'll go in and get them. Over and out!"

Daisy hoped no-one had heard them. Nobody, but nobody said, 'over and out' these days. She surveyed their surroundings. The only people who might have heard were an old lady pushing a two-wheel shopping trolley. She didn't count, but what about the young guy sitting on the car park wall, a bicycle leaning next to him? His deafness was far more critical. Luckily, he wasn't looking in their direction; the dark-haired head turned towards the sea.

"I don't know, Tony," her mum darted looks at Daisy. "I'm not sure we should be eating fish and chips."

By 'we' she meant Daisy again, worried that her body wouldn't be able to cope with the overload of carbohydrates.

"Well, needs must!" Tony refused to let go of that first-day-away-from work enthusiasm. "And we are on our holidays. Daisy, you will need to do an extra blood test or two. Is that okay?"

He put it as a question, instead of what it was—an order.

She nodded, and he smiled at her, winking when her mum wasn't looking. He took their orders and vanished into the shop, its door chiming melodically as he entered.

"I've never seen a castle in the middle of town before," Debbie remarked as they waited outside. She pointed at the castle behind them.

"Can we go there?" Matthew asked. His school was doing a project on medieval knights. Castles and battles featured often. A castle meant he could pretend to be gallant Sir Matthew, armed with a bow and arrow, shooting off the approaches of an evil baron.

"Mmm, of course." Daisy's mum had resorted to toe-tapping and darting anxious glances at the chippie. She'd be worried the food was taking too long. Daisy made sure her mum couldn't catch her eye. The constant fussing got on her nerves.

Tony emerged a few minutes later, holding steaming parcels of newspaper-wrapped food and cans of juice. He pointed at the grassy mound to the side of the Harbour car park. "I can see tables and chairs. Let's eat up there. The views are terrific."

Daisy wished she'd put on an extra jumper under her coat. It wasn't that warm.

Her dad homed in on a table under the huge beech tree in front of the small church that looked out onto the river. There were fishing boats anchored all the way up to the bridge on the left and the harbour smelled of dried out seaweed. The family sat down, and Daisy's dad handed out each parcel.

"Sausage and chips for you, Matthew, and a can of coke. A fish supper for you, Debbie, and one for me. You can share my coke. Battered fish for you, Daisy."

"Is there anything for me to drink?"

Tony bit his lip apologetically. "Sorry love. They didn't have any Tab or Diet Coke."

Debbie rummaged in her handbag, emerging triumphantly with a flask of water she had filled in the B&B.

"Here you go."

Matthew had eaten half of his sausage supper already. The chips looked especially good, doused with malt vinegar and salt.

Daisy sneaked her hand out and nabbed a couple.

"Hey!" Matthew's protest came out at the same time as her mum's, "Daisy love, not too many chips."

Daisy poked her tongue out, a gesture her mum pretended not to see. God, it was only three chips. Fish and chips without the chips were…well, not fish and chips. She compensated by eating all the batter and just half the fish. Her mum delved back into her capacious handbag, emerging this time with an apple. She handed it to Daisy.

The meal finished, Matthew repeated his request to

visit the castle.

"Oh, let's!" Tony leapt to his feet, gathering up the empty papers and cans and disposing of them in the nearby litter bin. "I love a good castle! And this one is Dhoon Castle, once the seat of the MacLellans. Fancy that! When I researched my family tree, a few years ago, I found MacLellans on my mother's side. Maybe my great-great-great grandfather built it."

Not enough greats, Dad. Daisy didn't bother to say it out loud. Her dad still thought she was as gullible as Matthew, ready to believe anything no matter how unlikely just because he said it with such authority.

Close to, Daisy didn't think it was a good castle. It wasn't that big for a start, and it didn't have a moat. The person who took their money told them that MacLellan had taken the stones from another nearby castle to build his. That cemented her opinion. The castle was a cheat, a second-rate fortress.

The visit didn't last long. There was not much to see, the bare bones of a place that had once housed master, family and servants and almost impossible to imagine. Matthew loved the supposed dungeon; his dad was a pretend prisoner jailed by the wicked Sheriff of Nottingham. Matthew as Robin Hood rescued him triumphantly.

"My mother's family were MacLellan's," her dad said as they left. The money-taker nodded, asking questions about where and when they had been born, polite, rather than interested questions.

They walked around the town. It did not take long. Daisy took stock: two butchers, one grocer, two newsagents, an ironmonger, a chemist, and a supermarket so tiny it didn't seem worthy of the name. Not one of them looked inviting.

There were two sweet shops, but her mum hurried them past those. Daisy spotted the jars of boiled sweets and brightly-coloured sherbet. Before her illness, sherbet was her favourite sweet treat. She liked to buy bags of the blue-coloured stuff, the kind that turned your mouth bright blue for hours afterwards.

The rest of the day stretched ahead. Two hours until dinner time. And then after dinner, what were they going to do?

Everything Daisy had thought about this holiday was right. Shit place, nothing to do and miles away from anywhere or anything exciting.

Tony stopped in front of the newsagents. "Right. Well, I'll need my newspaper."

As he bought a copy of *The Times*, Daisy's dad asked the newsagent his recommendation for dinner. The newsagent took the question seriously, firing off questions. A family of four, yes? Were the children fussy eaters? Daisy took offence at being labelled a child. Did they want Scottish food or something else?

Tony finished the conversation and looked pleased with himself. "Right. The newsagent told me there's a very nice Italian restaurant just over there." He pointed to a building above a coffee shop. It didn't look like a restaurant from the outside, but there was a sign hanging in the window: Bella Italia. Italian Home Cooking.

"Now, the man in the newsagents suggests we go for a drive. Debbie, are you happy to drive? I'd rather not do any more driving today."

Debbie nodded, and the four of them made their way back to the Braemar Quality B&B, as their car was parked outside. Daisy dragged her feet, hoping that Tony or Debbie would change their mind before they got back there or that they might let her away with not coming. A drive to look at yet more bloody boring trees and fields. Whoop-de-doo.

Approaching the house, she spotted a lace curtain twitch once more. Seconds later, Katrina opened the front door, bumping into them almost accidentally. She raised her arms up as soon as she saw them in an *"oh, it's you again!"* way. She didn't fool Daisy.

But her appearance triggered another reaction. Katrina had put on a black denim jacket over her print dress. Daisy's heart contracted with envy. Black denim.

She had spent a whole Saturday months ago trying to find a black denim jacket in London and hadn't seen one she liked. Now, she stared at the perfect example, slim-fitting, the cuffs worn and studded with gleaming metal buttons. Embroidered red roses covered the pockets.

"Did you get lunch?" Katrina called out.

"Yes, we did. Say thanks to your gran for the recommendation. Best fish and chips I've had in years!" To Daisy's dismay, Tony jumped in with a reply first. As Katrina seemed to be her age, Daisy felt answering her was her prerogative.

"Aye, I've heard folks say she does the best fish and chips in Scotland. If Alison had a bit more money, maybe she could advertise a bit more. Get people in and all that."

Business advice given, she lingered, scuffing her feet against the pavement.

"Do you want to come with us?" her dad asked. "We're going to look at the countryside."

At times, Daisy hated her dad. He was totally, totally embarrassing. No self-respecting cool girl was going to–

"Okay." Katrina skipped over, smiling. She stopped beside Daisy and nudged her side with her elbow. The smile she exchanged with Daisy changed from the polite one you gave adults to a conspiratorial grin.

Maybe Daisy's dad wasn't that bad after all.

THE GUY WITH
THE BIKE

Thankfully, Tony kept his terrible dad sayings to just "let's get this show on the road", as he rubbed his hands together and opened the back door of the car to let them in.

Sat in the back seat of the car in between Daisy and her brother, Katrina took charge of the outing, leaning forward so she could instruct Debbie. "You should go and have a look at the Dhoon."

"What's that, then?" Tony twisted so he could speak to her.

"It's a beach. It's got a shipwreck, aye? And the tide'll be in." Katrina sat back again, nudging Daisy once more. The nudges made Daisy hopeful. Was there more to this beach than Katrina was saying? Maybe it was like Brighton or even the beaches in Spain, scantily-clad teenagers (boys) parading up and down the sandy shores.

You could only hope.

Debbie ordered Katrina to belt up, embarrassing Daisy once more. Katrina, on the other hand, did so at once. "Aye, you're right, Mrs Walker. The roads around here arenae safe. Quite a few people have been killed because they werenae wearing their seatbelts."

Matthew's eyes widened. He was at the age where he'd figured out what dying was and that it could happen to his mum and his dad—and even to him. "Muuummm," he wailed. "It's too dangerous!"

Her mum and dad looked at each other. Tony turned around once more.

"Matthew, your mum's a careful driver. We'll be fine! And it'll be lovely to see the sea, won't it?"

Katrina nudged Daisy again. She nudged Katrina back, sure that she'd wound up her little brother on purpose.

The drive to the beach didn't take long with instructions barked out by Katrina; "left here, over the bridge, left here, slow here the road's twisty, a man's car exploded here years ago, but he was drunk at the time."

Matthew clapped his hands over his eyes at that.

The beach began to appear, stretches of sand, gorse and yellow-flecked rocks. The sea wasn't as blue as the water you saw in France or Spain, but it was a calm day, and the water looked glassily peaceful, the white foam-tipped waves gently hitting the shore and rolling back.

There were plenty of other cars in the car park. Daisy's hopes leapt. Maybe there was an amusement arcade or a pier.

Katrina led them to a sand track that took them to the beach, a long, narrow stretch of sand, book-ended by rocks. Daisy looked around her. There were houses on the rocks to the left-hand side and a lighthouse in the distance. Families with small children populated the beach's upper level.

There was no sign of an amusement arcade; only an ice-cream van in the car park hemmed in by yet more small children. The van was selling Mr Whippy's, the air-light, white sugary stuff Daisy had once adored before diabetes closed yet another door on her.

Tony took his shoes off and indicated that they should all do the same. "Who's for a paddle, then?" Daisy's mum and Matthew removed their footwear, but Daisy shook her head.

"I'll guard the shoes and bags," she offered. The rest of her family rolled up trousers and headed down to the water.

Left on their own, Katrina wriggled her toes into the sand. "Good idea not to," she said, gesturing at Daisy's family, all shrieking with laughter at the shock of the icy water. "Sellafield's no' that far away."

"What's Sellafield?"

Katrina's voice dropped to a whisper. "A nuclear plant. Your family will come back glowing green. Mind, maybe that'll make them live forever. There's an auld granny who swims here every day in the summer, and she's ninety."

Daisy didn't know if she believed that. She only swam in the sea if they went to France or Spain. Brighton was too cold, and it was like a hundred degrees warmer than this place.

Daisy turned to Katrina. "I thought this place might be…" About to say, 'exciting', 'cool', or 'full of teenagers', she stopped herself. Maybe Katrina did think the beach was exciting. She lived in Kirkinwall, and perhaps she had different expectations when it came to fun.

Katrina wasn't listening anyway. She had turned the other way and was waving at someone. The someone began to walk towards them. As he approached, Daisy cheered up. Now, this was much more promising.

She recognised him as the boy who'd been sitting on the

Harbour car park wall when they'd found the fish and chip shop. The one who, please no, didn't overhear her dad and his sergeant major impression.

He was a bit older than her and Katrina, eighteen or nineteen, maybe, and tall, thin and freckly. He looked familiar too, the big eyes, the ski-jump nose and the prominent top lip reminding her of someone. As unpromising as those features might be on their own, together they made him look distinctive.

Daisy tried her best not to stare. As clueless as she was about boys—an all-girls school didn't give you many ideas when it came to the opposite sex—she knew to stare was a no-no. She blinked and shifted her gaze.

"Alright, Kippy?" Katrina asked.

Kippy nodded, tipping his head to the side toward Daisy. "Who's this?"

"This is my new pal Daisy," Katrina said. "You can call her Your Royal Highness." It had sounded smart when Daisy said it earlier. Now, it was just…uncool. Mind you, Katrina saying Daisy was her pal made her glow with pleasure.

"Hello," she said, putting out a hand for him to shake. Katrina and Kippy exchanged grins, Kippy ignoring her hand. Daisy dropped it, feeling herself flush.

"I did tell you she was posh," Katrina said. "Daisy, this eejit is ma cousin, Alan Kirkpatrick, but we call him Kippy. He thinks it's because it's short for Kirkpatrick, but we do it because he smells like a kipper."

The 'cousin' explanation explained the familiarity. He did look like Katrina, who also had sharp features on a lean, lanky body. Daisy liked his big, blue eyes and the freckles made his face intriguing. Did they appear more in the summer? What did he look like in the winter?

Kippy screwed up his face, the movement joining together some of the more prominent freckles close to his nose. "Aye, whatever. Do I smell like a kipper to you?"

He leant in, proffering his throat for Daisy to take a sniff. She could make out washing powder and one of those nose-assaulting antiperspirants boys liked to use. Lynx, perhaps. Once the sting of the Lynx wore off though, it was warm and pleasant, and nothing like kippers. Younger brothers aside, Daisy never usually got this close to guys. She wished she could do something to make him stay where he was.

"You going to that party on Friday?" Katrina asked him as he stepped back. He nodded again, not taking his eyes off Daisy.

"Right. We'll come too," Katrina pronounced.

"I'll come and get you first," Kippy replied. To her acute disappointment, he broke the eye contact with Daisy. "I heard just about everyone's going. Should be a belter of a party."

Katrina nudged Daisy. "See? A bit of excitement for you."

Kippy looked at her once more, the eyes sparkling and mischievous. "Aye. Anything could happen."

Daisy's stomach flipped and turned over. When he'd said 'anything', the look he'd given her seared through her body. She could feel waves of heat radiating from her core.

"See ya." He sauntered off, back in the direction he'd come from where an abandoned bicycle lay in the sand. The heat left Daisy's body as quickly as it had come on.

"Think you'll be able to come?" Katrina asked as they watched him go. "There's no' much to do in this place, so we make up for it by having wild parties."

"What does 'wild' mean?" Daisy risked the uncool question.

Katrina smirked. "Sex, drugs and rock and roll. Chips, dips, chains and whips. The basic high school orgy type of thing. What else would it be?"

It took her a few seconds to get the Weird Science reference. Katrina's deadpan delivery was a perfect impression of Lisa, the woman created by two high school nerds. If you'd asked her last week to create the world's greatest best friend, Daisy thought she might have come up with Katrina. Cool, sarky, asking her to go to parties and with the benefit of good-looking relatives.

The holiday began to change shape and colour in Daisy's mind. A few hours ago, it had been flat and grey. Now, the sun popped out from behind the clouds, shining light and hope.

"So, can you come?" Katrina asked again. "As my new pal, I should introduce you to people around here."

My new pal. Daisy repeated it!

Her family were still paddling, Tony chasing her little brother and trying to splash him. The party was on Friday. That gave her three whole days to convince her mum and dad to let her go.

AN UNSUPERVISED EXCURSION

"Mr Walker! Are you enjoying your stay in our lovely wee toon?"

To Daisy, Katrina's question sounded unmistakably sarcastic, but her dad took the inquiry at face value. They were sitting in the Braemar Quality B&B's breakfast room the following morning. Tony had bagged them the best table, the one right next to the French windows at the back of the house that looked out onto the river.

Another couple—an elderly pair who'd exchanged polite hellos with them when they came in—were sitting at another table at the back. They looked as if they were a permanent fixture, watery eyes and mournful expressions unchanging as they sipped cups of tea.

Katrina, a white apron covering her flower print dress, deposited a rack of toast on the Walkers' table. She looked at Daisy, her eyes glittering at the invitation to join her in hoodwinking her father. The glance lasted a second or so before she turned her attention back to Tony.

"I am indeed, Katrina," her dad said, sharing out the toast between the four of them. "My grandmother came from here, you know. I've always wanted to visit the place. You're fortunate to live here, young lady."

Daisy winced.

"Oh, I am! Every day I say thank you, tae Jesus, for letting me stay here." Katrina's expression was strait-laced. Only Daisy caught the quick wink.

Having taken their tea and coffee orders and promising that the pre-ordered cooked breakfast of one sausage, one rasher of bacon and one egg was on its way, Katrina asked Tony what he planned to do with the family for the rest of the day.

"I'd like to get my bearings," her dad said. "I thought a drive out past the beach, as the man in the newsagents said there were some very nice walks out that way."

Daisy groaned inwardly. A walk! The pure, shitty hell of it.

Katrina nodded solemnly. "That's an excellent idea, Mr Double U! Or you could wait till ten o'clock and go out with Cameron on his boat. He takes the holiday-makers out for a wee tour of the coast."

Daisy's dad looked as if he'd died and gone to heaven. Katrina winked at her again. "I thought I'd take Daisy oot, and show her the sights if that's alright wi' you?"

Daisy sucked in a deep breath. Here was the sixty-four-thousand-dollar question, an unsupervised excursion with someone her mum and dad didn't know. She got no reply, as Tony and Debbie looked at each other, some rapid exchange of eye meets and body language going on. A yes/no thing hovered in the air between them.

Katrina poured out coffee for Daisy's mum and dad. Picking up the empty toast rack, she vanished suddenly behind the kitchen door, re-emerging seconds later with another one filled with wholemeal toast and a jar of sugar-free jam.

"My Gran bought it for you, 'specially,'" she said as she placed the jam in front of Daisy on the table. "Seeing as you're no' meant to eat sugar."

"Did she? How kind of her." Debbie picked up the jar and studied the label carefully, obviously checking if it really was sugar-free. Daisy glared at her. Taking the jam from her, she spread liberal amounts on a slice of toast.

Katrina performed the same sudden vanishing act once more, disappearing into the kitchen and coming out with the porridge, and cooked breakfasts the rest of the family had ordered the night before. She waited until they were all served before turning to Daisy's mum and dad.

Daisy cleared her throat. "Well? Can I? Go out with Katrina?"

"Well, that seems as if it might be nice for the two of you," Tony said. "It's just that–"

He didn't get the chance to finish as Daisy's mum leapt in. "You know Daisy has this health condition where she can't eat sugar, Katrina? Because she has diabetes? We have to be very careful with her."

She took Daisy's hand. Daisy stifled the instinct to pull it away.

"She needs to give herself injections every day, and she mustn't eat anything sugary. She won't feel very well if she does. But she also gets ill if she doesn't eat enough food or does too much exercise, and then she needs something sweet. Sometimes, though, Daisy doesn't know her blood sugar levels are too low, and that's dangerous because she might faint."

There was a yell from the kitchen. "Katrina? Get a move on, aye? There are dishes to do."

Katrina nodded solemnly. "The poor wee soul!" Daisy felt her gently kick her ankle under the chair. "Why don't you tell me what I need to do when I've finished breakfast, Mrs Double U? I promise I'll keep your wee lassie safe."

She smiled widely at Tony and Debbie, topping up both their cups with extra coffee, and left them. Daisy picked up her toast, took two mouthfuls and then began her argument.

The Case for Daisy Walker Going on an Outing Sans Parents.

"What did my mum say to you?" Daisy asked, dreading the answer. They were out on the street, breakfast completed and Katrina's work for the morning finished. Daisy hadn't felt up to listening to her mum explain her health condition to Katrina. She'd taken a shower to avoid hearing it.

Katrina smirked. "I need to take a lot of care o' you!" She nudged Daisy again. Daisy had worked out that Katrina used these nudges a lot. They were her primary form of communication. It was up to her to figure out what each different nudge meant.

This one, she guessed, was 'don't worry' and it was aimed at both her and her mum.

"Have you got your Dextrosol?" There was a sing-song note to Katrina's voice. Honestly, she sounded just like Daisy's mum, always checking that Daisy was armed with glucose tablets in case her blood sugar went too low.

"In my rucksack." Daisy nudged her back. They both laughed. Somehow, it wasn't as bad when Katrina asked it.

Daisy looked up at the skies. "Gosh, it's quite warm, isn't it? What sights are we going to see?"

She put the word sights in air quotes.

"The sights where you can buy decent music. Also, to see the sights you'll need a bike. You're tall enough you can borrow Kippy's."

She nudged Daisy. "Then, you can take it back to him after he's finished work and you, me and him can pal about together." Another nudge. "That's what you want, isn't it?"

Just Seventeen and the other teenage magazines Daisy read voraciously recommended a girl should never forget her friends. Swooning over a man was all very well, but girlfriends were crucial. She crushed the ignoble swell of happiness she'd felt when Katrina had mentioned Kippy.

"No. I quite like you too. I s'pose it's okay to spend time with you until then."

Katrina's eyes narrowed. Then she burst out laughing. "Yeah, that's right. C'mon then. Let's go get those bikes."

She led Daisy down a long street and then a close. Small houses dotted either side, the space between them so narrow occupants could pass each other stuff out of the windows if they felt like it. Next to the small house at the end of the close were two bikes leaning against the wall, both BMXs. Katrina pulled them straight and handed the bigger bike to Daisy.

"That's Kippy's," she said. "You're taller than me. It'll fit."

"Shouldn't we tell someone?" Daisy pointed to the front door, painted bright blue and decorated outside with plant pots containing brightly-coloured shrubs and flowers.

Katrina shrugged. "Nae need. C'mon. Let's get out of here."

Kippy's bike seat had needed lowering, but other than that it was a good fit. Daisy liked being on it, her hands on the handlebars he'd held and her bottom. She didn't allow her thoughts to veer too far in that direction.

Cycling wasn't something you did in London, not unless you were wearing a helmet and part of a supervised group. It was far too dangerous. Here, where the cars and lorries were infrequent, it was much more relaxed.

Katrina, she noticed, didn't bother with the Highway Code. She led the way, zig-zagging across the lanes, overtaking and undertaking other cyclists and the cars drawing up to junctions, and never bothering to stick her hand out to signal. Daisy almost left her behind when she turned right at one point.

"Exactly where are we going?" she called out. They'd left the town behind, cycling out past the sign that had welcomed Daisy and her family to Kirkinwall the day before and fields of brown and white cows grazing peacefully.

"The next big town! There's a Woollies there." Katrina sang out. "Move it, slowcoach."

It took all of Daisy's efforts to keep up with Katrina, who kept stopping, looking back at her and sighing loudly. No wonder her legs were so thin if she cycled these roads regularly. The thought motivated Daisy, who doubled her efforts and tried to control her breathing.

A few years ago, Daisy had been good at cross-country. She'd even represented St Mary's School for Girls several times. As soon as diabetes came along, her mum put a stop to it, too terrified of what might happen.

Daisy felt that lack of running and cursed her mother.

"Is it far away?" she asked, and the head in front turned from side to side.

Minutes later, and they were on the main road. It was nothing like London traffic busy, but there were a lot of lorries, and they roared alarmingly close. One overtook Daisy, sparing her only inches or so. The bike wobbled, the force of the gravitational pull so strong she toppled over, falling into the grassy verge at the side of the road.

There were enough grass and moss to break her fall, but she felt herself flailing, her arms and legs furiously flapping as she fell and then landed face down.

"Katrina!" The first was a shout, the second a scream, a desperate attempt to get the words heard above the wind and the roar of lorries.

The bike that looked as if it was so far into the distance it might never stop, halted, and Katrina placed two feet either side of the frame, turning her head backwards. Seconds later having cycled the wrong way down the road, she was beside Daisy, hauling her to her feet.

"Are you okay?" she asked, pulling the bike up and dusting off the bits of grass that clung to it.

"Ye-es," Daisy said, taking the bike back. "Can you go a bit slower, though?"

"I'll go behind you," Katrina said, "so you can set the pace. Off you go."

Five minutes later, Katrina's bike just about clattering right into the back of hers as she stopped, Daisy spotted the sign for the town, the one Katrina had promised was a vast improvement on Kirkinwall. Daisy was beetroot red, her breath coming in ragged bursts. She felt like flinging her arms around the sign.

As they cycled past the sign, she noted an expanse of water she guessed was a lake and then a long high street studded with shops. The afore-promised Woollies was there, and Katrina called out to her to stop when they got to the doors.

She shook her head when Daisy asked if they should lock their bikes, leaving them propped up against the railings next to the bank beside Woollies instead.

As she dismounted the bike, Daisy's legs shook. She felt decidedly unsteady on her feet.

The Woolworth's was tiny compared to the ones in London. Katrina headed straight to the music section and began flicking through CDs, muttering to herself. "Nah, nah, rubbish, shit…"

Daisy's legs weren't yet co-operating with her brain. They didn't seem to want to obey the 'stand up' command, trying to fold under her instead. She grasped the shelf, the movement causing Katrina to look up.

"What's wi' you?"

When Daisy didn't respond at once, Katrina stopped what she was doing and grabbed her arm. "Oh! This is what your mum told me about!"

She sounded excited, but also far away. Daisy felt sweat gathering on her top lip and trickling down her back and the sides of her torso. Gross.

"Kat—Kit-Kat! Kitty…" What was her bloody name, what was the name she said Daisy should call her? She tried to remember. The name began with a 'K', she was sure, but the rest of it flickered out of reach.

Katrina took hold of Daisy's arm and pushed her gently down to the floor. "Dextrosol, Daisy?"

Daisy shook her head. "Not, not…no hypo," she said, her chin slumping onto her chest. Katrina crouched beside her and began to rifle through her jeans pockets and the backpack.

Finding nothing, she stood up. "Stay here. I'll be right back!"

Their actions had attracted the attention of two older ladies nearby. "Do you think she's drunk?" one asked the other, pointing at Daisy.

"Not...no..." Daisy muttered. It must have come out louder and angrier than she thought, as woman number one took her friend's arm, and they both hurried away, shooting Daisy a dirty look over their shoulders.

Katrina was back, holding handfuls of pick and mix. "I didn't know what to get to you, so I just went for the ones covered in sugar," she said, kneeling next to Daisy. She'd picked cola bottles, jelly babies, shoestrings, bonbons and fizzy chips.

"Not...no..."

"Shut up!" Katrina said, pushing a cola bottle into Daisy's mouth. "You're hypo. Eat. Your mum said sometimes you don't know when you're low."

By the time she'd forced the third cola bottle into Daisy, the shop's manager had appeared. He'd brought a security guard with him too.

"Right, you two!" he barked. "You'll be paying for those sweets, however many of them you've eaten. We don't tolerate shoplifters here, and we'll be calling the police to deal with the two of you. Get up!"

NO-ONE'S EVER HIT ANYONE FOR ME

The security guard—a man who looked as if he could pick up Katrina and break her in two—began to take the sweets from Katrina's hand.

She responded by punching him in the stomach. His eyes widened comically, and he let out an "Oof", dropping the sweets he'd managed to take from Katrina and doubling up.

"Right!" the manager bellowed, stepping in between the security guard and Katrina. "That's enough! I'm calling the police now to charge you with assault and theft."

"No!" Daisy shouted, her mind finally pulling itself out of the swamp it had sunk into. "No! Not theft. I'm…"

The effort of talking exhausted her. She held out her left arm with its Medic Alert bracelet.

Katrina folded her arms. "My friend's got diabetes. Her blood sugar level was low, so she needed sugar, and she didn't have any on her. I got her some sweets because otherwise, she would have fainted and DIED."

It was a bit of an exaggeration, but the manager's expression softened, and he held out a hand to Daisy.

"Oh, oh…well. Let's get you into the back office and get you something to drink. Johnny, can you get some more sweets for the young lady? No charge, of course!"

Daisy grasped his hand and pulled herself up slowly. Katrina smirked at the security guard, who glowered back at her.

Woolworth's back office was a small, windowless room strewn with paper. The manager pressed two cups of tea on them, plenty more cola bottles and a promise that there was no harm done to the security guard. One wee lassie could hardly hurt a big, beefy guard, could she?

Daisy wolfed down too many sweets, the sugary coating of them sticking to her lips. The manager wrapped up the remaining cola bottles and handed them over, telling the girls to take care of themselves.

Outside the front of the shop, Daisy burst into laughter, the effort of it causing her to double up, hands on thighs.

"I can't believe you punched that security! You nutter," she stuttered, the words coming out in fits and bursts. Then, "No-one's ever hit anyone for me before."

Katrina smiled at that.

"Shall I give Kippy a call?" She pointed at their bikes. "Mebbe you shouldn't cycle back. Kippy can bring the work van. We can put the bikes in there."

Daisy agreed, relieved at the prospect of not having to cycle back but dismayed at the thought of Kippy seeing her. She could feel sweat drying on her body, and she knew her face was scarlet.

Katrina must have seen something in her face. She held out a powder compact and a lip gloss. "Here you go. Put a bit of this on."

"Where did you get that?" Daisy asked. The makeup looked suspiciously new, packaging still in place.

Taking her bike from where it lay against the wall, Katrina looked back at her and grinned.

"I nicked them when I took the sweets."

And with that, she pointed at the other bike. "C'mon. I'll phone Kippy at his work."

"You stole my bike."

It was an accusation, but a friendly one. Kippy had picked them up at the park by the loch twenty minutes after Katrina called him from the public phone box just outside the park. Daisy wasn't sure how he'd gotten away with it. It was the middle of the day, after all, but the van had driven into the car park, horn honking loudly and startling the pensioners and small children playing nearby.

Kippy, Katrina told her, was an apprentice. He worked for McCallum's Painting & Decorating, a small Kirkinwall firm. The boss let him drive the work's van, even though he was yet to sit his driving test.

Throwing open the door, Kippy jumped out. Daisy silently thanked Katrina for her makeup stealing tricks. Kippy looked…amazing. Even dressed in overalls liberally coated with splashes of paint, those big blue eyes and the tall lankiness of him was beautiful. She felt her belly tighten, and she pushed her lips together hoping the gloss made them look inviting.

"Sorry… I, er…" She wished for wit and quick thinking. "It's a great bike!" Sadly, the wish went unanswered.

"I said it was okay for Daisy to borrow it," Katrina said, wheeling the two bikes over to the van. "You don't need your bike when you're working."

"How come you're too lazy to bike back then?" Kippy took the bikes from Katrina and loaded them into the back of the van which was already chock full of ladders, tins of paint, rollers and trays.

"Daisy had an incident," Katrina announced solemnly, once the bikes were safely squashed into the van and the back doors closed. Daisy turned, shushing her. Sweating buckets and collapsing in a Woolworth's store was hardly glamorous.

Katrina poked her tongue out at her. "Well, you did." She turned back to Kippy. "She's got diabetes and she wasnae feeling very well. I didn't think she should cycle back."

Kippy glanced at Daisy. "Are you okay now?"

"Yes, thank you. Katrina punched a security guard who was trying to arrest us," Daisy threw in. The 'arrest' thing was maybe an exaggeration, but Katrina's over-dramatics were catching.

Kippy shook his head at that but then grinned. "What did you dae that for?"

"I had to get sweeties into this one's gob quickly, so I helped myself to the pick and mix. The security guard tried to take them off me. Accused me of stealing."

Katrina's voice had gone up at that in fake outrage.

"To be fair," Daisy said. "He wasn't wrong there."

Kippy shook his head again. His younger cousin's appalling behaviour probably wasn't news to him. He wrenched open the door to the passenger side of the van and told them to get in.

Katrina insisted Daisy sit in the middle. The van didn't have enough room for three people up front, and Kippy's arm touched hers every time he changed gear. She wasn't a driver herself, but Daisy thought he shifted them more often than he needed too.

She angled herself slightly so that the arm came into contact with her breast and hoped that he noticed her nipples had hardened. The delicate brush of arm to nipple sent powerful messages to her groin.

"You're driving Miss Daisy," Katrina said, "so watch your driving."

Again, Daisy was no expert, but Kippy drove very fast, and he took the corners at a dizzying speed, the van almost tilting on its side as they sailed around them. If the nipple brushing hadn't distracted her, she might have found herself screaming.

They were back in Kirkinwall ten minutes later. "The party's an all-nighter," Kippy said as he dropped them off. "And there'll be gear there."

"Good," Katrina said, jumping out her side. "We'll be there. Once we've figured out how to get Miss Daisy in."

"Oh, it'll be fine. My mum and dad will be totally cool with it," Daisy said, breezily, dismayed that Kippy might think she was the sort of girl who needed to ask her parents if she could go to a party, even if it were true.

And what was gear anyway? Painting gear? Tools? Instinct warned her to keep her mouth shut. It was probably an uncool question.

The van drove off, and Katrina nudged her. "No, they won't be. We'll just no' tell them, okay?"

OUTRAGEOUS PLANS

Katrina's part in helping Daisy in Woollies went down a treat. She curated her story carefully. Out went the bike ride and the near miss with the lorry that had sent Daisy hurtling into the grass verge. Also missed out were the security guard punch and the threats to call the police.

No, instead Katrina and Daisy had travelled there by bus. Once inside, Daisy had started to feel unwell. Katrina had force-fed her sugary sweets; the manager had been alerted and had allowed them to help themselves to as many cola bottles as they wanted.

Her cousin, an experienced van driver, had then picked them up and driven them back. Taking the road extra slowly because of the precious cargo he carried.

A sanitised version of what had happened, but one that had her parents nodding along in approval. Debbie still looked faintly anxious—*see, I let you out of my sight for a second, and this is what happens!* —her eyes had narrowed when Katrina dropped in the precious cargo bit. It was a tad OTT.

But Tony heaped praise on Katrina. How smart thinking she was to realise Woolworth's Pick and Mix was just the thing for someone suffering from a low blood sugar episode!

Perhaps, and he said this tentatively, checking out Debbie's reaction at the same time, it would be lovely for Daisy to spend more time with her new friend?

Yes, yes, yes. Daisy mentally crossed everything, fingers, legs and toes, jumping for joy inside when her mother nodded slowly. She said okay to the plan, so long as Daisy always made sure she had her Dextrosol with her, and that Katrina knew what to watch out for.

But spending more time with her new friend and going to a teenage party at a house where parents were absent? Two different things entirely.

Katrina waited for Daisy the next day, promising Tony and Debbie they were only going to hang about the town, and she'd return their daughter to them in time for lunch. Having agreed, Tony said he'd come with them part of the way as he wanted to pick up his newspaper. He didn't get as far as the newsagents, however; stopping instead at the local solicitor's office.

"See you at twelve, Daisy?" It was half-hearted, though. Her dad's attention seemed riveted on the pictures in the window of the office.

Daisy nodded fervently, and Katrina grabbed her hand. "The park, over there," she pointed at the hills beyond the houses at the edge of the town and waited until they were out of Tony's earshot.

"I've been thinking about the party," she said as they headed along the High Street. Thankfully, the day was dry and warm again. Hanging out in town wasn't appealing when the rain pissed down.

"I know," Daisy said. "You told me I shouldn't tell them about it. Sneak out. I don't know how I'm going to manage that."

"Easy," Katrina said as they headed up the hill that led into the park. "You tell them you're ill and you go to bed early, stuff the bed with pillows or something and then sneak out the back way. That room's got a two-way door with another room that my Gran usually locks. I'll mind and leave it open for you."

It was a solution of sorts, but it wouldn't work. Daisy was sharing a room with Matthew for a start, and her mum would check up on her repeatedly, her head bobbing back and forth behind the door to the room. She'd heard too many horror stories of diabetic teens who died in their sleep. Katrina nodded at the explanation. Daisy sensed the whirring of a mind trying to puzzle out a problem.

They'd reached the bench at the top of the park. From there you could see the swings, the slides and an overview of the whole town, roofs, church spires and the pastel-dotted colours of the houses.

Katrina leant back, elbows up on the back of the seat. "I think I know how you can do it. Depends on how much you want to go to this party."

She turned her head there. "As I said, the parties are great round here. Nae parents, nae rules, lots of music, dancing and all the other stuff."

All the other stuff was what interested Daisy. At fifteen, her life experiences were sadly lacking. She longed to emulate the effortlessly cool Katrina, cycling the streets without bothering to look out for other traffic, punching security guards and going to wild parties. It was so devil-may-care and grown up.

Katrina began to explain her plan. It seemed fool-proof, but…oh, could she do this? It was also totally and utterly out-rageous. But was the plan safe and what if they got caught?

Standing outside the little solicitor's office on the street corner, Tony marvelled at the house prices pictured in the window. They reminded him of the game Monopoly, the sums of money mentioned were like those paper bills you gathered and then used to buy the plastic buildings and hotels. Unreal.

The morning visit to the town's newsagent was now a reg-ular pre-breakfast routine. He had developed a rapport with the newsagent—*call me Archie, Tony*—who was happy to keep him a copy of The Times every day. There wasn't much of a demand for it here, the locals preferring the Glasgow Herald or the Daily Record.

Archie liked talking about Kirkinwall and its charms to those not from the area. Tony was a willing listener, and he asked lots of questions too.

What should they go to see today? That's what usually started it, but then he moved to generalisations.

Did the town get lots of tourists? Did the visitors spend lots of money in the area? Was there anything that could be done to get more people to come? It seemed a shame that more people didn't know about the charms of Kirkinwall and the surrounding area.

Archie took his questions very seriously, ruminating over answers as he puffed on a pipe. He gave thoughtful, measured replies.

In the solicitor's window, one picture caught Tony's eye—a three-bedroom townhouse on the High Street. A photograph of the rear showed a long narrow garden stretching back to the water. Tony had never lived near water. He fancied that deficiency was something he should put right.

He reached fingers out to touch the picture, unaware that inside the solicitor's office, the secretary could see him. She knew the photo he touched. The house was her dream home, too. No wonder the strange man wore an awed expression.

An idea had started up in Tony's mind at the outset of the holiday, the tiny seeds of a plan.

By the time three days were up, the seeds had germinated. It was no longer an idea, but a compulsion. Tony had worked it all out. And he knew exactly how he would do it. The money was already in place, thanks to a fund he'd set up some years ago. In the back of his mind, had he always known this opportunity might come? Perhaps so.

Tony was a smart man. He knew about risk and reward. He thought things through. Decades of not pursuing risk, of weighing up its consequences and discarding it, were behind him. Now, he wanted a change. There were chances here, chances to make a difference and bring benefits to many. He saw himself standing at a crossroad, one path worn and familiar, the other untrodden but the horizon twinkling in the distance.

The details of what he would do sparked up in his head, tiny electrical currents that sent electrons flowing back and forth between Mackies, the Gordon Arms, the town's artistic past and more. He felt them flash, each building or new project lighting up—all that glitters can be gold.

It was foolproof, he decided and then corrected himself. Such a plan could never be entirely foolproof, but years of working for the Metropolitan Police, one of the biggest law enforcement agencies in the world, gave him inside knowledge.

He would need to work out how he could persuade Debbie to agree to his plans, but Tony had charm and persuasion by the bucket load. That would be the least of it. And he had seven days to do so.

Tony put a foot down firmly on the untrodden path. He pushed open the door to the solicitor's office, step one of outrageous plan about to be enacted. "Hello there!" his voice boomed out. "I'm interested in one of the properties you have in your window. Number 26, The White House? Do you have a schedule I can look at?"

SCOTTISH GENES

Bella Italia was a terrific place, Daisy reckoned. The small Italian restaurant in Kirkinwall welcomed the Walkers with open arms. So far, this was their third visit in a week, and the place was never full, even on a Friday night as it was now. No wonder they liked the generous-tipping Londoners so much.

The restaurant didn't go for the whole check-print, table-cloth thing, but Mateus Rose bottles turned into candle holders were positioned in the centre of the tables, and red, green and white bunting hung around the walls. The waiter and the chef were Italians, though, and the two of them exchanged regular, heated exchanges they didn't seem to care if customers heard.

Katrina's instructions in her head, Daisy encouraged her family to go for pizzas. And dough balls. And garlic bread. Nobly, she refused all the suggestions she'd made, sticking to a small bowl of pasta with a tomato and bacon sauce, and salad.

The meal dragged on for ages, an interminable pause

between the first course and second. Then, her dad insisted they go for the hazelnut and chocolate gelato as he said he was in a celebratory mood, so allowing Daisy a small spoonful. At last, Tony stood up, and a waiter materialised seconds later with the bill and little shots of an almond liqueur he pressed on her mum and dad.

It was only half-past seven.

Walking back to the Braemar Quality B&B, Tony began yawning, patting his stomach at the same time. "Goodness, that was filling, wasn't it? I feel as if I couldn't eat anything for days."

Daisy's mum said something similar, and Daisy felt her hopes soar. It looked as if they might just pull this plan off.

Back at the B&B, Katrina swung the front door open. "The Double Us!" she said, smiling at all of them. "Have youse had a nice night?"

She ushered them all into the B&B's living area, efficiently whisking away coats and bidding them to sit down. She reappeared a minute later with a bottle of whisky and one of coke, and a little glass dishes filled with cream and raspberries.

"Would you like a wee nightcap of this lowland malt, Mr Double U? No' one you can buy in the shops, and I got a coke for Matthew."

Her dad, Daisy could tell, wasn't drunk, but he wasn't sober either. He took the bottle off Katrina and whipped off his glasses so that he could read the label.

"Goodness, well I should try this, shouldn't I?" he said, returning the bottle to Katrina. "I've Scottish genes, you know. My grandmother was a MacLellan and from this neck of the woods."

Katrina added solemn approval and pressed the little

dishes on them too. Freshly-made cranachan it was, she said, a very Scottish pudding that her granny had made that afternoon. Katrina made a huge play of refusing to give any to Daisy. Cranachan, she said, was far too sweet. It had too much honey in it.

Matthew helped himself to two, and Daisy swallowed hard in alarm. Katrina, though, was ahead of her, whisking away the second dish as quick as you like.

"I'll save it for you for tomorrow. If you eat all that sweet stuff before you go tae bed, you'll never go to sleep!"

It wasn't an argument that was going to win over a nine-year-old boy, but it made her look good in his parents' eyes.

Tony persuaded Debbie into having a dram too, and they sat there, the armchairs of the Braemar B&B hugging them as they sipped the whisky. Katrina had told her she reckoned it would take five to ten minutes to work, but to Daisy, the seconds stretched out. She watched them, trying not to be too obvious.

The little carriage clock on the mantelpiece chimed half-past eight, and Tony began to yawn. Debbie's eyes had drooped, lids dropping slowly over eyeballs, flicking open again, and then doing the same thing again. Matthew had curled up on the sofa, eyes closed.

"Gosh," Debbie said, "I'm exhausted, Tony! I think I'm going to have to go to bed."

Tony murmured agreement, muttering that maybe the whisky was a lot stronger than the kind of drink he usually took. He turned to Daisy, his expression apologetic.

"Your deadly dull family need to go to bed, Daisy. I'm sorry."

Daisy swallowed back guilt, the emotion conflicting with colossal excitement that had made her tremble, counting down the minutes until her mum, dad and little brother were safely tucked up in bed, and she was free.

"Dinnae worry, Mr Double U," Katrina's sing-song voice again. "Me and Daisy can watch a film. Youse should go to bed."

Daisy waited until she could hear the doors to the bedrooms upstairs open and close, footsteps walking across the floors above them and the creak and squeak as bodies sank into mattresses.

Katrina held up a palm and Daisy slapped it.

"Right, time to party, eh?"

CHIPS, WHIPS, CHAINS AND DIPS

Daisy had stored the clothes she planned to wear to the party earlier. She pulled the plastic bag from under the sofa, and Katrina started to strip off too, telling her to be quiet, as Mrs Burnett was in the room along the corridor, watching TV.

The thought struck Daisy, how come I'm not bothered about getting half-naked in front of Katrina? For the last two years, she'd hid her body carefully from her classmates, too conscious of those throw-away remarks that got passed around the girls' changing rooms.

"Gosh, I love your chunky thighs! Mine are so bony, aren't they?" or, *"I'm so jealous! I wish I didn't care about body hair."*

Katrina had the kind of body that would be the envy of all those bitches, legs so skinny there was a thigh gap you could fit a hand through. About to tell her, Daisy changed her mind. Maybe she hated her thinness.

Katrina's party outfit was far better than Daisy's. She'd

pulled on a short denim skirt and a cropped bright red tee shirt, the hem of which touched the bottom of a scrawny rib cage. The best bit was the fishnet gloves. Daisy had settled for jeans with Converse trainers and a sparkly tee shirt. It made her look slimmer if she didn't tuck the tee shirt in.

She tilted her head to look at Daisy's get-up, screwing up her face.

"I look shit, don't I!" Daisy wailed.

"Not shit. Just a bit goody-two-shoes." Katrina straightened her head and began to sing the words to the old Adam and the Ants song. She stopped abruptly when she saw Daisy's lip tremble and pushed her back into the armchair.

"Right, get your head down. Bend forward."

She knelt, pulling her fingers through Daisy's hair. Taking a can of hairspray from her bag, she sprayed Daisy's hair liberally, pushing her fingers through the hair and tugging it out.

The appearance reflected in the mirror was much more pleasing. Daisy's light brown hair stuck out in a halo around her head. Strict school rules meant Daisy wore plaits, bunches or a bun that flattened her hair against her skull. These did nothing for a round face like Daisy's. The halo flattered, though. It made her face look smaller and sharper.

"Tuck your tee shirt in, too!" she ordered. "Trust me; baggy tee shirts make you look fatter, not slimmer."

Daisy obeyed. It was right, the tucked-in tee shirt was far more flattering, even if it made her feel vulnerable, the outline of her bottom clear to see.

They let themselves quietly out of the front door. The sun was just beginning to set, casting their shadows in front of them as they headed east along the High Street and towards the harbour square.

"What about Kippy?" Daisy asked, keeping her tone as casual as possible.

"I invited you to this party," Katrina reminded her sharply. "You're not to go off snogging Kippy or anything."

Daisy shook her head, flattered that Katrina thought her the kind of girl boys like Kippy wanted to snog at parties. She hadn't snogged anyone in her life. The thought of kissing Kippy terrified and thrilled her at the same time.

"We're meeting him along the way," Katrina added, and nudged her. "He was really keen to know if you were going to the party."

Oh, the warm glow of it all. 'Really keen'. Had any boy ever been excited about her going to an event? Not that Daisy knew. She felt the corners of her mouth tipping upwards, even when she told her facial features not to; it seemed they didn't want to listen.

She wondered how you got to be like Katrina. Were you born like that or did your experience teach you life lessons girls like Daisy were yet to learn? She tried some questions. Was Katrina still at school? No. How old was she? Sixteen. Was her job working at her gran's B&B?

Katrina rolled her eyes at that one "No, you eejit. I just help ma gran out. I'm gonnae be a hairdresser."

"You'll be good at that!" Daisy blurted, impressed. She didn't think she'd ever liked a hairstyle as much as the one Katrina had just given her. As it happened, Daisy liked the idea of being a hairdresser. Her mum went to an expensive London salon, staffed by glamorous, other-worldly creatures who wielded scissors dizzily fast. She'd told her mum that aspiration once. It hadn't gone down well.

"Aye, I've got an apprenticeship at Dulcies," Katrina pointed at a building opposite the harbour square, the sign in the top floor window surrounded by posters of women with bobs that cloaked razor-sharp cheekbones. "I start September. Don't want to stay there, though. I want to go to London."

Daisy heard the longing in her voice.

"You could stay with us!" she exclaimed, delighted at the idea.

She imagined Katrina meeting her from school. *"Oh… you mean Katrina!"* her imaginary conversation with her London school friends Lisa and Dana went, as she saw them stare at her. *"She's my Scottish friend. She works in the Trevor Sorbie salon."*

In the scenario, Katrina was dressed as she was now leaning against a wall, one foot placed half-way up, so her knee jutted out. She was smoking too, blowing out rings that drifted slowly upwards before disappearing. It was part Olivia Newton-John in *Grease*, part Madonna in *Desperately Seeking Susan*.

When Lisa and Dana fell on Katrina, impressed, she looked them both up and down. *"C'mon Daisy, let's get out of here. This place is lame."* As she left, Daisy looked back apologetically at Lisa and Dana. They stared at her in envy.

"What about you, Your Royal Highness? Are you still at school?" There was a mocking tone to Katrina's question as if she knew the answer already.

"Yes," Daisy muttered. "Still at St Mary's School for Girls."

"An all-girls school?" Katrina's reaction was incredulous. Daisy wished she'd kept her mouth shut.

"Are you all carpet-munchers then?" In response to Daisy's blank look, she clarified further. "Lezzies."

This didn't enlighten Daisy either. "Oh, for God's sake. Lez-be-uns," Katrina enunciated impatiently.

"No!" Daisy spat. At her Church of England all-girls school, accusations of lesbianism were the ultimate insult and thrown around liberally. She was practised in furious denial.

"Who's a lezzie?" Kippy had appeared, his bicycle coming to a squeaky stop in front of them.

"No-one!" Daisy cried. "Not me."

This, her third meeting with him, and he was better looking than she remembered. Eyes, skin, hair and everything about him joining together perfectly. The vision of him swam in front of her. She could feel her hands move, almost involuntarily. They wanted to touch that beautiful, freckly skin.

Suddenly, she felt the nerves that had been making their presence known all day intensify, her stomach fluttering madly. What would this party be like? Would Kippy want to snog her? And if he did, what would she do?

She cursed her mum and dad. Why had they sent her to an all-girls school? If she'd gone to a mixed school, she would know about snogging. Some girls at her school practised on each other, but Daisy knew that asking Lisa or Dana would be a mistake from which she would never recover.

"Good," he said, dismounting from the bike. He held a plastic bag that looked as if it had cans and bottles in it. Daisy's nerves jangled further. Alcohol was one of those teen rites of passage things she was yet to do, and her mother had already read the riot act on why teenage diabetics shouldn't drink.

Katrina, heading now for the bridge past the Harbour car park, pointed beyond the bridge. "The party's over there. A friend of Kippy's. Sometimes my friend. His ma and pa have gone to Largs for their holidays.

"I told Daisy here it's going to be a chips, whips, chains and dips kind of party, Kippy. We dinnae want to let her down, eh?"

Kippy laughed, his eyes seeking out Daisy's. "There will be chips and dips. Dunno about the rest."

She smiled back anyway. "Not your basic high school orgy then."

"Mebbe. If you're lucky."

Kippy's remark made Katrina snort. "Alright, pipe down you two. And hurry up. We're wasting valuable drinking time."

With that, she beckoned them both onwards. Daisy glowed inside. The exchange she'd had with Kippy had made her skin tingle. The night ahead looked oh-so-promising. She asked who would be there and Kippy reeled off a list of names. They all sounded like nicknames. Daisy couldn't tell if they were the names of boys or girls, and she didn't like to ask.

It was quickly apparent where the party was taking place, the sound of music reaching them as they crossed the bridge.

They were at the venue a few minutes later, a semi-detached house at the end of a road. Loud music pumped out of the open windows, and there was a group sitting in the garden, smoking and drinking cans of beer. One of them stood up as he saw them.

"Kippy!" His voice rang out, and he staggered forward, clapping Kippy on the arm. "Alright, Kitty?"

"It's Katrina," Katrina muttered, shoving off the arm he tried to drape over her shoulder.

"Aye, and who's this?" He turned his attention to Daisy, blasting her with beery breath.

Introductions made, he told them to make their way into the house, saying Dod was out the back. Inside, the air was thick with smoke and the noise overwhelming—music playing on a stereo in the living room—and chatter.

The house wasn't big, but Daisy had never seen a home

so crowded with people. Girls sat on the stairs, chatting and laughing. Girls and boys stood jam-packed together in the hallway, while glimpses into the living room and kitchen revealed a sea of heads.

They'd not got any further than the front door.

"I think we'll stay outside," Kippy said, and Katrina nodded. Retreating, he led them around the side of the house to the back garden. There were people there too, two girls and a boy sat on the grass smoking a roll-up.

"Kippy, man!" The boy held up a hand. "Want tae join us? Special party privileges for the inner circle, ken?"

He pointed at the two girls sitting either side of time who giggled.

"I'll stick wi' the beer, Dod. Great party, by the way."

By this, Daisy took it they were in the presence of the host. He didn't seem bothered by the number of people or the mess they were making. Daisy had gone to a party back in June where parents weren't present. The girl holding it had been uptight the whole time, making people take off their shoes and shoving coasters under mugs and glasses as soon as anyone put them down.

Dod struggled to his feet. He looked Kippy's age—eighteen, Daisy guessed, short but powerfully built, his dark eyes taking in her and Katrina, especially Katrina. He had a slow, lazy grin and his face settled into the smile as if the muscles there performed the movement all the time.

"Ah'm just doing weed," he said, waving the roll-up back and forth, grin in place. Flakes of tobacco fell out, littering the grass in front of him. "Ah'm up at five the morn."

"Out on the boat?" Kippy said, and Dod nodded slowly, taking in an enormous drag of the roll-up.

"Are you going sailing?" Daisy asked. Her audience stared

at her in disbelief, and Daisy cursed herself. What had she done wrong now?

Katrina broke the tension, bursting into gales of laughter. "Dod, this is my new pal, Daisy. We call her Your Royal Highness. She's dead posh, but we like her anyway."

Dod grinned at her, a beam that made his eyes crinkle into slits "Well, Your Royal Highness. Ah'm no' sailing tomorrow. Ah'm going out on a fishing boat where ah will work ma bollocks off. That's testicles to you. But ah will get paid well for it, and then mebbe, just mebbe ah'll be able to take Katrina oot."

"In your dreams, Dod," Katrina's reply dripped scorn.

He shrugged and then signalled to the two girls still sitting on the ground, who both leapt to their feet. The three of them went back into the house, braving the crush of the kitchen. Daisy thought she could hear him, "Am ah goin' sailing!" and more laughter. It was mortifying.

"Dod's an eejit," Katrina said, settling herself on the recently vacated ground. "Take no notice."

Kippy sat down beside her and Daisy followed suit. He took three cans of beer from the carrier bag and offered them to her and Katrina. Katrina accepted one but stopped Daisy's hand.

"Daisy can't drink," she said. "She's got diabetes, remember?" About to object, Daisy realised she was relieved. There were too many things about this party that made her nervous. Not having to drink alcohol made life easier.

Kippy accepted the explanation without asking any questions. Daisy watched him pull the tab on his can of beer and drink, his throat moving rhythmically up and down as he did so. She longed to touch it, the skin looked inviting, and she could smell him; that same smell she'd noticed when she'd first met him.

Katrina drank her beer too, but more slowly.

"What's London like?" she asked.

"Big, noisy, crowded, exciting. Sometimes."

"I bet you go to the cinema all the time," Katrina mused, her tone envious. "And you see all the latest films as soon as they come out. Do you go to gigs, too? And nightclubs?"

Oh dear. Daisy did go to the cinema a lot, but gigs and nightclubs weren't yet allowed. She muttered an indiscriminate "mmm-hmm" hoping it would discourage further questions along such lines.

"And what about the shops?" Katrina continued. "Is the Chelsea Girl in London ginormous? And Clock House. And you've got Portobello Market." By now, her tone was reverential. Daisy didn't want to admit that she'd only been to the market twice and never bought anything.

Kippy had finished his beer. He stood up. "Do you want to dance, ladies?" he held a hand out to Daisy, but Katrina knocked it away. "No. We're talking. And the music's shite."

"Suit yoursels." He wandered off, Daisy sighing to herself as he left.

"Don't worry. You can dance with him later," Katrina nudged her once again, teasing and serious at the same time.

She stretched herself out on the ground, head propped up on an elbow. "We should hang out together for the rest of your holiday. Will your ma and pa let you?"

"Yes," Daisy said. It was her holiday too, and her mum and dad would want her to enjoy it, wouldn't they? "I didn't want to come here on holiday. I thought it would be shit."

"It is shit," Katrina said, "but now you've got me, it'll be better." She raised her eyebrows suddenly, her attention caught by something over Daisy's shoulder.

"Ssh…look!" she whispered. Daisy glanced behind her. A couple of party-goers were taking advantage of the garden's relative privacy. There was a small shed at the back, its sides almost enclosed by a head-height overgrown hedge. The boy was pushed up against the side, his eyes closed. The girl was on her knees in front of him, her head pushed into his groin. They hadn't realised the bird's eye view Katrina, and Daisy had from where they sat.

"Is she…?" Daisy turned back to Katrina, her eyes wide.

"Sure is," Katrina smiled. "That lassie is known as Blow Job Bob. Her real name's Belinda. She's very popular."

The music had changed—from pop to something that sounded cooler. "Is that the Pixies?" Daisy asked, and Katrina nodded approvingly. "Yeah, Kippy must have changed it. We can go in now. Anyway, I don't want to watch the rest of Bob's performance."

She hauled Daisy to her feet and set down a half-drunk beer can.

Behind them, she heard the boy groaning. She hoped that kind of thing wasn't expected of girls in general. Where would she start?

I WANNA BE ADORED

Inside, the house seemed even busier. It took ages to push past the bodies jammed in the kitchen and lined in the hallway to get to the living room. Daisy saw Kippy, his lanky figure placing him above most people's head height. He raised a hand, his fingertips touching the ceiling and beckoned them through.

The floors felt sticky underneath. Stood next to Kippy, Daisy noticed his smell had changed. Now, there was the washing powder, Lynx and beer—a sour, yeasty scent that she quickly decided she liked. It was a new combination, unique to Kippy and imprinted the overall impression of him on her mind.

Two girls had edged their way next to them, their smell overwhelming that of Kippy. Daisy recognised it at once—Hubba-Bubba, Elnett hairspray and Impulse, scents she associated with the girls' toilets at her school and ones that didn't bring back happy memories. Daisy guessed they were the same age as she and Katrina, although the heavy make-up they both wore made them look older.

One girl dug her elbow into the other's side and grinned broadly. "Knock-knock!" she announced loudly, smirking in turn at her friend and Katrina.

Beside her, Daisy felt Katrina stiffen.

The other girl repeated what her friend had said. "Knock-knock, Katrina," shouting the words this time, her face creased up mischievously.

"Up yours, Nicola. That joke's so old it's gone mouldy." Katrina moved off, beckoning to Daisy to come with her.

What was that about? The girl called Nicola who'd made the remark pursed her lips together and widened her eyes. "Ooh-ooh! Touchy!"

Katrina glared at her and stuck her middle finger up defiantly. "That lipstick makes your teeth look yellow. You coming, Daisy?"

Nicola screwed up her face but shot a hand across her mouth nevertheless.

Daisy's first loyalty was to Katrina, not Kippy, but she felt overwhelming happiness when Kippy followed them both back out to the garden. Other partygoers had decided the same, the warmth and the crowds driving them outdoors. Belinda and her partner had vanished.

"Are you okay?" Daisy asked Katrina, who shrugged.

"Those two stupid bitches have been making the same jokes for years. It's not even funny." She didn't elaborate any further, sitting on an old swing at the back of the garden and ordering Daisy to take the one beside her. Kippy began to push her gently, alternating between her and Katrina.

The hands on her back were gentle, a small push, a little warmth.

In the adjacent garden, separated only by a fragile-looking

fence, stood an old man. Dod, who'd also come back outside, saw him and waved enthusiastically in response. The old man smiled slowly and raised up his walking stick, waggling it.

Daisy held her breath. Yikes, was this a complaint? Would the police be called and, *oh my goodness, people here were doing drugs if her mum and dad found out…?*

"Gimme one of those," Dod pointed at Kippy's bag, lying at his feet. Kippy pulled out one of the cans. Dod took it and sauntered over to the fence.

"Alright, Bobby?" he shouted, and the old man nodded, that same slow smile still in place. Dod thrust the can at him, and the old man took it.

Dod took a roll-up from the pocket of his shirt and proffered that too. The old man's smile was broader this time.

"Dinnae tell Kathleen!" he said, his voice loud and hoarse.

Dod put his fingers to his lips and turned back. The man went back inside his own house.

"Deaf as a post," Dod told the back-garden partiers. "Perfect neighbour, aye?" He laughed again, a joyful, infectious sound that couldn't offend you, even when the laughter was at your expense, Daisy decided.

Katrina was sitting on the ground once more; her long legs stretched out in front of her. Dod sat next to her and put his arm around her. She pushed it off, but when he took her hand instead, she didn't pull away.

Daisy found herself wishing Kippy would do the same, but they seemed to be stuck, her on the swing, him pushing her, his warm hands making all-too-brief contact with her back. Why break that spell?

"You on holiday?" Dod asked her, and she nodded. "Where d'ye come from?"

When she said London, he looked at Katrina. "That's

where Katrina wants to go. I dinnae think ah fancy it myself. But if the love of ma life wants to go there, then ah've gottae go, haven't ah?"

Katrina rolled her eyes. The move cemented what Daisy felt about Katrina. She was the cat's pyjamas. Some young man declares you the love of his life, and you just roll your eyes. Then there was the guy who had tried to put his arm around her when they'd first come in, and the looks she attracted as she moved from place to place. She seemed to have guys falling over themselves for her.

Dod had laid himself out, head propped up in one hand as he told them stories of life on a fishing boat. Daisy noticed that people approached their group from time to time, spoke briefly and quietly with him, an exchange would take place and then they left.

The music had changed again, a track Daisy thought was the B52s. Dod got to his feet, hauling Katrina with him. "You have tae to dance with me to this one, Kit-Kat."

Someone did call her Kit-Kat after all.

They disappeared, swallowed up in the throng of people inside the house.

Kippy moved from behind her and sat down on the spot Dod had just vacated. Daisy took that as an encouragement and sat down next to him. They weren't alone—people stood or sat in small groups in the garden—but Daisy felt as if they were in a bubble, the thin skin of it insulating them from everyone else. She sat as still as she could. Moving too much might burst the bubble.

Kippy took several gulps of beer. Perhaps he was as nervous as she was.

"How long are you staying in Kirkinwall for?" He edged closer to her. Sat opposite Daisy and cross-legged too, his dark-denim covered knees almost touched hers.

"Ten days. Well, six days now, but almost a week!" Emphasis on the 'almost a week'. Funny that. When her mum and dad told her and Matthew their summer holiday in the depths of nowhere would last ten days, Daisy had stared at them, aghast. Now, she wished they were there for a month like they did when they went to France.

"You're not like the girls here," he observed Daisy as he said it. His left knee pressed against her.

With great daring, Daisy dropped a hand to his knee. "Is that good or bad?" *Did 'not like the girls here' mean not like Blow Job Bob? Was that a good thing or a bad?*

"Good," Kippy said. "You're so pretty. Smart, too."

I'm not pretty; I'm not smart. Daisy bit back her automatic response and let joy spread its way through her body instead. It tingled through her veins. She leant forward at the same time as he did, their foreheads touching and their eyes locking together.

"I think you're so–"

Whatever she was going to say was abruptly interrupted. Katrina stood at the back door, arms folded.

"Lovebirds! Time to come in."

Kippy pulled back first. "C'mon then. Let's go and dance."

Kippy had taken her hand to pull her to her feet and not let go of it. He guided the two of them into the house, Daisy revelling in the feeling of her hand in his. For a thin guy, his hands were surprisingly large, the skin dry and warm.

They joined Katrina and Dod swaying together in the living room—there was no room for anything else—to the Stone Roses' *I Wanna Be Adored.*

Kippy sang the lyrics to her, Daisy unsure if he meant he wanted adoration or thought those were the lines she'd like.

Who wouldn't want to be adored?

She confessed that when she'd first heard the song, she'd thought Ian Brown wanted to be a door. Kippy burst out laughing at that, then cocked his head to one side to listen properly.

"Aye, right enough." From then on, he changed the words to I Want to be A Door and added some lines of his own further developing the scenario. The bubble of happiness around Daisy expanded.

Five songs later, Katrina appeared in front of them, telling Daisy it was time to go. When Daisy opened her mouth to protest, she shook her head.

"Don't be daft, Daisy. What if your ma and pa wake up, and decide to check up on you?"

Thanks to the loud music, the exchange had gone unnoticed. Neither Kippy nor any of the other party-goers had heard the shameful truth that Daisy had parents who would do that kind of thing.

"I'm off home!" Katrina announced loudly. "I promised Gran I'd help her get the stuff ready for breakfast." She nudged Daisy as she said it, the reason for their leaving early cleverly disguised as Katrina, rather than Daisy-driven.

"D'ye want me to walk youse home?" Dod shouted over the music, his eyes half-shut. He looked as if he might fall asleep on the spot and Daisy wondered how on earth he was going to manage to get to sleep in a house still full of energetic party-goers.

"Nah," Katrina said. "Kippy'll see us safe." She nudged Daisy again, harder this time. "C'mon."

Despite his evident exhaustion, Dod managed to grab Katrina before she left the house, pulling her into a snog that went on for ages.

Stood outside on the street, Kippy caught Daisy's eye and looked away hastily. Was he thinking about doing the same thing, Daisy wondered hopefully.

At that time of night, the road was quiet with only the odd car passing them on the way. To Daisy's right, the sky was a dark blue velvet, the street lights of the town unable to tarnish it with their sodium glow.

"Is Dod your boyfriend?" Daisy asked. The snog should have confirmed it, but her new friend did not seem to play by standard rules.

"No!" Katrina didn't break her stride. She seemed determined to march them home quickly, mindful perhaps of the promise she'd made earlier. "No way." She was several feet ahead, so Daisy couldn't tell if her question had annoyed her.

"I'm going places. Dod has lived here all his life. He loves living here. He'd never move to London. I'd just be leading him on if I was his girlfriend, wouldn't I?"

There was a snort from Kippy, who cuffed his cousin lightly on the head. "She just lets Dod kiss her and sleep with her from time to time. That's no' leading him on at all. The heart-breaking wee bitch."

Katrina did stop this time, repeating the gesture she'd treated Nicola to earlier that evening.

Kippy smiled at Daisy and took her hand, banishing all thoughts on the nature of Katrina and Dod's relationship.

Katrina turned, noticing the hand holding straight away. "How come I'm stuck with you two lovebirds?" Another rhetorical question, Daisy decided, delighted that Kippy didn't dispute the term lovebird.

Back at the Braemar, all the lights were out apart from one downstairs room that Daisy worked out was the guests' living room. That must mean that her mum and dad were still safely stuck in the land of Nod.

The three of them stood in an awkward triangle. "See you tomorrow, then?" Katrina eventually volunteered. Daisy nodded, closing her eyes briefly in relief when Kippy nodded too.

"Better give her a kiss then," Katrina folded her arms. "Make it quick, though! We don't want her pa coming out with a shotgun!"

Kippy leant forward, kissing Daisy on her cheek, his other hand cradling the side of her face. The lips felt as if they were branding her, the heat penetrating her skin, muscles and bone. The seconds ticked by, one second, two seconds and then all too soon it was over, Kippy standing back, eyes sparkling, and cheeks flushed.

Daisy wondered if her cheek would ever feel the same again.

GETTING UP
TOO EARLY

"Let's check your mum and dad," Katrina suggested as she and Daisy crept up the stairs as quietly as possible. Her gran, she said, had ears on elastic even though she was in her sixties.

The door to the Walkers' senior room was closed. Katrina opened it as slowly and quietly as she could, and they peered in. Two tousled heads lay on the pillows, one face up and the other turned to the side. Her dad was snoring, and her mum gave out tiny snuffles from time to time. They were okay, thankfully.

In her room, Matthew lay on his side, letting out the same noises her mum had made.

It seemed as if Daisy and Katrina had pulled off the perfect plan.

Daisy woke up the next day, glowing.

Brushing her teeth in the bathroom, she thought her face

had changed. It looked brighter, the skin clearer. "I've been kissed! I've been kissed!" The words sang in her head, her mind longing to add, "I've got a boyfriend, I've got a boyfriend," but that didn't feel sure yet.

Tony and Debbie yawned their way through breakfast, while Matthew moaned that they'd made him get up too early.

"Are you okay, Daisy?" Debbie said. It had taken her until now to ask, proof that what they'd unintentionally ingested last night was taking its time to wear off. Typically, she'd have been knocking on the door at six o'clock in the morning, demanding to know how Daisy felt and if she'd done a blood test yet.

Katrina chattered to them both, pouring out coffee into mugs that were much bigger than the bone china teacups the Braemar Quality B&B usually favoured. She'd also given them a full jug of orange juice and replaced the tiny jam pots with a jar of honey.

"Och, once you've got some coffee and toast and honey in you, Mr Double U, you'll feel brand new," she said, pushing the toast rack in their direction.

Daisy stared at her, panicky. Were they okay, her parents? Temazepam wasn't that dangerous, was it? Her nanna took it from time to time, and there were one or two mums, parents of girls at her school who were said to live on the stuff.

Katrina smiled back at Daisy, her eyes bright, but even so Daisy could sense she was worried. Daisy took two half slices of toast and liberally spread them with butter and honey, handing them to Matthew.

"Gosh, well that's the last time I'm drinking whisky for a while, eh Debbie?" Tony said, rubbing his eyes and knocking back his second coffee. "Obviously my Scottish genes are nowhere near as good as I thought if it makes me feel this bad."

Debbie closed her eyes briefly and then opened them wide again. "But Matthew didn't –

"Aye, the fresh air too, Mrs Double U!" Katrina's voice was sing-song. "Folks from the city often notice they sleep very well when they come here. Mebbe the pollution from a' that traffic keeps you awake, aye!"

Granny Burnett had appeared behind Katrina with plates of bacon and egg. She dumped them in front of the Walkers.

"I've heard that," she said. Only Daisy saw the searing look she gave her granddaughter. "Get back in the kitchen. You've got dishes tae wash up."

When the Walkers eventually finished their souped-up breakfast, Tony suggested they all go for a walk to energise themselves. About to agree, Daisy stopped herself as Katrina came out of the kitchen. She was white-faced.

"Oh, hiya, er… Daisy, can I show you something? Is that okay, Mr Double U? Mrs Double U?"

Debbie nodded, the movement of her head looking as if all her energy concentrated on that one thing.

Daisy followed Katrina into the kitchen, a room she'd not seen so far as a guest of the B&B. It was surprisingly large, a Raeburn stove taking up space along with a Belfast sink and a huge fridge. Guests' dirty plates littered the table in the middle.

Katrina stopped, tipping her head forward to whisper. "Sorry, Gran made me come and get you," she whispered, the end of the sentence coming as Mrs Burnett stomped her way into the room. The old woman was a scary woman when an-gry, as was the case now. She grabbed hold of their arms and pulled them, so they both stood in front of her.

Daisy had heard the saying if looks could kill plenty of times, but this was off the scale. Mrs Burnett started at the top, looking just over their heads and then swept her gaze downwards, stopping at chest-height.

It was even more impressive because she couldn't be more than five foot tall.

"You gave your mum and dad and your wee brother Temazepam." Now her eyes moved back up again, unblinking as she stared at Daisy.

"I...I, um..."

"Oh, dinnae bother making up some lie, little Miss. And I ken fine who came up wi' the idea. I've already spoken tae her about it. She'll no' be doing that again in a hurry."

Daisy couldn't see Katrina's face, but she could sense the expression on it. There could only be one person in the world that Katrina was afraid of, she suspected, and that was Mrs Burnett.

"So, dae I tell your mum and dad what you did?"

"Oh, Mrs Burnett, no, please no! I'll never do it again. I've been feeling terrible all morning; I was worried when they were so tired. I didn't think it would be that bad, and I just wanted to go to that party. I didn't do anything naughty at the party, I promise. I didn't drink or smoke or anything, and the thing is my mum would have been so worried, and instead, she was—"

Granny Burnett held up a hand. "Shut up! That's still no' a good reason. I won't tell your mum and dad, but. You. Are. Niver. Gonnae. Do. That. Again, are ye?"

As she said it, she pointed, pressing the finger onto Daisy's chest after each word. She had surprisingly good fingernails, oval-shaped and painted red.

"D'ye ken, when I found oot what had happened, I was

gonnae put the pair of youse over my knee and skelp you," she said, stepping back and folding her arms. "This yin," she tipped her head to the side at Katrina, "might think she can get away wi' murder, but she can't.

"Now, get oot of my kitchen before I change my mind."

She backed up her threat too, hitting Daisy hard enough on the bottom as she left that she stumbled.

Out in the now-deserted breakfast room, she turned to Katrina. "How did she know?"

"They were her bloody Temazepam, weren't they?" Katrina muttered. The paleness was still there, and something else Daisy sensed. Maybe it was that Daisy had seen her, belittled, treated like a child and threatened with a spanking. Nothing like the cool Katrina she'd encountered so far.

"When your ma and pa started going on so much about how tired they were this morning, Gran checked her packet and saw tablets were missing. Then she remembered that I'd said I went to a party last night, and she figured it out."

Daisy nodded, then from seemingly out of nowhere, a giggle bubbled up. It started with a smirk, moved into a grin and turned to full-on laughter. Katrina was at first bemused, and then the bubble became contagious, the two of them howling.

"You… you made me drug my parents!"

"Aye, and you let me!"

"Would she really have spanked us?"

"Probably!"

And that set them off again.

Maybe Mrs Burnett heard them as she made a start on cleaning out the fourth bedroom, whose guests had checked out earlier.

Maybe, she smiled too.

LIPSTICK, POWDER AND PAINT

Daisy's family seemed to have recovered well from their inadvertent drug taking. By the end of the day, Tony remarked how well he felt, relaxed and refreshed. Her mum said one or two things about calmness, putting it down to being away from streets full of traffic and pedestrians moving at one hundred miles an hour.

Racked with guilt, Daisy had spent the next two days with them. The afterglow from the party, though, underlined the guilt, scored it out in the end. She'd drifted behind Tony, Debbie and Matthew as they explored some of the towns and villages nearby, uncomplaining when her dad insisted on a visit to yet another dull and dreary museum, its exhibits stuffed animals, old paintings and random bits of metal said to come from Iron Age settlements.

She saw nothing, her head full of Kippy and THAT kiss. But an after-glow only gets you so far. By the Sunday night, she started to wonder, what now? Had that kiss made her and Kippy boyfriend and girlfriend, and if so, shouldn't he get in touch with her? Call her, or come to visit?

By the time it got to Monday, she was frantic. She'd spent the night before wakeful, her mind going over and over everything Kippy had said to her and analysing the way he had looked at her. What did it all mean?

In the morning, Katrina laughed and joked with Mr Double U, as she now insisted on calling him. Breakfast was the usual this morning, no extra coffees, or toast loaded up with butter and honey to shake them awake. Had he seen the salmon jump at the hydro-electric place? Did he know just how much money a whole wild salmon was worth? Everyone in the town knew it very well.

"I was wondering, Mrs Double U," she turned to Debbie, angling the pot to pour out tea. "Would it be okay for Daisy to hang about wi' me, this afternoon? I thought we could go for a walk down by the river, and that."

Debbie shuffled uncomfortably. The question had apparently put her on the spot. And memories of that hypo, even if her daughter had been rescued, were still fresh.

"I know what to do now," Katrina announced solemnly. "Daisy goes this funny colour when she's no' feeling well. And her speech goes all funny. And," she put down the teapot and ruffled about in her apron, pulling out a packet of Dextrosol tablets and flashing them in front of Debbie triumphantly.

"I bought these, so I'm prepared!"

They were blackcurrant ones too, Daisy's favourite. She raised two cautious thumbs-up so that only Katrina could see them. Did Katrina's suggestion mean that…that (please, God) her cousin would also be involved?

In the end, Tony took over. He over-rode her mother's

objections, saying Daisy deserved some fun this holiday too. If Daisy could find it in her to keep her ancient old mum and dad company for a few hours or so, she could meet up with Katrina after lunch.

Daisy joined Katrina nodding furiously. Four hours of museum visiting, countryside driving and walks, and she was free. Free!

Katrina picked her up outside the Braemar B&B at one o'clock. "Let's go," she said. "My place. We can play music, chat and stuff."

And…and your cousin, Kippy. Trying to play it cool, she said nothing to Katrina as they headed along the High Street, but her new friend was one step ahead of her. Kippy had been working away, she said casually. It sometimes happened, as there wasn't that much work in a town as small as Kirkinwall. He was due back that afternoon. Maybe she saw Daisy's rapid blinking; the compute of words to the brain and the reaction they created. *Yes, yes, yes!*

They walked past the Academy, the secondary school Kippy and Katrina had both attended. It looked tiny to Daisy, a dark, red-brick building that extended backwards in a long column. They continued past sports grounds, hockey and football pitches where several small groups of children played, their games uncoordinated and unconnected.

"Here," Katrina had turned into a road just past another school building. The semi-detached houses on the street were wooden, dark strips of timber stacked on top of each other. She let herself into Number 42.

"I'm home!"

The house smelled strongly of cigarette smoke, and a TV blasted out Australian voices in the front room. There was a grunt of acknowledgement, but Katrina shook her head and pointed at the stairs.

"My mum doesnae care," Katrina told Daisy as they made their way upstairs, "so long as you don't bother her."

Her room was fabulous. Daisy's heart contracted with envy once more. It wasn't big, but it was well set out. A large poster took up much of the door—Beatrice Dalle in the film *Betty Blue*, chin held in her hands and sulky look to her face—while other posters covered up most of the walls. The Athena tennis girl, hand itching bare arse, the Joshua Tree, and Rosanna Arquette and Madonna squeezed in together pouting at the camera.

A mauve duvet topped with a red velvet blanket covered the bed. In the corner of the room was a ghetto blaster on a dressing table, the shelves beneath it stacked with tapes.

Katrina cocked her head, letting herself out of the room and returning seconds later with Kippy.

"I can hear that squeaky bike of a mile away," she said and grinned at Daisy. The loveliness of a friend who seemed to want your happiness as much as you did. *"I've never had this,"* Daisy thought, *"not the friend, not the…guy."* And not the sheer, joyful lovely happiness of it either.

He stood in the doorway, his eyes flickering over her and down again. Katrina gave an exaggerated sigh. "Oh, go and choose us some music, you soppy git."

Kippy stepped past Daisy, smiling at her briefly as he did so. She noticed the quick glance. Was it a check-in, an attempt to find out what she thought before he did anything?

He scrutinised Katrina's music selection, finally handing over a tape.

Katrina had pulled Daisy onto the bed beside her, the two of them sitting on its far end, legs dangling over the side.

"Oh, alright then. House of Love okay with you, Daisy?"

Daisy sensed a test. "Yes. Hannah is my favourite song of all time. The guy on the street with a loud cut and all that."

Katrina grinned. "Me too. Dod says this is the perfect song to get stoned to, and he should know."

She stuck the tape in the ghetto blaster, and Daisy thanked the gods for her musical education courtesy of a short-lived friendship with a music geek a year before.

Katrina took down a metal box from a shelf above her bed. She opened it up, revealing a vast assortment of make-up and brushes. There were eyeshadows in every colour, lip palettes, blushers and pots of glitter.

"Let me make you up, Daisy!" she coaxed. "Kippy's rubbish to practise on."

He scowled at that. "You *promised* you'd never tell anyone."

"Daisy doesn't mind. She's from London. Guys wear make-up down there, and no-one gives a shit," Katrina said, gesturing to Daisy that she should lie down and place her head in Katrina's lap.

Daisy smiled at him, doing her best to look open-minded. To her surprise, she found the thought of him in make-up strangely attractive. He had big eyes and big lips—just what all the girls in her year at school craved. Made-up, such eyes and lips would look incredible.

"I want to be able to do make-up as well as hair," Katrina told her, studying Daisy's face carefully and picking multiple items out of her box. "Then I can get into TV and films."

It was soothing to be made-up by someone else. Katrina had a light touch. She used a lot of products, but only tiny amounts of them. When she'd finished, Daisy sat up not knowing what to expect.

The results were incredible. Holding the hand mirror,

Daisy stared at her unfamiliar self. Katrina had applied a tiny amount of foundation to her cheeks, hiding the redness and lined her eyes with purple kohl which looked much better than the usual black Daisy used. She'd applied a turquoise shadow to the lids and purple mascara to the eyelashes. She'd also done something with a blusher that made Daisy's face look much slimmer, finishing off the look with a light pink gloss.

Kippy's reaction made it all worthwhile. "Oh, wow. That's amazing," he said, sliding across the floor on his bottom so he could stare at her carefully.

They were both artists in their separate ways, Daisy decided.

"I could make you matching pairs," Katrina said, idly. She held up make-up and looked at her cousin. Watching Kippy, Daisy noticed agreement then refusal cross his face.

"Go on," she told Kippy. "I bet you'd look fabulous."

He shrugged, an exaggerated movement she supposed meant to tell her and Katrina he did this reluctantly. "Okay then. But if you two ever tell anyone…" The words were fierce. Daisy smiled at him and then Katrina. She loved being part of people's private lives.

Kippy took up the position Daisy had relinquished. He stretched out on the bed, his head on Katrina's lap. *They're cousins,* Daisy's brain told her heart, the latter organ fluttering with jealousy anyway. *Cousins!*

She distracted herself by talking. "You're so smart, Katrina. You should come and live with us in London. I bet you could get into any fancy salon you wanted. And end up doing hair for Princess Diana or something!"

Head bent, a concentrated expression on her face as she blended eyeshadow on Kippy's eyelids, Katrina let out a sigh.

"Not her! Her hair's terrible. Though maybe I could give her a good hairstyle. For once in her life."

She held out two Kohl pencils for Daisy to inspect. "Brown or black?"

Daisy took the pencils from her and studied them carefully. "Brown. It looks better with blue eyes."

The finished product was something else. When Katrina had made Daisy up, she'd improved Daisy's appearance entirely. Everything looked exaggerated—her eyes whiter and rounder, and her lips glossy and more substantial.

Kippy, though. It was like seeing someone else altogether. Daisy had thought right. Those eyes and lips were perfect for make-up. But what Katrina had done to him made him… The eyes were ginormous, framed with thick lashes they reminded Daisy of birds of prey. They fastened on her, and she felt trapped. Katrina had painted a dark mahogany gloss onto his mouth, some of which was stuck to his front teeth, reminding Daisy of vampires. It made her want to shuffle backwards on the carpet.

"Gosh," she said, unwilling to say what she meant. "Different!"

Kippy rolled his eyes, the movement making him look himself again.

Katrina's expression changed from a scowl to something else—knowing, perhaps. "You two should snog," she said. "See if it's any different."

Oh, oh, oh. Her first snog. And with someone she fancied so much he made her stomach clench and her heart pitter-patter. Yet, fully made-up, she didn't find him attractive after all. He seemed repulsive, scary even.

But she didn't get a choice. Kippy had lowered himself to the carpet beside her. He put a hand on the back of her head and pushed it to his. Daisy, her eyes fluttering madly, was aware of the smell of him—turps, that Lynx body spray he wore, the waxiness of the make-up, and something warm and undefined. She closed her eyes, her last vision that of dark lips and hawk eyes closing in on hers.

A tongue pushed against her lips and she opened them. What a peculiar feeling, someone else's tongue in your mouth. She felt it explore her gums and her tongue, and gave in. It was a like a dance, the two tongues slithering and moving together.

Suddenly, something else started. It had begun earlier that day when Katrina had mentioned he'd been away working, but now was free to come around and see them. *I want you; I want you…*

What was that 'want'? Did it mean, I want you to like me? Or did it hint at something more? *I want you inside of me…* the shock of the thought almost made her pull away. Yes, that was what she wanted, imagining something her mum had told her about in a hideously embarrassing chat when she was thirteen.

The man puts his penis into the woman's vagina, and then he moves it a few times, and he ejaculates—that is, fluid called semen comes out of his penis inside the woman.

Gross then, and now…suddenly appealing.

"Alright, break it up!" Katrina's order sounded bored. "Time for you to pack your bags and head home, Miss Daisy!"

Kippy pulled apart first. She thought she saw something different, something in his eyes that lit up. Was it, *I want you back?* Oh, the roller coaster he put her through! It soared to great heights; it dipped, so your stomach dropped out. She'd waited for him to kiss her or take her hand earlier and he hadn't done anything. Katrina had used her paints and powders to create what seemed like a different person, and he'd stuck his tongue in her mouth and fastened hawk-like, greedy eyes on her breasts.

Katrina stood up. "We're off back to the B&B." She extended a hand to Daisy. "If you're lucky, me and Daisy will hang out with you tomorrow too."

Analysing his reaction afterwards, Daisy finally decided it was caution, or wariness perhaps. It wasn't reluctance, no, not at all.

AN INTEREST IN RELIGION

Back at the Braemar, Katrina said they should go out to the beach one evening, her, Daisy, Dod and Kippy.

She hadn't seen Daisy's family come into the living room behind her, just in time to hear the last word.

"Who's Kippy?" her father asked.

Turning to face Daisy's dad, Katrina treated him to her best, sweetest smile.

"Mr Double U! And Mrs Double U. How nice to see you! Kippy is my cousin. His real name is Alan, but we all call him Kippy because his surname's Kirkpatrick."

Her dad had folded his arms in best intimidating father fashion. Were Katrina's charm effect and Daisy's luck about to run out?

"He's a good Jehovah," Katrina added. "Like me. We were talking to Daisy this afternoon about the lessons Jesus can teach us."

Daisy's mum put a hand in front of her mouth. Daisy thought she was trying not to laugh.

"You're Jehovah's witnesses?" Her dad sounded sceptical.

"Aye. Well, kind of."

Mrs Burnett had also appeared, her arms folded too. "Kitty? What are you telling people?" She had positioned herself next to Tony and Debbie, an alliance of adults against teenagers.

Katrina had lost some of that usual insouciance. There was a tell-tale pinkness to her skin.

"I'm telling them about, er, my past, Gran." Mrs Burnett's granddaughter changed her tone. The voice didn't sound quite as breezy. "We were Jehovah's witnesses, but we left a few years ago. My mum didn't like it very much. I still pray to God every day, though."

"Terrible people, Jehovah's," Mrs Burnett added. "They're no' keen on people leaving them. Ma daughter was daft to get mixed up wi' them in the first place." She shook her head. "Still, this yin has turned out not bad, considering. My grandson's alright too."

It took Daisy a couple of seconds to work out by 'grandson' she meant Kippy. Help had come from an unexpected quarter.

"I hadn't realised you were interested in religion again, Daisy," her mum piped up, her eyebrows tilted upwards in what was probably disbelief.

Daisy had flirted with it briefly as a pre-teen when it had been fashionable among the girls in her year at school. It had been a short-lived fixation, quickly brushed off when she realised the Bible Study group they'd joined took a hard-line stance on any kind of fun.

"I'm thinking about taking Religious Studies as one of

my 'O' levels. Alan and I discussed it." Daisy held her mum's eyes. Months of saying "I'm fine!" when asked so many times during the day what her blood sugar levels were doing was good practice for lying to her parents.

Her mum raised her eyebrows. Then she smiled. "Of course. We're going back to the Bella Italia this evening. Would you like to join us, Katrina?"

Katrina agreed enthusiastically, saying she'd never been there. Left alone with her once her family had gone to their rooms to get ready, Daisy asked the all-important question.

"Were you really a Jehovah's witness?"

Katrina grimaced. "Yes, until I was twelve. All I can remember is being dragged round houses all the time and asking people to read stuff. Then my mum left my dad and decided we should stop being Jehovah's too. When that stupid cow Nicola made that 'knock-knock' joke at the party, that's what she meant. Nobody ever lets you forget anything here."

Daisy didn't know much about Jehovah's witnesses, but they occasionally came to their door in London. Her mum always said, 'no thanks' politely but firmly. Once or twice, she'd seen teenagers dressed in awful, old-fashioned clothing in their company, and felt very sorry for them.

"Is Kippy one too?" she asked.

"No! And I don't pray every day either. Lucky my gran didn't give me away, eh?"

Daisy laughed. "You're so cheeky. I can't imagine you as a Jehovah."

"I've worked hard not to be," Katrina replied. She pointed at herself.

"Do your family get dressed up for dinner or anything? Suits and stuff? Isn't that what posh people do? 'Cause I don't have anything that smart."

DAISY, DAISY, GIVE ME YOUR HEART, DO

How could ten days have flown past so quickly? The time had raced by, as if hours and minutes had been speeded up just like when you fast-forwarded a videotape, the people moving across the screen in double-quick time.

It was the last day of Daisy's holiday. Tomorrow, she would pack her rucksack and say goodbye to the Braemar. Who could have guessed that it would only take a week or so for her to feel so differently about those Scottie dog ornaments? Hideous at first and now so dear to her, symbolising the place where she'd found friendship, freedom and first love.

She'd spent the last couple of days wriggling out of as many family trips as she could—her mum and dad occasionally insisting she come along, but mostly leaving her free to team up with Katrina. Kippy worked through the day, but he joined them in the evenings. They hung about at Katrina's house or in the town. Sometimes Dod was there too.

Daisy was never on her own with Kippy, but she supposed she didn't need to be. He held her hand, he sat beside her, and he always kissed her at the end of the night. Sometimes, his hands explored her back and moved down to her bottom, and when he broke away from her, he would look at her. Analysing the look endlessly, Daisy decided it was questioning.

And whatever the question, her answer would be 'yes'.

"Do you promise you'll write to me?" Daisy asked Katrina now, an oath she thought she wouldn't believe even if her friend swore she would.

"Write what?" Katrina replied. "*Dear Daisy, today I helped my gran out and served some cock-suckers their breakfast. Then, I went to Dulcie's and swept up all the grey hair they'd cut off the pensioners in for their half-price Wednesday haircuts.* You'll die of boredom before you've even finished reading it."

She and Katrina sat on one of the picnic benches on the Moat Brae staring out at the river. Most of the boats were in—Dod had appeared a few hours ago, stinking of fish, filthy and so knackered, he told them, he could sleep for a week—and there was a crab fishing competition taking place. Daisy could see Matthew and her dad, peering hopefully at their net dangling in the river.

"Are they using chicken as bait?" Katrina pointed at Tony and Matthew.

Daisy shrugged. "No idea."

"Chicken's the best," Katrina stood up. "I'll tell them."

She bossed everyone around—Daisy, Kippy and even Daisy's mum and dad. They all accepted it, Daisy thought as she watched Katrina hurry over to Tony and Matthew. She couldn't hear the exchange, but she saw Tony nod enthusiastically and head off in the direction of the little supermarket, no doubt in search of chicken.

Tony and Debbie knew nothing of the real Katrina. Her mum and dad told her how much they liked Katrina and what a mature and responsible young lady she was, Tony repeating this in a tone of wonder that made Daisy bristle. Not so surprising, was it, that Katrina, the B&B owner's granddaughter and about-to-be trainee hairdresser was a grown-up?

The actions Katrina had carried out when Daisy's blood sugar had dropped so low after the cycle run they'd taken to the Woolworth's in Castle Douglas had elevated her to sainthood status in Tony's eyes.

Naturally, her parents didn't know about the swearing, the parties, the stealing, the lies she told them all the time, and the virginity she'd lost when she was thirteen years old, something she'd dropped casually into conversation one day.

Her parents' opinion of Katrina had afforded Daisy more freedom than she'd ever had in her life. Even if diabetes hadn't made her mum so paranoid, her existence in London seemed cossetted, wrapped in cotton wool; Debbie knew where she was most of the time. The options were school, after-school activities or with her friends. She and her friends were allowed out by themselves, but nine times out of ten, her location was known.

Her time in this small, seaside town had been fantastic. When she got back to school, Lisa would boast about her holiday. Her family had gone to Florida for three weeks. No doubt she would talk about the theme parks they'd gone to, the American boys she'd mingled with and the parties by the pool.

"I'll be able to boast too!" Daisy hugged the thought to herself. *I met this girl, this fabulous girl. We spent almost my whole holiday together. We went to parties where people were drinking tonnes and smoking weed. I met this boy and I…*

Katrina returned, taking the steps up to the Moat Brae two at a time. "I might miss you. Just a little bit. Not much." She gave Daisy the usual nudge as she sat back down beside her.

"I might miss you. Not much either, if I'm honest." Daisy kept the words light to stop herself crying. If only she could take Katrina back with her to London, she might finally gather enough courage to dump Lisa and Dana forever.

Daisy's friendships at school had suffered because of her illness. When she'd spent so much time in the hospital, and at home, because she was ill, shifts had taken place.

Lisa and Dana had drawn closer together. When she was with them, they talked about films they had seen, clothes they'd bought, parties attended, or times spent hanging out together at the shopping malls—Daisy hadn't been part of any of these occasions.

And then there was that remark. Some months ago, the three girls had talked about the 'O'levels they were taking next year. Daisy dreaded hers. Exams were important, so she was told. And you had to work hard for them.

"What exam are you worried about the most?" Daisy asked Lisa.

"Home economics," Lisa grimaced. Her expression changed suddenly, from a scowl to a broad smile.

"I was doing nutrition homework last night, and my mum decided to help. I got her to quiz me about sugar. You'll never guess what she said!"

She looked gleeful; the 'never guess' bit obviously literal. "She said, 'Stay away from sugar. It will make you fat, spotty and give you diabetes. Just like your friend Daisy.' Sorry!"

Daisy swallowed hard several times, trying not to cry.

When she repeated Lisa's, or rather, Lisa's mother's remark

to her mum, Debbie called the woman a bitch. Swearing was something Debbie never usually did in front of Daisy and Matthew.

"The stupid woman's got it wrong, Daisy," she said. "You've got type 1 diabetes. It's an auto-immune condition. Nobody knows what causes it. It's certainly not because you've over-eaten sugar. Maggie's mixed you up with people who have type 2 diabetes. Even then, she's not, strictly speaking, right. Excessive sugar consumption isn't the only cause."

Her mother hadn't, however, refuted the fat and spotty part of the sentence. The thought of returning to St Mary's now made her feel sick.

"I suppose we should do something special tonight," Katrina said. "You could come to mine. I'll get Kippy and Dod too. Or we could cycle out to the beach, have a wee bar-becue. We'll say goodbye to you in style."

"Alright then," Daisy said. She'd been worried Katrina would settle for a hasty good-bye tomorrow morning, whip-ping her dirty breakfast plates away and shouting "Cheerio, Daisy!" over her shoulder.

Katrina was as good as her word. Later that afternoon, she arrived at the B&B. "Hello, Mr Double U! Did that chicken trick work?"

A mistake. Tony launched into a detailed description of he and Matthew's crabbing triumphs. Katrina nodded along enthusiastically, expertly diving into a pause in the conversa-tion a minute later.

"Am I allowed to kidnap your daughter, Mr Double U? I'm gonnae miss her, so I want to spend the last night with her."

Tony looked charmed. "Of course, Katrina, of course! But not too late back, eh?"

"I'll make sure of that, Mr Double U," Katrina said solemnly, holding up two crossed fingers that he couldn't see.

Freedom granted, the two of them rushed out onto the street, Debbie's cries of "have you got your Dextrosol?" echoing behind them.

"Around the corner," Katrina said. "Dod's taking us all out to the beach."

Dod was parked on the next street, his car an old banger but a car nonetheless. Kippy was in the front next to him, and they both waved at her.

"C'mon, c'mon ladies. Party at the beach!" Dod said. He had already started smoking, the sweet-sharp smell of it filling the car. As they drove off, turning right past the Tolbooth, he waved cheerily at a man stood in his garden. Katrina tutted and told him not to push his luck. The man, she informed Daisy, was the local policeman.

"That fat prick does nothing off duty," Dod said, waving again. The man glared at them but stayed where he was.

It was the perfect evening for a trip to the beach. The day had been hot and still. Now it was pleasantly warm, and only a few clouds broke up the blue sky.

An old couple walking a dog were the only other people there. When they saw Dod's car pull up and four teenagers spill out, they hurried back to their own car and drove off.

Dod announced they needed driftwood to build a fire. Katrina offered to help him find it, and the two of them began to scour the line of trees that backed the shore.

Kippy tilted his head. "Come for a walk with me?" Daisy took his hand, and he pulled her towards the car park area behind the beach, out of sight of the others. He glanced over his shoulder. No-one could see them.

He pulled Daisy towards him, pressing her tightly against

his chest and abdomen. Daisy, her arms around him, could feel those skinny ribs. Just as his first kiss had left what felt like a permanent mark on her skin, the ribs seemed to imprint themselves. Maybe every time she held her arms out, she would sense the press of bones on biceps.

"I'll miss you, Kippy," she said, her words muffled. "I wish I didn't have to go home tomorrow."

"I'll miss you too," he murmured back.

"Will you? Is that true?" Daisy had hoped for some bigger, better declaration. Books, films and magazines promised her that young men were champing at the bit for the right opportunity to declare their undying love. All they needed was a deserted beach, the sun setting in the sky and alone time with their girlfriend—a scenario just like this one.

Kippy didn't say anything. His head was on top of hers. Daisy told herself he promised undying love in his mind.

"Better no' stay here too long," he said. "They'll take the piss out of us." He dropped his arms and stepped back, keeping hold of her hand. The scenario wasn't playing out as Daisy had imagined.

"Don't you want to kiss me?" she asked, dismayed the squeakiness of her voice.

He bent his head and kissed her, a light peck on the lips.

Daisy closed her eyes briefly, then kissed him back doing what he'd done to her when he'd been covered in makeup. She pushed his lips open and thrust her tongue in, waiting for him to respond as enthusiastically.

The response was there. It just wasn't as…good as the last time.

Kippy drew back. "Woah, there Tiger!" He grinned at her. Then, he surprised her again. The arms went around her once more, and he pressed her to his hips. "Feel that?" 'That' was something Daisy had heard about—the stiffie, the boner, the hard-on, the erection—but was yet to experience up close.

"Oh, wow!"

He'd taken her hand and unzipped his jeans. "Want to touch it?" When she didn't respond, he guided her hand in anyway. Daisy felt layers of cotton and the warm hardness through it. Daringly, she pushed her fingers through the gap she found in the material and touched skin.

Kippy's head rested on top of hers once more. He groaned, "Keep going," and undid his belt and the jeans. They slid over thin hipbones and down to his knees. Daisy watched in fascination as his cock jumped out, standing out at a right angle.

He took hold of her hand again and folded it around his cock. "Move your hand up and down," he whispered, then, "No, slower than that!"

A few minutes later, his groaning intensified. Daisy's hands were sticky, coated in a viscous liquid.

"That was incredible," Kippy murmured into her hair, "amazing!" He kissed her, and this time it felt fantastic again, Daisy's stomach somersaulting as her mind silently ordered Kippy to do things. *Feel my boobs, kiss my neck, put your fingers between*—

But the silent orders went ignored.

"We'd better get back," Kippy said, taking her hand. "The others'll think we've…" He didn't finish, waggling his head from side to side, and rolling his eyeballs instead. Daisy laughed. It hardly mattered if she got a reputation for 'that sort of thing', as a teacher at St Mary's had once warned, preaching on the dangers of allowing boys liberties. Daisy was leaving tomorrow. She hoped what she'd just done with Kippy would make him think of her fondly after she left.

Dod and Katrina had managed to start a fire and sat

around it. They greeted Daisy and Kippy's return with cat-calls. "Did you give her one, my son?", a question neither of them bothered to answer.

As the sun dropped, everyone's face took on a sharper, more defined look—their faces shadowed and highlighted by the flames. Kippy looked spectacular. She could see the fire's reflection rippling in his eyes, and the shadowing made his high cheekbones stick out even more. The flames did the same thing to Katrina's face, making the family resemblance clearer than it was usually.

"You won't forget me, will you?" Daisy asked them all, suddenly anxious. "And any of you can come and visit me in London whenever you want. I mean it." She had already pressed her phone number and address on Kippy and Katrina, writing the details down on several pieces of paper in case they lost one.

Dod grinned at her. "You're in the inner circle, Your Royal Highness." He stood up, pulling Kippy with him and making the two of them bow, their arms sweeping out in front of her.

"How could we ever forget you?" He flopped back down beside the fire, as did Kippy.

"He'll no' forget you," Dod continued, tipping his head towards Kippy, that big, lazy smile back. "Ah've never known him pay so much attention to a lassie."

Katrina's face took on a mischievous cast. "Aye, that's right Daisy. We were beginning to think he was a poof."

Her cousin cuffed her, the blow hard enough to push her over onto her side. Katrina laughed, kicking out at him as she lay in the sand.

She began to sing the words to the old song. "Daisy, Daisy, give me your answer..." By the time she'd got to 'I'm half crazy', Dod had joined in, Kippy shaking his head and joining in too once they reached 'the love of you'. They sang the whole song to her, Dod making her laugh when he put on a high falsetto.

The love of you. Kippy had sung those words, love of you.

I love you, right?

Daisy burst into noisy tears.

THE GIRLS OF SUMMER

"Will they or won't they come?" Daisy wasn't sure if the party on the beach the previous night counted as her official 'good-bye'. She hadn't asked outright (uncool), but she'd made sure everyone knew what time she and her family were hitting the road the following morning.

In the last ten days, Daisy had bargained a lot with a higher power she wasn't sure existed. This morning was more of the same, "Please, please let them be here when I go!"

Katrina didn't usually do Friday mornings. A sour-faced middle-aged woman had served them their breakfast, grunting in response to a request for more toast. Daisy, her eyes and ears on constant alert, found her gaze darting between the door and the window.

There was no sign of them. The car packed up and the bill settled, she stood outside. Her dad was anxious to get going. If they set off now, they'd manage to avoid hitting Birmingham and surrounds at peak rush hour. Daisy pleaded, "Please, just a couple more minutes! I think Katrina…"

She trailed off. There they were, coming towards her from the opposite end of the High Street she'd been watching all morning. Uncool or not, she took off, a spring that made her mother wince and worry about its lowering effects on Daisy's blood sugar levels.

Far enough away from the rest of the Walkers to make any conversation too hard to overhear, Daisy only just stopped herself from flinging her arms around Kippy. Or Katrina; it seemed an equal battle played out in her mind as to who she was going to miss the most.

"Here," Katrina said, handing over a small package. In it was a little Scottie dog that nodded its head. Only a fortnight earlier, Daisy would have thought it a crap present. Now, it was a different thing imbued with poignancy and meaning.

"Don't cry!" Katrina said, watching as Daisy turned it over in her hands. "You did enough of that last night."

When Daisy had burst into tears on the beach the night before, everyone had been kind. Kippy had pulled her into a hug and murmured, *"Ssh, don't cry,"* repeatedly. Dod had rolled another joint and asked her if she wanted him to sing *Daisy, Daisy* again, while Katrina told her off for being a soppy git. She smiled nicely as she said it, though, and handed her a tissue she took from her jeans pocket.

Clinging to Kippy, Daisy willed the words, *please don't find another girlfriend* into his brain, at the same time as knowing how useless the plea was. Kippy was so gorgeous and so talented, why would he ever remember her? If only she were older, then no-one could make her do anything, or take her away from wherever she wanted to be.

She could drop out of school, move to Kirkinwall, get a job at Mackies selling people fish and chips—all possibilities that would keep her where she wanted to be.

What if I never see them again?

"Do you promise you'll write to me?" she said now.

Katrina had already told her she would have nothing exciting to say, while Kippy, well, Kippy was a boy. Maybe she should ask him instead to send little postcards, paintings he'd done himself. If he signed them, *love Kippy x* that might be enough.

"Or phone?" she asked before the silence got uncomfortable. Phoning was more managable for most people. If you did it after six pm or at the weekend, long-distance calls weren't too expensive. As she'd already handed out extra post-it notes with her number on them, it wasn't a point she could press. She was beginning to sound needy.

Clingy, the teenage magazines promised her, is not a good look.

Katrina hugged Daisy. "Bye-bye, Your Royal Highness." She stepped back so that her cousin could take her place. His hug lasted longer, the kiss a tender touch of the lips to the top of her head. When he stood back, he held onto her hand, their joined hands dangling between them. The real goodbye had probably taken place last night.

A car horn blasted behind them—it could have been 'hurry up'; it could have signalled disapproval of the kiss.

Daisy dropped Kippy's hand and tried not to look over her shoulder as she made her way to the car. Matthew smiled sweetly at her as she got in. "Are you sad, Daisy?" he asked. "Were they good friends?" The question floored her, and she used the excuse of fastening her seatbelt to duck her head and hide her eyes.

Kippy and Katrina stood in front of the Braemar, waving until the Walkers' car was out of sight.

Waving furiously back, Daisy wondered how they felt

about her leaving. Perhaps Katrina and Kippy were used to visitors, people coming and going. Was it part of living in this small town that you formed intense friendships with tourists, but you always kept the knowledge that they would be leaving at the end of August in the back of your mind? Maybe they thought of her in a Don Henley way. His song referred to boys, but she could be one of the girls of summer. Once the summer was out of reach, they regarded her that way too.

Sometimes, though, life likes to surprise you. The Walkers car drove over the Tongland Bridge, Daisy trying her hardest not to weep as she watched the small town shrink behind her.

"Daisy, Matthew," their dad began, his eyes watching them in the rear-view mirror, "would you like to live in Kirkinwall?"

She and her brother stared at each other in disbelief, united for once.

"Live in Kirkinwall?" she asked at the same time as Matthew said, "Can we stay in the castle?"

Their mum turned around, her expression pensive.

"It's not definite, but your dad and I have been talking about it. We think it would be good to live somewhere quieter and safer than London."

Daisy's heart began to race. She wished she could force the car to do a U-turn and go back to Kirkinwall, where she would push open the door, spill out onto the street, find Kippy and Katrina and yell, *I'm coming back, I'm coming back!*

"I'd love to live there!" she burst out so loudly, Matthew put his fingers in his ears. "That would be amazing!"

She saw her mum and dad exchange smiles. "That wouldn't be anything to do with a particular young man, would it Daisy?" Tony asked.

She knew they didn't believe the Jehovah's Witness references Katrina had made when her mum and dad overheard them discussing Kippy, but she was still circumspect with what she told them. He was nineteen, and she said seventeen. She made no mention of beer drinking or friends that smoked weed and stuck a metaphorical two fingers up at the local policeman.

Her dad had teased her about his name. *"Kippy, Kippy? Why on earth is he called that?"*

"Daisy and Kippy up a tree," Matthew sang out now. "K-I-S-S-I-N-G!"

And the rest, Daisy thought.

Her dad and mum began to explain the plan for moving to Kirkinwall. They'd need to find out about schools and how easy it was to go from the English curriculum to the Scottish one—that was the most important thing. Daisy didn't get why that should be so crucial, but she kept quiet. Moving to Kirkinwall HAD to happen. She mustn't argue with her parents' reasoning.

Her dad would stay working in London for a while, her mum explained, while she would move to Kirkinwall with Daisy and Matthew and see if she could get a job locally.

The house he had in mind wasn't the castle or even on the same street as the castle, her dad added, apologising to Matthew, but it was nearby. They could rent out their London home for a while, to see if things worked out.

"When would we move here?" Daisy asked, her mind rushing through various scenarios of what living in Kirkinwall would be like for real. All of them involved Katrina. Her imagination stopped short of Kippy, however, though her subconscious jigged up and down at the thought of being so close to him all the time.

Again, her mum and dad exchanged glances.

"We were thinking about October. We will need to get

you into a new school as soon as possible if you're to sit your exams next year."

Daisy hugged herself with joy. Would any service station they stopped at have a payphone? She wanted to phone Katrina and Kippy as soon as possible. October was only five weeks away, four if it meant the beginning of October. She would mark the date on the calendar on her bedroom wall and cross off every day until October.

She had to wait until they got back to London, late that night. Kippy wasn't in—that information made Daisy twitch, was he out with another girl? But Katrina was.

"Katrina!"

"Your Royal Highness? Did you forget something, because if you left anything behind I've nicked it already?"

"No, no, nothing like that. We're going to live in Kirkinwall! We're moving there! In October! Just five weeks from now!" Daisy could hear all the exclamation marks in her speech. She suspected she was destined to talk like that for a while.

"I told you this place is a shithole. Why do you want to move here?" Daisy had hoped for a more enthusiastic reaction.

"I was going to come and live with you in London! Y'know, when I get a job in a posh nob salon that does all the hairstyles for the rich and famous." Now, Katrina sounded genuinely put out.

"We're not selling the London house," Daisy said. "Just moving to Kirkinwall for a while to see how we get on. Maybe we'll end up back in London anyway."

She crossed her fingers against it. London, who wanted it when there were cool friends to hang out with and lovely, angular boyfriends to kiss?

"Oh," Katrina said. Daisy heard someone behind her talking. The cheery Mrs Burnett, no doubt, wondering why her granddaughter was taking so long. "My gran says, did your dad look at the White House on the High Street?"

Katrina's question took Daisy by surprise. Her dad said he'd only asked the solicitors about the place. He hadn't looked at it.

"Yes," Daisy said, unsure of whether she should be admitting it or not. She sensed openness might be a way to make Katrina (and maybe her gran) keener about the Walkers' move to Kirkinwall.

"Yeah, they did Gran." Then, "Nice house, that. Make sure you tell your ma and pa to let you have the top floor bedroom."

"I will. I can't wait." Daisy let her last sentence hang there. Can't wait to move, can't wait to be in the White House, although it was a very grand name for a terraced townhouse in a tiny town, so few people had heard of. Can't wait to be in Kirkinwall. What did she mean?

There was a pause at the other end. This time, Daisy heard Granny Burnett bark orders. "Kitty, off the phone! There's folk needing breakfast!"

"I cannae wait either," Katrina said. Was there a smile Daisy could hear in her voice? "Let me know when you're coming."

THE BEST FISH AND CHIPS IN SCOTLAND

October 1990

Tony was proud of his flyers. The logo he'd got one of his designer friends to create for the shop was especially pleasing. The word Mackies was entwined with fish and paintbrushes, alluding to the town's fishing and painting past.

Archie at the newsagents had been just as enthusiastic when Tony showed him the logo. "Aye, aye—this looks very good. I suppose you know a lot of designers and folk like that, Tony?"

That remark flattered Tony more than anything else. Back in London, accountants tended to have a reputation as the dullest of the dull. Here was someone who thought he was part of an exciting, glamorous crowd. No need to disappoint him.

"An excellent idea to reinvigorate the chip shop, Tony!"

Archie added. His eyes kept returning to the flyer in his hand. He held it delicately as if it was something precious.

"I've been saying for years that this town needs more investment in tourism. We don't want the tourists to ignore this part of the world, but we have to give them something, apart from the castle and the museum!"

Archie made an excellent co-conspirator. When Tony first mooted the idea of plugging some money into the town's fish and chip shop, Archie offered to act as the go-between. He'd sound out Alison at Mackies—discreetly, mind! —and see if she was up for the idea of a loan to improve the premises.

"Your fish and chips are by far the best I've ever tasted!" Tony began his meeting with her, the two of them sat in the small tea shop on St Mary's Street drinking the breakfast brew and eating scones. "There's no doubt about that. But I wonder if some extra money might help you make more of your shop?"

Alison cocked her head to one side. She was in her early thirties and had been running Mackies for the last ten years, taking on the business from her father. She made a living, but only just, and it was demanding work. You relied on the summers and visitors. A couple of very rainy Julys and Augusts the last few years had done for her.

"Sometimes I dinnae think I'm cut out for business," she said with a sigh. "Aye, the extra money would be good but what would I dae wi' it?"

Tony smiled. "I have some ideas. Do you want to hear them?"

In truth, Alison's question filled him with joy. He had more than a few ideas. If he explained them with charm, he suspected Alison would give him a free hand. She was the perfect person to start his programme, the Tony Walker

Project as he'd begun to call it in his head.

"Now, I think you have room for expansion of the premises?" He pulled out a plan of the shop and its surrounds.

Mackies was in an old building that had once been part of the small shipyard in Kirkinwall. The fish and chip shop took up only a tiny part of the premises, the rest of it used for storage by a nearby garage and mechanics.

"We could give them smaller spaces, and create somewhere for people to eat, sit in. Do you know what I mean by BYOB?"

Alison, who'd been nodding along slowly up to this point, shook her head.

"Bring your own bottle! It means you don't need to worry about getting a licence. People bring their own beer or wine. And of course, with some extra money we could…" he paused, wondering how to put it tactfully.

"Make the place look nicer?" Alison smiled at him. "I know it's no' the bonniest."

That was an understatement. The sign Mackies was missing the 'k', the lino inside the takeaway was tatty, and the shop's overhead fluorescent tubes highlighted the general lack of care. The place wasn't dirty. It was just somewhere that hadn't seen a lick of paint in a long time.

"Yes! Precisely. Alison, I want to make Mackies recognisable. Do you know about branding?"

Alison shook her head again.

"Well, take Coca-Cola! Think of the letters used in the Coca-Cola sign. You only need to see a tiny bit of that sign to recognise the world's most famous drink. We could do that with your shop, Alison. We could create a distinctive look that people see, a look that makes them say to themselves, 'Ah, Mackies, the best fish and chips in Scotland!'"

Alison looked thrilled by the prospect, sitting up in her seat attentively. "The best fish and chips in Scotland! That would be great.

"Is it a loan, like? The money for making Mackies better?" Now, she sounded sharper.

Tony shook his head and did his best to look as trustworthy as he could. "I see it as more of an investment, Alison. My family and I are very committed to our new hometown. Did Archie tell you my mother's family comes from this area originally?"

He paused, allowing Alison to signal Archie had told her.

"So, I put some money in. You and I become partners, but I'm quite happy to wait for Mackies to start making serious money before I take any share of the profits. I'm sure McArthur, Middleton and Brown can draw up the paperwork for us." He named the small solicitors' office in the town.

Alison buttered the second half of her scone and added some strawberry jam, lifting it up in a toast to Tony.

"Aye, do your worst, Tony. Here's to a new Mackies!"

The next stage of the Tony Walker Project was a dedicated bank account, set up in the name Kirkinwall Enterprises. Tony left Alison imagining a new, prosperous business that drew the crowds and headed across the street for the small bank.

Banks were very different in small towns. Here, people knew you by name, and they smiled. The queues were only ever one person long, as was the case today. Once, the man in front of him had finished, Tony began his usual charm offensive. The teller's name badge said, 'Lucy Anderson'. Tony went for her second name. People were more informal these days, but maybe that was just in London. Best to be safe.

She told him to call her 'Lucy' anyway. Everyone else did.

He explained what he wanted to do—set up a business account and allow two or more people to withdraw from it. The plan was that it would fund several companies after a while. Here was some of the money for it.

And this was the point of no return. Handing over that cheque he'd made out to himself and seeing what Lucy Anderson made of it.

She didn't bat an eyelid.

Lucy led him to a little room, bare and windowless, but furnished in the bank's colours. She pulled out sheets, sliding them across the table to Tony. He could fill in this kind of information in his sleep. Forms successfully filled in, he pushed them back across the table. Lucy widened her eyes then. He was a Lord? Tony flashed her a conspiratorial grin. Yes, he had that title, an ancient one, but he preferred only to use it for paperwork. Otherwise, like Lucy, he wanted her to use his first name.

Lucy nodded at that. Weren't posh people lovely? The credit cards for the account would take a couple of weeks to come through, she said. Did that give him enough time?

Tony told her that was fine. He'd thought ahead about that as well, withdrawing enough cash to allow Alison to begin the refurbishment of Mackies. Now, that young man Daisy liked. Didn't he work for a local painting and decorating firm and wouldn't they appreciate the business?

HEY GORGEOUS, WANNA GO FOR A RIDE?

As she'd promised herself in the car when her mum and dad told her they were thinking of moving the family to Kirkinwall, Daisy had circled the date in red on the calendar in her room.

At the end of each day, she scored out the number. September the fourth didn't change that quickly to September the fifth, and neither did it hurry itself to get to the seventh, the eighth or the ninth of the month. The date of the move felt branded onto her arm, the first thing she thought of when she woke, the last number she saw as she closed her eyes to sleep, the gesture did little anyway.

Press the pen as hard as you like, the seconds, minutes and hours will still string themselves out as slowly as they can.

Nevertheless, there was plenty to do back in London. Daisy was in school for a few weeks, even though it seemed pointless. Then, there was the house to pack up, prepare for strangers coming in. Short-term tenants had been found for their London home. Debbie roped her and Matthew into extensive tidying up duties. If it surprised her that her once sullen teenage daughter did it all without complaining, she didn't say anything.

Tony would lease a flat close to his work and travel up as much as he could. At some point, he hoped to make Kirkinwall his home too.

As Daisy suspected, the letters didn't materialise. Katrina and Kippy must have reckoned they were off the hook. Why write to someone who was about to move to the area anyway? Daisy would have liked a letter or two, especially something from Kippy. She contented herself with a few phone calls, always ones she made rather than received.

But then phone calls were expensive, she told herself. And she was the daughter of a man who made a lot of money.

Katrina made her laugh with stories about the customers at Dulcie's. She'd started her apprenticeship and was hard at work sweeping the floor and making people endless cups of tea. Exciting, it wasn't, she moaned. At this rate, she'd be allowed near a pair of scissors in time to collect her pension.

Frustrating for someone who'd been cutting the hair of anyone who'd let her for the last few years.

The Kippy calls were far more…unsatisfactory. He spent hardly any time at home, for a start. He was out working all day, or he was off somewhere with work. And his leisure time, the hours that haunted Daisy as she imagined predatory girls sliding up to him, their hands and fingers brushing warm, freckly skin. Again, getting hold of him was difficult.

The only way it worked was if he was at Katrina's house or the Braemar B&B.

Their conversations didn't have the jokey ease of her chats with Katrina. She fired questions at him, all trying to elicit how he felt about her and if he was still single.

"What had he been doing? Had he been busy at work? How was Dod? Did he…did he know it was now only three/two/one week until she moved, the newest resident of Kirkinwall…?"

Kippy only became animated when she asked after Dod, relating daft anecdotes about parties he'd thrown, jokes he'd made, ways he'd thwarted the local bobby. She kept up those questions, then, pleased that he sounded so cheerful when she did so. The words flowed smoothly, and the conversation seemed less like the kind of chat a maiden aunt has with her nephew.

Her mum told her to pack lightly, clothes and just whatever else she needed. They would take some, but not all their possessions with them. The London tenants were due to move in a week after the Walkers left.

Daisy didn't sleep the night before. Excitement fizzed through her. In her head, she'd played through her reunion with Kippy countless times. It took various forms. Sometimes they ran through the fields of waist-high corn to meet each other. Or he appeared at her new home, banging furiously on the front door. *Daisy, Daisy are you there?*

She'd even created a scenario where he was on a motorbike, a hulking, exhaust-fumes-spitting beast of a machine that roared into the Harbour car park, spinning around before it came to a stop in front of her. He took off his helmet, shook out his hair and smiled at her lazily. The smile was Dod's, but Daisy gave it to Kippy in this fantasy. His eyes glittered. They swept over Daisy, taking in every bit of her body.

"Hey, gorgeous! Wanna come for a ride?"

Subtle, it wasn't.

Her mum and dad took turns to drive up the motorways and the dual carriageways north, their car followed by the Pickford's' van that held their furniture and the other belongings they needed for their new home. This time, when her mum asked her when she'd last done a blood test, Daisy didn't need to disguise lethargy or aggression.

"Just done one, Mum!" her voice sang out, "and it was all right!"

Thanks to quiet roads and perhaps the force of will of someone desperate to speed the car up, the Walkers made good time. Did the town look different, Daisy asked herself, her face glued to the window?

In her mind, perhaps she'd made a little greener, the skies bluer and the whole more of a shortbread tin picture of a place than it was. Today, the sky was overcast and grey, and she didn't remember the ugly industrial buildings on the outskirts. The tide was out too, and the boats in the harbour looked tired and rusty.

As their car made its way along the High Street to Number 26 the White House, pedestrians watched its progress. The Pickford's van was probably the giveaway, announcing the arrival of new residents.

By the time the car and the van had come to a stop, there was a little crowd outside the White House. Mrs Burnett was one of them, arms folded as usual. Daisy crossed the road.

"Hi, Mrs Burnett! Does Katrina know I'm here?"

And your grandson. Pride held her back from asking that, though.

Mrs Burnett's expression didn't change. She reminded Daisy of those warnings: if you don't change your look, your face will stick that way—an encouragement to always smile. Mrs Burnett wore her habitual grimace.

"Aye, she does. I'll send her along later."

With that, she turned away.

As promised, Katrina appeared later that evening. A knock on the door sounded out at six o'clock. The Walkers were busily unpacking. It turned out that unpacking took longer than packing. There were endless decisions to be made about what went where.

Matthew answered the door. "It's Katrina!" his voice sang out. Daisy gave up on sorting out her books and clothes and ran down the stairs.

"You came!"

Her first sight of the town in six weeks had disappointed. Katrina didn't, though. Her hairstyle was different, the blonde hair tied in a high ponytail, little artfully curled tendrils hanging about her face. She wore black cargo pants and a bright red lace top.

Stood at the bottom of the stairs, Katrina rolled her eyes. "Aye, you daftie! Are you in the top bedroom?"

Daisy's mum and dad had emerged from their own unpacking. "Our first guest!" Tony exclaimed, rubbing his hands together. "Should we do something to mark the occasion?"

Daisy looked at him, horrified. Surely, he didn't mean to hijack her friend's first visit? She and Katrina should spend as little time with her parents as possible.

Debbie took Tony's hand. "Let's leave them to it, Tony," she said. "Why don't you girls both come down at seven o'clock for dinner. Is that okay?"

"Mm-hmm!" Daisy grabbed Katrina's hand and dragged her up the stairs behind her. Katrina complied, dashing up behind her, giggles barely suppressed.

Daisy had commandeered the top floor, just as Katrina had told her weeks ago. Katrina looked around her. The third floor had a bedroom, a bathroom and a living room. All the rooms were tiny, but to Daisy, it felt like a home of her own. Katrina explored, holding out a hand to touch the walls from time to time, and nodding to herself.

She came to a standstill in the middle of the bedroom, its floor covered in Daisy's unpacked clothing, books and music.

"I'll help you decorate," she announced folding her arms in a way that made her look just like her gran. "We could paint this place together, mebbe get Kippy to help if that's no' too much like a busman's holiday for him."

About to object because painting didn't sound fun, Daisy nodded enthusiastically at the mention of Kippy. "Alright then. You choose the colours, right? You and Kippy are artier than me."

It seemed only fair that Katrina should decide how Daisy's new rooms were to look. She was going to spend a lot of time there after all. The house showed off the Walkers wealth; something that didn't make Daisy comfortable.

In London, her friends had all been the same. They too were the daughters of accountants, and lawyers, doctors and company directors, and they lived in homes like Daisy's, complete with garages, driveways, dining rooms and additional bathrooms. Here, she stood out—a too-rich oddity. If telling Daisy what to do with her rooms made Katrina more comfortable around her, it was a tiny price to pay.

Katrina began to pick clothes off the floor, tutting at most of it. There was a small, in-built closet and she hung up tee shirts, jumpers and jackets.

"He's working. You know that, right?" She threw the remark over her shoulder, watching for Daisy's response.

"Oh, yeah?" Daisy's heart soared. She'd been waiting for Kippy to arrive ever since the Walkers' car had pulled up outside Number 26.

"Aye. He's in Ayr. Some big job his firm landed. He'll be back Sunday, though. You just have to put up wi' me until then."

Sunday was two days away, an aeon. On the other hand, hadn't she already waited six weeks? Two days was a blink of the eye. It gave her time to make herself feel like a resident, the kind of girl who hung out in the Harbour Square car park waiting for guys on motorbikes to roar their way into a stop in front of her.

"Good," she said, joining Katrina in front of the closet. "Okay then, I can tell you're dying to do it anyway. What clothes should I throw away and what should I keep? And you'd better tell me about Kirkinwall Academy, seeing as I'm starting there a week on Monday once the October holiday has finished and I'm crapping myself about it."

YOU'RE GOOD, LITTLE MISS

Having stayed with Daisy until 10pm that night, Katrina turned up early the next morning. She had started working at Dulcie's, the hair salon, but she was allowed every fourth Saturday off.

She appeared pushing two bikes, one of which Daisy recognised as Kippy's.

"You won't be cycling too far, will you?" Debbie asked. "If Daisy does too much exercise, it affects her—"

"I know, Mrs Double U! Poor Daisy might have a wee hypo. We're no' going far, I promise. Mebbe she should eat a banana before she goes or something just to be on the safe side. They're dead sweet, aren't they?"

Debbie smiled at her. "That's a smart idea. Daisy?"

Daisy didn't think it was such a great idea, given that bananas gave her the dry heave. There was something about the texture of them, that awful, repellent sliminess.

Nevertheless, she plucked one from the kitchen's new fruit bowl and stuck it in her rucksack, smiling as reassuringly as she could.

Out on the street, she hopped on Kippy's bike and sent a silent thank you to him for the loan he probably knew nothing about.

"What's the plan for today?"

Astride her own bike, Katrina pointed ahead of her. "We're off to find some fun. Follow me."

She set off, pedalling furiously. It looked as if Daisy might need to eat that banana after all. She followed Katrina as she headed down the High Street, along St Mary's Street and out towards the Tongland Bridge.

Ten minutes later, Katrina turned right, up a steep hill that wound its way up from side to side. At the top was a hotel called the Star Tavern, its sign in bright neon and a red T hanging above the door.

The fun bit was not evident.

Katrina got off her bike, leaving it leaning against one of the walls surrounding the hotel's small car park.

"C'mon," she said, dismissing Daisy's question about locking up the bikes.

Daisy followed her around the back of the hotel. It looked prettier than the front; a conservatory looked out onto a large beer garden dotted with tables covered with large umbrellas. The garden was walled, and there were flowers and shrubs in abundance covering the walls. There were no customers, but through the glass, they could see a lone waitress dressed in the regulation black dress with its white collar, cuffs and apron setting out salt, pepper and vinegar on the tables in the conservatory.

Katrina opened the door. "Hiya, Morag!" She took a

condiment tray from the waitress's trolley and put it on one of the tables. "How are you?"

The waitress was about her mother's age, Daisy guessed. The woman gave an exaggerated sigh, pushing her hands into the small of her back.

"Fucking knackered is what I am," she said. "Place was open until 1am last night because we had a dance on. Then, half the locals decided to stay for a lock-in. I've had two hours' sleep. I'm too old for this shite."

"Me and Daisy could finish this off for you," Katrina said. "We could help wi' the prep for lunch too."

Morag studied them both carefully. "Does this one know anything about hotel work?" She pointed at Daisy.

"Aye, she's from London. She's worked in some of the big hotels down there."

Morag looked at Daisy again. Daisy smiled as broadly as she could, hoping Morag wouldn't ask her the names of those so-called big hotels or what she'd done as a supposed waitress.

Morag sighed again and started to remove her apron. "Thanks, Katrina. Mick's in the kitchen. He'll tell you what to do."

And with that, she walked off.

As soon as she was out of earshot, Katrina turned to Daisy. "You don't mind, do you? I help out here sometimes. Morag's a friend of my mum. She helped us a few years ago. Mick's her son. He's just finished catering college."

Something about the way she said 'Mick' made Daisy study her more closely. Katrina had stretched out that one syllable and her voice had softened. Daisy smiled to herself. A little something more to add to her stock of information on Katrina, Kirkinwall's High Princess of Cool.

"No, I don't mind. My mum and dad said they wanted to

unpack and then do a bit of exploring. I didn't fancy that." She quite liked the idea of helping a hotel prepare lunch for its guests. A part-time job was something else Debbie had ruled as out of the question when diabetes came along.

They finished putting the salt and pepper on the tables. Katrina led the way into the hotel, which smelled overwhelmingly of old cigarette smoke. Underneath that, Daisy made out cooking smells. The conservatory was in front of a lounge bar, velvet-covered chairs and stools surrounding tables of four, and dark wood panelled walls. It was warm and cosy, the type of place you could imagine people wanting to overstay their welcome.

From there, they made their way down a small corridor to a door marked staff only. Behind it was the kitchen, a radio blaring within.

"You shouldnae be smoking in here!"

The chef—Mick, Daisy guessed—was a bit older than them. He wore chef's whites over jeans, a lit roll-up between his lips as he sliced onions in record time.

He took the roll-up out. "I'm not smoking," he said. "This is for medicinal purposes. Do you want a bit?" He held the roll-up out to Katrina, who shook her head. "Not just now. We're here to help you out. Me and my new pal, Daisy. Your ma's knackered."

Katrina's voice had changed slightly again, and she hadn't taken her eyes off Mick. Even with her devotion to Katrina's cousin, Daisy could appreciate that Mick was the best-looking guy she'd ever seen. He was tall, the same height as Kippy, and he shared his mother's blonde hair and blue eyes. The tendons in his forearms rippled as he continued to chop onions, the movement oddly mesmerising.

"Help me out?" Mick leant back against the table and

took another drag on his roll-up. He looked them both up and down, a lazy, lascivious sweep of the eyes that lingered too long at chest height.

"Okay, put pinnies on," he pointed at aprons hanging on a hook on the door, "and wash your hands. You can peel potatoes and chop them up into chips. Make sure they're thick cut."

Surprisingly, it did turn out to be fun. Daisy and Katrina sang along to the music on the radio, Mick poking fun at their taste in music. He named obscure bands and then mocked them for not having heard of the musicians. He made himself another joint when he finished the first one, but Katrina refused the offer once more, to Daisy's relief. She needn't feel obliged to either, and she had no wish to make a fool of herself.

"I'm gonnae try out a new dish of the day today," Mick said. "Would you two taste it for me?"

The dish he presented to them looked beautiful, reminding Daisy of the food you got in French restaurants. When she told him this, the grin he gave her split his face in two. The dish was seafood crepes, thin pancakes folded over a creamy sauce with prawns and scallops and garnished with watercress in a balsamic dressing.

Daisy took a generous forkful. It was as delicious as it looked, and she didn't need any encouragement to take another mouthful. Katrina's response wasn't quite as enthusiastic, but she told Mick the dish was great anyway.

"Are you from London?" Mick asked Daisy, who nodded. "Do you think people in London would like that dish?"

It was easy enough to work out what he wanted her to say. "Totally."

"Mick wants to go to London. Be a famous chef in one of those Michelin-starred restaurants there," Katrina piped up.

That was where he triumphed over Dod, Daisy guessed. Here was someone else who had big dreams of going to the city.

Morag had wandered into the kitchen. She helped herself to some of the seafood pancakes. "Needs a wee bit more salt and pepper," she said. "We'll be lucky if we sell two of these. Naebody wants this stuff. They want fish and chips, or pie and chips. And that's it."

She turned to Katrina and Daisy. "You two helping with the lunchtime rush, then?"

Stood next to Daisy, Katrina gave her a discreet nudge. "Aye!"

Morag nodded. "Okay, thanks. There are some spare uniforms in the cupboard. And tie your hair back too."

Morag's prediction proved right—at least for the first half-hour. None of the lunchtime customers looked at the specials board and asked for the seafood pancakes.

When a large group of well-fed and well-dressed old men came in, Daisy pounced.

"Hello, gentlemen! Isn't it a beautiful day?" Her mum and dad might claim not to recognise this super-charming version of their daughter.

A large man dressed in an old-fashioned tweed suit and smelling strongly of pipes beamed at her.

"It is indeed, young lady! We've not seen you here before?"

"I'm new," Daisy said, "just like today's menu! Our chef has been working hard all morning to prepare new and delicious dishes for you to try out!"

Across the room, she saw Katrina stare at her, incredulous at first and then grinning broadly.

The large man looked at his companions and back at Daisy. "Well, young lady we usually go for the steak pie. Do you want to recommend something else?"

Daisy nodded vigorously. "Can I suggest the chef's seafood pancakes? They're made from the freshest, local seafood encased in a creamy sauce. I had them for lunch myself, and I thought I'd died and gone to heaven."

Morag had joined Katrina. Both were shaking their heads.

The large man smiled. "Seafood pancakes, eh? And what would you recommend we drink with them? Usually, we all have a pint of 80 Shillings with our pies. I'm not sure that would be the best choice for seafood pancakes."

There were snickers from the man's companions.

Daisy smiled at them all and plucked the menu from the large man's hands. Tony was an incredible wine snob. He made a great fuss of choosing wine whenever they were in French restaurants. If you could order a bottle of white wine from a French sommelier and not have him sneer at you, you were doing well he always said.

"Well, sir, I recommend the white Burgundy," she replied, crossing her fingers behind her back. "It's a good partner for the creaminess of the sauce."

As it happened, the white Burgundy was the most expensive wine on the list.

The large man took the menu back from her. He narrowed his eyes, fixing Daisy with a gimlet-eyed look.

"Oh, you're good, young Miss!" he said. "Two bottles of white Burgundy, then. I hope this dish lives up to expectations."

Most of the table ordered the seafood pancakes, apart from one man, who told Daisy apologetically that seafood always repeated on him.

Back in the kitchen, Daisy leant back against the door and let out a deep breath.

"Top London hotels, eh?" Morag said. "You know that man's a councillor, aye? Councillor Murdoch, the local Tory.

He's the stingiest bugger there is. He'll put the bill down as expenses."

She left the room, taking a large set of keys with her, muttering that she couldn't remember the last time anyone ordered white Burgundy and wondering if it was still drinkable.

"Thank you!" Mick picked her up and whirled her round, as much as it was possible to do so in a confined space. He was surprisingly strong.

He planted a kiss on her cheek before setting her down. Anxious that Katrina wouldn't read anything into it, Daisy stepped away from him quickly.

"They havenae said they liked it yet," Katrina said, her eyes boring into him.

Mick scowled at her. "Shut up, Catty."

She stuck her tongue out, and he slapped her arse. It looked like a hard slap to Daisy, but Katrina only smirked.

They left the hotel an hour later, leaving Mick whistling happily to himself as he cleared up. He'd sold ten times the number of seafood pancakes his mother had predicted. The hotel's guests that afternoon had included a French family who'd eaten the pancakes, their eyes round in wonder. British food had a terrible reputation in France, Daisy knew. The Frenchies must have got the shock of their lives when they bit into Mick's pancakes.

"Tell your mum and dad I took you on a tour of the countryside," Katrina said, as she threw a thin leg over her bike. "We cycled for an hour or so, and then did some walking. They'll like that."

"So, I don't tell them you made me work for free next to a chef who was smoking weed and who kept offering us a toke, then?"

Katrina stared at her, and then laughed when she realised Daisy was joking. "Aye, best not to, eh?"

A TRIP AND A FAVOUR

The cycle ride back was marginally more comfortable, start-ing as it did downhill. It was still a challenge to keep up with Katrina who cycled as if she was jet-fuelled, and in no time the gap between her and Daisy widened.

A horn beeped loudly as a van sailed past her, almost making her fall off her bike. An arm waved at her from the passenger side, but the vehicle didn't stop. It beeped again at Katrina when it passed her.

Katrina stopped her bike to wait for Daisy to catch up.

"That was Kippy," she said. "They must have got that job fin-ished early. We can stop at his work on the way back. Want to?"

Yes and no. Yes, Daisy was desperate to see him, but all her happy imaginings of their romantic reunion hadn't looked like this. At the very least, she should be dressed in her most flattering outfit and wearing some make-up.

Kippy, Kippy, Kippy.

"Okay then." She'd just recovered her breath. The thump-ing heart was still there, though, its thuds joined by weird fluttering's in her belly. She gripped the handlebars hard, try-ing to stop the trembling.

Katrina turned right ahead of her, cycling past the houses and down towards the industrial estate. She had slowed, allowing Daisy to keep up with her. They stopped outside McCallum's Painting & Decorating portable cabin. The van was parked alongside, its back door wide open.

Kippy got out of the passenger seat of the van. He wore his painting gear—those dirty white overalls splashed with various paint colours. As if he'd sensed her, he looked straight over to where she was, a slow smile starting up.

He held up two fingers, signifying how long he'd take, and she nodded. The heart thumping hadn't stopped, and she shivered, cold and unbearably excited.

Having dumped tins of paint, brushes and ladders in the cabin, he wandered over.

"Hey. You're back then." He stood in front of her, and the view of him shimmered in front of her. She had to fight the inclination to put a hand over her eyes so that she could stare at him properly. He looked much, much better than she remembered.

"Yes. It's brilliant to see you."

The words fell into the space between them. Daisy wished she could take them back. She suspected Katrina was rolling her eyes.

"It's good to see you too." At that, he opened his arms wide, and Daisy fell into them gratefully. There was that smell she remembered, paint, turps, washing powder and Lynx. She took big sniffs of it and let it transport her straight back to the beach and the summer. And what she had done to him at the time. Did he think of that too, now he held her in his arms and was she expected to…?

Oh. Love. Boys. Guys and what they think. Trying to make sure your inside self never pushed past your outer layer and started embarrassing you. Who knew?

He dropped a kiss on her head. "I see you nicked my bike again."

"Oh, er... sorry about that, I—

He laughed at her then, telling her he wasn't bothered, and he was ninety-nine percent sure he knew whose idea that had been. Katrina screwed up her face. "Aye, whatever. Guilty as charged."

He pointed at the van. "I told Lenny, the boss, I'd go to the cash and carry for him, pick up supplies. Do you want to come with me?"

"Yes," Katrina said. "Your Royal Highness?"

Daisy hovered uncertainly. She did, of course, but she'd already been away from home for five hours. Her mother was probably frantic by now. Admitting you had to check in and get permission, though; mortifying.

"We'll take the bikes back first," Katrina announced, "then, you can come and pick us up. At the top of the High Street."

Kippy mumbled a few 'bossy boots' comments, but agreed, saying he'd meet them in five minutes.

Cycling as fast as she could to catch up with Katrina, Daisy saw her stop ahead outside Number 26.

"Thought we'd better tell your ma where you're off to."

She was in the White House before Daisy could object. Yes, Debbie needed to know Daisy hadn't collapsed in a fainting fit somewhere, but she was hardly going to like her daughter disappearing in a van with a young driver who fancied himself as Stirling Moss.

She needn't have worried. Debbie received an edited

version of the truth. Katrina's mum had offered them a lift to Dumfries. They were going to mooch around the shops, and they'd be back later. In time for Daisy's tea, Mrs Double U. I guarantee it.

To seal the deal, she produced the unopened packet of blackcurrant Dextrosol tablets she'd bought for Daisy in the summer, promising she'd keep observing Daisy carefully. Debbie nodded reluctantly, calling out that dinner was at seven pm and they'd booked a table at Bella Italia.

The engine revving impatiently, Kippy and the van were parked down one of the little side streets, thankfully out of sight of the White House. Katrina opened the passenger side door, bowing and sweeping her arm forward. Daisy was obviously meant to sit next to Kippy.

Kippy had since passed his test, Katrina told her. His driving, however, was no less scary. Daisy watched the needle on the speedometer sail way past 70mph as they left the town. Just like before, he hurled the van at corners full throttle, changing the gear only at the last minute and accelerating out of them so fast, Daisy found herself thrown against him repeatedly.

He shifted the first time she did it and then didn't bother, a small smile playing on his lips. Underneath the overalls, he wore a tee shirt, and Daisy found herself studying his bare arms. They were as liberally freckled as his face and coated in fine hairs. When the van jolted again, she allowed her arm to touch his. The skin felt hot.

As they approached Dumfries, Katrina told her cousin he could drop her and Daisy off at the town centre so that they could go to the shops. There was even a Next here, Katrina told Daisy, her voice suggesting that was impressive.

"I need someone to come wi' me," Kippy said. "Help me

load up the van."

Katrina wrinkled her nose. "Not me! Daisy will go with you."

Perhaps she'd read Daisy's mind. When Kippy said he needed assistance, she'd held her breath. Wandering around a store looking for paint had never seemed as exciting.

Katrina dropped off with a promise to pick her up in an hour's time. Daisy found her hands shaking as she got back in the van. What should she say to him? She racked her brains and wished she knew more about football, usually a fail-safe topic to discuss with guys. The more important thing, however, was getting Kippy to kiss her, or hold her hand. Something that felt more solidly 'boyfriend' than a hug and the faint press of lips to her head.

Kippy didn't seem that bothered about talking. He smiled at her briefly when she got back in the van and then drove off. They headed back out of the town and to an industrial estate.

The car park outside the cash and carry was busy. As Kippy locked the van, his eyes narrowed. Following his gaze, Daisy spotted two guys also wearing paint-splashed overalls making their way across the car park towards them.

Kippy moved closer to Daisy, startling her when he draped an arm around her shoulder.

"Do me a favour, aye?" He whispered the words.

"Kippy, man!"

Up close, Daisy realised the two men were about Kippy's age. They were grinning at him, but the smiles had a wolfish quality to them that felt threatening.

"Davy. Ewan. How's it goin'?" Kippy's voice sounded clipped. The arm around Daisy pulled her closer.

"Fine, aye," The one called Davy said. "Who's this, then?" He nodded at Daisy, not taking his eyes off Kippy.

"Ma girlfriend. Daisy."

Gosh. Goodness. Great. She supposed that was what the arm around her was meant to show but hearing Kippy saying 'girlfriend' was lovely. She'd asked for proof, and she had it. But, what did you do when someone introduced you as his girlfriend? Again, this wasn't a familiar situation for Daisy. She decided to go with a general introductory phrase.

"How do you do?"

They grinned even more at that.

"What are you, the Queen?" Davy smirked. "Mind you, if anyone likes a queen, it's this one." He'd turned away from Daisy and stood, so he faced Kippy.

Kippy scowled at him. "Aye, whatever."

To Daisy, it seemed like the four of them were stuck firm, their feet planted in the ground as the air stilled around them. Something was wrong, and they needed rescuing. Kippy had asked her to do him a favour, after all. Helping him would surely make him like her even more, wouldn't it?

Daisy shifted her head, the movement drawing she and Kippy tighter together. His hand brushed against her breast, and she watched Davy's eyes fasten there too.

She stepped out from under Kippy's arm and took his hand. "C'mon then, let's get the paint, Kippy, you big stud. Then you can take me to bed or lose me forever."

She'd always wanted to use that Top Gun line.

It worked. Davy and Ewan's eyes widened. Davy's jaw even dropped open.

Inside the store, Kippy let go of her hand. "Thanks for that," he muttered. "I was at college with those two for the painting apprenticeship. They were always taking the mickey out o' me."

He flushed, the pink making him look even better—his eyes whiter and more prominent.

Why did they take the mickey out of him? The admission made him seem less scary. No that wasn't right. Daisy wasn't scared of him, but she wasn't used to eighteen-year-old young men. Her incarceration at St Mary's School for Girls since the age of eleven hadn't equipped her for boys. How did they work? What did they think? When he told her that other people had made fun of him at college, she felt better.

The male species? They're not that different after all.

"Anytime!" Daisy said, and then cursed herself. Did she sound too keen?

Kippy had taken one of the large trolleys and was pushing it towards the paint supplies section.

"Am I…am I your girlfriend, then?" He'd sounded so definite when he'd said it a few minutes ago, but Daisy wanted it confirmed. People often said different things in front of others.

"Do you want to be?" He threw the question over his shoulder, turning his head too quickly for her to work out his expression.

"Yes, I do."

Kippy had stopped in front of a display of gloss paints, picking up and putting down cans. Having found what he was looking for, he moved in front of Daisy and pulled her into him, so that her head was pushed up against his chest. She could hear the thumps of his heart. Did it echo her own, the fright she'd experienced when she said 'yes', and he didn't reply?

"There's a wee vacancy for a girlfriend in ma life. You can fill it if ye want." A whisper, the words muffled in her hair.

He let go of her too quickly, but the moment had scattered itself like magic dust all over Daisy. She glittered and glowed.

THE ART GUY

Love made you a much better person, Daisy realised.

Now, she was the sort of girl who spent the whole of the next day helping her parents unpack the various boxes and bags they'd brought with them. It made her smile and giggle a lot, and it even induced her to play board games with her little brother, even when he insisted everyone play Monopoly for the fourth time in just two days.

The family togetherness lasted until Monday evening. "Pick me up at Dulcie's just after five," Katrina said. "And then we'll go and meet Kippy."

Just as well she had Katrina organising her love life for her. Kippy hadn't said anything about meeting up again, and Daisy didn't yet remember her new phone number so that she could force it on him.

She had her bicycle with her, but she walked alongside Daisy as they headed for the industrial estate. Kippy and another worker strode out of the cabin bang on five thirty. They wore the air of people who'd been let out of jail.

Daisy observed him, checking out his reaction as he saw her. Gratifyingly, he looked pleased, parting from his mate as he strode over to them.

Stood in front of them, Daisy wondered if he should kiss her or something. Should she kiss him? She stepped forward, pushing herself towards him trying to kiss his cheek, just as he had done the other day.

At the last minute, he moved out of the way, turning to grab his bike from where it was fastened to a railing. Daisy stumbled forward clumsily into the space he had left. She felt herself become red-hot, an uncomfortable heat that rose from her gut up her chest, neck and cheeks.

Kippy whirled around. "Are you okay?" Thankfully, he didn't seem to have noticed the attempted kiss. Katrina, though, wore a hyena grin. She pushed her lips out, an exaggerated pout that was clearly meant to be an impression of a kiss. Daisy shot her a dirty look.

"Want to do something with us, Kippy?" Katrina asked, to Daisy's relief.

About to swing his leg over his bike, Kippy paused. "Aye, alright then. But I need to drop a bottle of turps off somewhere first."

"Fine. We'll come too. You can give Daisy a backie."

Backies, or riding behind someone on a bicycle were much harder than they looked. But the thrill of it was something else. Every hundred yards or so, the bike wobbled and Daisy and Kippy would both fall to the left or the right, legs jerking out to stop them clattering to the ground.

It broke the ice. Daisy found herself laughing hysterically, while Katrina mocked them both. If Daisy'd taken a backie from her, she said, they'd have been there in half the time.

Pressed up against his back and clinging on as tightly

as she could, Daisy relished the closeness. The smell of him flooded her senses and the bones of his back pushed against her, moving continuously as the pedals whirled round.

They'd gone past the primary school and all the shops on St Mary's Street. Kippy had yelled out to Katrina, who was in front, as usual, telling her to turn left. He headed up a hill, the slower pace of it making the bike steadier.

Even so, it was a remarkable feat of endurance to be able to bike up a hill with someone else's weight behind you. Daisy found herself blushing. He was panting hard, probably wishing he didn't have such a heavy lump behind him.

He stopped two houses before the top of the hill. They were in a nice bit of town, Daisy reckoned. It overlooked the river, fields enclosed by trees to the right and panoramic views all around. The house he'd stopped in front of was huge. It had a sweeping driveway, a double garage and was three storeys high.

Katrina had dropped her bike just in front of the iron gate. There was a deliberate thud to the drop, the bike pushed down and abandoned in an exaggerated way. Contemptuous, even.

"What are we doin' here?" she asked. "I hate Snob Hill."

Kippy, his breath still coming in pants from the upward climb, reached into his pocket and pulled out a key.

"This is Aul' Carlton's place. He gave me the keys."

As explanations went, it told Daisy nothing. But Katrina nodded at it, holding her hand out for the key. "Cannae wait to see this."

Inside, the place was beautiful. Daisy had been worried about how posh her new place looked to Katrina, but Aul' Carlton (whoever he was) seemed to be the owner of a *Hello!* magazine home. They walked past paintings on walls, on tiled marble flooring that made footsteps echo, deep noisy clacks.

Kippy seemed to know his way around. The hallway segued into a central space, light dusting of paintings, ornaments mounted on plinths and sumptuous fabrics draped everywhere. A spiral staircase dominated the place, the top of it illuminated by an atrium.

"Fuck me!" Katrina said, "I had nae idea Aul' Carlton was that rich." She fingered the velvet drapes that hung below a brass model of an otter standing on its hind legs. The otter was firmly attached to its stand. Otherwise, Daisy wouldn't have fancied its chances of remaining there.

"Son of some lord," Kippy said. "Carlton isnae his real name. His father didnae like him very much when he was alive, but when he died, he didnae have any other weans, so all the money went to Aul' Carlton anyway."

He pointed at the staircase. "Up here. I need to clean some paint brushes."

Daisy and Katrina followed him up the stairs, up past the first floor and the second. At the top, he turned right and along a narrow corridor, its décor and carpet not quite as luxurious as the floors below.

He came to a halt at a narrow set of stairs. "The attic, aye?"

Daisy had stopped so abruptly Katrina bumped into the back of her. "What's up there?" she squawked, mortified when they both turned, astonished at the sound of fright.

Katrina reached for the stair rail. "Flowers in the Attic, probably. Brothers shagging sisters all locked up there, while their nasty granny and papa whip them."

She narrowed her eyes and moved in front of Daisy. "Sinners!"

It was bellowed out so loudly the only thing Daisy could do was burst into hysterical laughter. Of course, she'd sneaked the *Flowers in the Attic* book out of her mother's bedroom. And read the incest bit, appalled and fascinated at the same time.

Did that really—was that even—

They followed Kippy up the narrow staircase. The luxury thing had vanished completely. Here, the wallpaper flaked from the wall and the carpet was threadbare. At the top, Kippy pushed open an old, wooden door, its surface tattooed with wide open grooves.

He flicked a light. They were in what looked like a studio. A skylight added illumination to wooden floors flecked with tiny splotches of paint. Canvases in makeshift frames leant against the walls, face down, so the pictures weren't visible.

"Oh, we are honoured, Miss Daisy!" Katrina exclaimed hands held palms out. She spun around, the outline of her body picked out by the setting sun that let itself die out through the skylight.

"We are in," she faced Daisy, "Kippy's studio. Get us!"

"Sod off, you wee bitch!" Kippy had whirled, his position changing from staring up at the skylight to glaring at his cousin.

"Ooh-ooh, woah. I'm so sorry, Princess."

If ever there was someone who looked least like the picture of apologetic, she stood in front of Daisy now. Katrina had rolled her eyes repeatedly, folded and unfolded her arms several times and let out plenty of deep sighs.

Meanwhile, Kippy scouted the room, picking up the odd chalk that lay on the floor, and turning any painting that faced outwards towards the walls, and putting brushes into jam jars he filled with the turps.

"My cousin here," Katrina's voiced dripped sarcasm and

scorn, "thinks he's a real painter, not a painter and decorator. An art guy, like."

Daisy took in the canvases, the dripped paint floors and the easel in the corner. Well, duh. Shoulda, woulda, coulda saw it sooner. Kippy, there in the middle of the room, moved lightly from foot to foot, dancing his way about the studio. Maybe he needed a paintbrush in hand and then he'd bounce higher, waiting to paint his next masterstroke.

She called out, sort of brave. "You like drawing and painting, then?"

Kippy nodded.

"Aul' Carlton was the art teacher," Katrina added. "He was devastated when his star pupil said he wasn't going to art school." She smirked. "The old perv fancied you, didn't he?"

Kippy flushed and swore at her again.

Daisy recognised furious denial when she heard it. Maybe Kippy had suffered the same problem as she had at her all-girls school—that ever-necessary need to deny you were gay. Even being the subject of an old man's lust was suspect.

Aul' Carlton had retired, it turned out. He spent his winters in the south of France and had told Kippy he was free to use the studio during those months.

There was an easel in the corner, covered with a sheet. Kippy refused to let Daisy or Katrina lift it up, muttering about work in progress.

Daisy pulled forward one of the canvases leaning against the wall, turning it so she could look at it properly.

"God, these are amazing! I mean it." Daisy had thought she might have to fake enthusiasm for Kippy's work, but there was no need.

Kippy didn't do landscapes, but he painted lots of scenes from Kirkinwall. From her short acquaintance with the town, Daisy recognised a lot of them. They were like cartoons, but great ones.

Here, people were sitting on a picnic bench on the Moat Brae, the boats anchored in the harbour. There was the bridge, lined with people watching boys jump off into the river. In another, people queued outside Mackies, the fish and chip shop.

She loved that one. It was full of detail—people talking to each other as they queued. She thought she recognised some of the faces. The old woman with her arms firmly folded was Mrs Burnett, surely? He'd even painted a fat ginger and white cat in that one, running off with a large fish in its mouth.

"Do you like my stuff?" Kippy asked, his voice low doubtless to prevent his cousin hearing.

"Yes," Daisy said. "I think you're brilliant." She placed the canvases carefully back against the wall.

Katrina held a smaller picture in her hands, her eyebrows raised. "This is an interesting one. You havenae got the tattoo right, though."

At that, Kippy tried to grab the picture from her. Katrina laughed, holding the drawing behind her back and standing against the wall to stop him taking it from her. She slid it out from behind her and passed it to Daisy.

"What do you think, Daisy?"

Oh. Goodness. The picture wasn't what Daisy had been expecting. It was a charcoal sketch of Dod—the lines blurred and yet the outline so vivid against the paper, the figure almost leapt out. He was slouched in a chair, smoking a roll-up. Daisy recognised the half-closed eyes and the lazy grin, perhaps the most distinctive part of him.

He was also half-naked. He wore overalls that had been turned down at the waist. The tattoo Katrina mentioned was an anchor. It covered his chest and came half-way down his stomach. The overalls were low down, so low that Daisy wondered if the dark shading there was supposed to be pubic hair.

"Don't take the mick," Kippy said, grabbing the paper out of Daisy's hand. "Aul' Carlton telt me I needed to do life pictures, right? Dod wouldnae strip completely, so I draw him like that. He doesnae mind posing anyway. He smokes and starts talking shite. I have to concentrate on what I'm doing so I dinnae say anything and just let him speak."

"Perfect for the both of you then," Katrina said. "I've had enough art. Let's go." She began to descend the stairs, beckoning Daisy and Kippy to come with her.

Out on the street, Daisy asked Kippy what he liked about painting. Her art classes at school hadn't been enjoyable, but she remembered liking still life, putting together little tableaus of what their teacher called representations of their lives and finding ways to reproduce them.

"People," he answered at once. "You could line a hundred folks up and find something different in all of them, even if we are a' Jock Tamson's Bairns."

He grinned at Daisy's confusion. "We're a' the same. Mind, I think mebbe you'd be better to draw than Dod."

Katrina turned around to face them. "Watch out, Daisy. He's trying to get you to strip off, the dirty sod!"

Kippy only smirked, smacking his cousin lightly on the back of the head. "Dinnae listen to her. She's only jealous, 'cause I've never asked her to model for me. She's too ugly."

Katrina stuck her tongue out, the confidence of someone who could tell a blatant lie when she heard it.

Daisy smiled at Kippy, her mind distracted by the 'trying

to get you to strip off' comment. Was that the case, oh please yes? If she were brave, she could use this opportunity to offer him the life painting experience he needed. *"I wouldn't mind stripping naked for you, Kippy!"* she heard the courageous part of her say. *"I'll take everything off, not just my top half."*

"No, don't, Daisy!" *the imaginary Kippy said back to her.* "I *don't know if I'll be able to control myself."*

The words stayed in her head.

THE INNER CIRCLE, KEN?

She spent most of her evenings the following week with Katrina. Frustratingly, Kippy headed off to Glasgow on the Tuesday for another big job. This time, though, he did arrange something with Daisy.

"I'm back Friday night. Dod's not out on the boat, either," he said, dropping his arms and stepping back. "His mum and dad are away, so he's got an empty again. We could go there. You coming?"

He asked his cousin too, and Daisy pushed down an unworthy feeling of disappointment. She had hoped that their reunion on Friday might be more personal and intimate, involving just the two of them. On the other hand, wouldn't it be lovely to spend the evening with friends?

"I'll see if Mick can come too," Katrina said, her words a little too casual.

Kippy stared at her hard. "Aw, c'mon. That's rubbing

Dod's face in it, isn't it? It's no' fair to him. Anyway, Mick'll be working."

She looked as if she wanted to argue with him but then changed her mind.

Number 26 seemed to take a long time to furnish just as Debbie wanted it to look. Tony left on Friday morning, as he needed to sort out his new living arrangements in London. Their former home had been rented out, and he wanted to find a flat somewhere near his workplace.

"I'll need to work for a few more months," he told them all. "But I'll come up here as often as I can. And fingers crossed, I'll be able to move up here permanently at some point."

Debbie relaxed her grip on Daisy, but Daisy helped around the house as much as possible. She went to the antique shop with her mum and helped pick out some quaint shelving and chests of drawers for the rooms. They visited the local primary school where the kindly Mrs Sharp catching up on paperwork while the children were on holiday made them very welcome and asked Matthew lots of questions.

Daisy half-wished she was going there herself. It seemed far less intimidating a prospect than starting a new secondary school. Her arrival there had been sorted out by phone weeks beforehand, the call lasting a long time as Debbie went through the logistics of moving someone who'd studied in another country and ensuring her daughter missed nothing out.

"Can I go to Katrina's on Friday night?" Daisy asked her mum as they washed yet another batch of unpacked glasses. She crossed her fingers behind her back, figuring it was better not to tell her about Dod and his empty house.

Her mum moved onto stacking plates in the cupboards above the sinks. "Just Katrina, eh?"

Throw the dog a bone.

"Um, I think her cousin Kippy, Alan that is, will be there too. I quite like him."

"Are you courting, then?"

Honestly, who said that these days? Courting. Maybe Daisy should call Kippy her gentleman caller from now on. That might be an idea. Gentleman callers sounded very respectable; they were not the kind of guys who drank, smoke and asked for hand-jobs in deserted car parks.

"Yeah, I think so."

To her surprise, her mum hugged her at that. "It's difficult to work out what young men think, isn't it?" and Daisy found herself nodding along. Difficult? Impossible, she reckoned, but maybe this was universal. All over the country, teenage girls looked at the faces in front of them, screwed up their own and wished they could read those minds.

"Oh, go on then," Debbie said as she released her. "Make sure you take your stuff with you and don't forget–"

"My Dextrosol, I know. I'll be back by half-ten, eleven?"

Dod's old banger of a car parked a safe distance from the house. Although he only lived a ten-minute walk away, Katrina had insisted he pick her and Daisy up, chauffeur style. She sat in the back of the car, patting the seat beside her. Kippy was in the front next to Dod.

Gratifyingly, Dod appeared pleased to see Daisy.

"Your Royal Highness! Ye've come back to join the inner circle, aye?" he asked. When she agreed, yes, she had, he said they were really thrilled to see her. Kippy flashed her a grin that Daisy hoped meant the same too.

Dod favoured the same mad driving style as Kippy, and they were back at his house in minutes. It looked entirely different without the hordes of people as if it was somehow smaller, rather than larger. He let them all in the door. The floors felt sticky underneath, and there were empty bottles and cans, full ashtrays and dirty plates everywhere. He appeared to have been making the most of his parents' absence.

Dod opened the kitchen door out into the small garden. Although it was mid-October, the temperature was warm enough for them to sit outside. The garden was in the same state as the inside of the house—empty cans and bottles, cigarette butts littering the pathway and a lawn badly in need of a cut.

"When's your ma and pa back, Dod?" Kippy asked over his shoulder as he kicked his way through the cans and bottles.

Dod shrugged. "Monday. Ah've got loads of time to tidy up. Eh…" he glanced hopefully at Katrina and Daisy, "Ah don't s'pose…?"

Katrina pushed her way past him, plonking herself down beside Kippy and beckoning Daisy to join them.

"You don't s'pose right, Dod. Daisy and me will not be helping you tidy up this mess. It's dead sexist to ask us just because we're lassies."

He shrugged. "Worth a try." He sat down too, taking a packet out of his pocket and smiling at them all.

"Anyone want to get stoned?"

In for a penny.

"I haven't smoked weed before!" Daisy burst out, then cursed herself for being so uncool.

Dod grinned at her. "Ah didnae think you had, your ladyship. We want tae welcome you to the inner circle, ken? Even if you do have funny ideas about boats and what you do on them." He burst out laughing at that.

"And luckily, you're with a master who'll see you right."

He winked, his tongue darting out to lick the edge of a cigarette paper he joined to another one and laid flat on the ground in front of him.

Katrina pushed herself up from lying back on her elbows. "I don't think she should. Daisy's got this health condition, and I'm supposed to be looking after her."

If Daisy had closed her eyes just there, she might have thought Katrina was her mother. She suddenly wanted to try drugs very much indeed. On the other hand, what if she did it wrong? And made a fool of herself in front of Kippy, gorgeous Kippy? Kippy's expression was impossible to read. She couldn't work out the look he gave her meant, *"yes, try it"*, or *"I don't care if you do or you don't"*.

Katrina sighed. "Okay, well I've got a plan B. First, you must do a blood test, Daisy."

The blood test intrigued Kippy and Dod, who both wanted to try pricking their own fingers with her lancing device. A macho thing, Daisy guessed. It was a safe bet they pretended it didn't hurt too.

"Between four and eight!" She held the stick up triumphantly, evidence of blood sugar levels in the normal range. Katrina snatched the bottle with its comparison chart from her and checked the stick herself.

"Okay then. Second, you're no' going back to the White House tonight. Can I use your phone, Dod?"

He nodded, and she got to her feet. "Daisy, I'm going to speak to your mum. I'll tell her you're staying with me tonight."

Daisy followed Katrina into the house and the hallway. Katrina held the receiver to her chest as she waited for someone to pick up. "Trust me. But you'll need to speak to her too."

Her voice changed, the words coming out breathy and girly. "Mrs Double U? It's Katrina here. I hope you and Mr Double U are settling in fine to your new life in Kirkinwall."

There was a short silence, and some mmm-hmm's from Katrina.

"Mrs Walker, can Daisy stay with me tonight? We're going to watch Pretty Woman and do face masks. I know I've got to be careful, Mrs Double U. I just made Daisy do a blood test and guess what it was!"

Another pause.

"It was between four and eight! I'll make her do a blood test before she goes to bed tonight too. I'll make sure she eats right too. What should she have for her tea? Baked potatoes? I can do that."

Daisy counted silently, one, two, three…

"Aye, she's here! I'll hand her over."

Katrina winked and passed the receiver over. Daisy found her mum remarkably relaxed. Maybe she'd had a glass of wine or two, and all the usual worries she experienced when it came to her oldest child had vanished. She made Daisy promise to do lots of blood tests, but she didn't ask for Katrina's phone number.

Thankfully. Seeing as Daisy wasn't actually at Katrina's house.

With a final admonishment to make sure Daisy kept a jar of jam beside her when she went to bed, jam being useful if you woke up in the middle of the night with low blood sugar levels, Debbie agreed, astonishing her daughter. Daisy had expected a firm 'no' and an order to be home by half-nine.

It had been far simpler than Daisy would have guessed.

Katrina high-fived her as she came off the phone. That wasn't enough for Daisy. She flung her arms around Katrina.

"Thank you, thank you, thank you!"

"Get off me! You're no' at your all-girls school now." Nevertheless, Katrina looked pleased. Her eyes glittered, and she couldn't stop a big grin.

Outside, Dod was talking about a Prodigy gig next month he wanted to go to in the nearby big town, Kippy joining in with how they would get there and who else was going. They looked up as Daisy and Katrina joined them, Kippy raising his eyebrows in a question.

"Plan B is go," Katrina said, dropping down beside them. As Daisy sat down next to her, she nudged her hard. "Let the debauchery begin!"

PLAN B

Daisy couldn't help herself. As plan B began to unfurl itself, what she thought about the most was…

…how worldly-wise she would seem to Lisa and Dana. And not just Lisa and Dana. St Mary's School for Girls had a strict hierarchy. At the top of it was lower sixth, not the oldest girls in the school, but the ones in the first year of AS and A levels. They were worldly-wise girls. They ignored the school's no make-up rule, adjusted their uniforms, shortening skirts and dumping ties in bins, and skived off lessons to queue for gig tickets.

Daisy totted up what she'd done over the last few months. *"I went to a party where people were doing drugs. And a girl was giving a boy a blow job in the garden in front of everyone. I pretended to be a waitress and made an important man spend lots of money."*

The internal voice said the next bit more quietly. *"A gorgeous guy snogged me. I figured out how to make him…very happy."*

And now she was about to do drugs. Her coolness

quotient was about to explode, surely?

Creating the perfect joint was apparently a serious business. Daisy, Katrina and Kippy watched in silence as Dod took out a small, brown lump and flicked his lighter. It looked precarious to Daisy, the flames dangerously close to his fingers. Seconds later, he put the lighter down and rubbed the lump, tiny grains flaking off and into the tobacco he'd put on Rizla papers.

He rolled the paper incredibly slowly, stopping and starting. "God, sometime this century would be fantastic, Dod," Katrina muttered. The utterance had no effect on their host, who told her you couldn't rush greatness.

At last the joint was ready. And their little group had company.

"Are ye smokin', Dod?"

Leaning on the hedge that separated the two gardens was the old man who'd taken the beer from Dod the night of his party.

Dod looked up. He shook his head and then smiled. "Aye, we are. You want tae join us, Bobby?"

Bobby needed no further encouragement. There was a small gap between the hedges at the bottom of the garden, and he wriggled his way through it.

"Dinnae–"

"—tell Kathleen!" the four of them chorused, and he started to laugh, an odd, wheezing sound.

Kippy got to his feet and disappeared inside, emerging seconds later with a foldaway chair. Bobby accepted the offer gratefully.

"Daisy's a dope virgin, Bobby," Dod announced, much to Daisy's embarrassment. Bobby smiled, though. "Ah was too, till this bad jin introduced it to me."

His accent was much thicker than the others. Daisy nodded politely. She'd understood the 'Ah was too', bit, but nothing else.

Dod lit the roll-up, taking in a huge breath. Daisy kept her eyes glued to him. She was going to do this right. Thankfully, she and Lisa had tried smoking last year. Neither of them had liked it, but at least she'd been able to do it without throwing up.

"Daisy, have you ever heard of blowback?" Dod asked. He'd lowered himself to the ground carefully, lying flat, eyes watching the slow drift of clouds and darkening skies.

Daisy shook her head. Kippy took the joint from Dod's fingers. He inhaled deeply, a movement Daisy thought was the sexiest thing she'd ever seen. His eyes closed, his chest rose, his chin tilted upwards. The eyes opened, and he turned to face Daisy.

"Open your mouth," Dod said. "He's goin' tae breathe into it. Just swallow."

Daisy did as she was told. Kippy fastened his lips on her, those lips that had burned their way onto her cheek and lips for the first time six weeks earlier. Now, the burn was different as he breathed into her mouth, a puff of acrid smoke that caught her suddenly at the back of the throat.

For a few seconds, Daisy panicked. All instincts told her to pull back. She was conscious of their audience—Katrina, her expression guarded, Bobby who couldn't care less, waiting for them to finish so he could get his turn, Dod, still watching the skies.

She swallowed, sniffing hard at the same time to help her breathe. The taste wasn't pleasant, but she'd have put up with far worse to keep Kippy's mouth on hers. He pulled back and grinned at her.

"Ach, you'd better do it again," Dod said. "Just to make sure, ken?"

Kippy took another deep inhale. As Daisy knew what to expect this time, her mouth met his halfway. She kept her eyes open too. Kippy blinked rapidly, but then the eyes looked back into hers. The smoke hit the back of her throat again, and she swallowed slowly. Their lips stayed in place.

"Alright, alright, break it up." Dod sat up, plucking the joint from Kippy's hand and passing it to Bobby, who took great greedy inhales himself, telling them cannabis helped with his arthritis. After that, it was Katrina's turn. She took one small, shallow puff herself before handing it back to Dod.

Was something supposed to happen? When did it happen? When the joint reached Kippy again, Dod decided Daisy had fulfilled the first part of her dope education. Now, she was qualified to take a toke herself. She aimed for a halfway approach, an inhalation longer than Katrina's but not as deep as Kippy's.

As the joint continued to make its way around their small circle, she felt her legs and spine soften. She and her mum had gone to yoga lessons last year, her mum saying it could be a mum and daughter thing they could do together.

At the end of the class, the teacher made them all lie down in what she called the corpse pose. She would tell them to imagine each part of their body melting into the ground. It always made Daisy want to giggle. The silly, excessively slowed-down voice the instructor used didn't help. The old ladies in the class who farted as they over-relaxed their pelvic floor muscles sent her into silent hysteria.

Now, though, she had no problems imagining her limbs melting into the earth underneath her. It felt so soft and comfortable, good enough to curl up foetal style.

"You okay, Daisy?" Dod grinned at her. "Nothin' can touch ye now, eh?"

She smiled back at him. Lovely, lovely guy Dod. It was a pity her mum and dad were so over the top about education. No doubt they would think he wasn't suitable company because he was only a fisherman and just because he did a bit of weed. Daft prejudices!

"Daisy, tell them what you think the words to I Wanna Be Adored are!" Kippy said. He put a hand on her head, stroking her hair.

"I want to be a door!" she said, giggling. The group laughed too, even Bobby who said modern music was shite and there has been nothing worse listening to after 1956. Kippy and Dod tried to come up with alternative lyrics. They both sang along, changing the words as they went. It seemed extraordinarily funny.

Kippy hadn't moved his hand. As the minutes passed, Daisy pleaded with the universe to keep her locked in place for as long as it could.

"Anyone hungry? Ah'm starving." Dod stood up, stretching his arms above his head. Bobby muttered about the mysterious Kathleen and got out of his seat, stumbling as he did so. He dismissed the cries of "are you alright?" with a wave of the hand and wriggled back through the gap in the hedge.

"Who's Kathleen anyway?" Daisy asked once Bobby had shut his back door.

"Naebody knows!" Dod said. "His wife, his sister, his daughter? Ah've never seen her." That made the four of them all laugh again.

Kippy helped pull Daisy to her feet. Katrina threaded her arm through hers. "C'mon then, drugs queen! I promised your ma I'd make sure you ate something."

As she steered her towards the kitchen, Daisy realised she was hungry. The hunger felt like hypo hunger, the sharp, sudden pang that made you want to stand in front of the fridge and eat its entire contents.

Inside the kitchen, she turned to Katrina in panic. "I think I'm…" she didn't need to say anything more. Katrina whipped out Daisy's blood testing equipment once more. "Do a blood test," she ordered, pushing Daisy onto the one chair in the room.

"Oh, I'm all right." The two of them studied the test. Katrina nudged her hard. "You daftie. You've got the munchies, that's all."

Dod had buttered what looked like a whole loaf of bread. He'd also found an eight-pack bag of crisps and several chocolate bars.

"I've got the Scooby snacks. Let's watch telly."

It took Daisy until eleven o'clock to realise that the plan was for her and Katrina to stay the night. The dope made this idea slightly less terrifying than it might have been. When Dod eventually switched the TV off and went outside for a last smoke with Kippy just after midnight, Katrina caught hold of her arm.

"Are you okay? We can sleep in the same room if you want. You don't have to stay in the same room as Kippy. And if you do sleep with him, don't think you have to do anything with him."

Where to begin? Most of her wanted to give in to Katrina's easy opt-out, to fall asleep while chatting and giggling, and exchanging silly confidences. And what did you do with a guy in bed, anyway? Snuggled up together under a duvet in a strange house, she could have asked Katrina. Then, the next time she would be prepared, the details already sketched out in her head.

Dod walked back in and threw an arm around Katrina. "Gonnae join me, sweetheart? Been a while, aye?"

Katrina flashed Daisy an apologetic look mouthing 'are you okay?' again.

Daisy nodded, and the two of them vanished upstairs. Kippy was back to, his usual smell amplified by smoke. He held a hand out for her. "I think we're sleeping in the box room," he said, and she followed him up the narrow staircase, heart thudding hard.

The room was as tiny as it sounded. There was a single bed, separated from the wall by about twelve inches of space, and a small chest of drawers.

She sat on the bed, unsure of what to do next.

Kippy sat beside her. "Are you okay? Katrina told me I had to take care of you."

He put an arm around her shoulder, taking care to make sure his hand avoided her breasts. Daisy leant into him.

"I'm fine… I—"

What to say now? The earlier relaxed feeling was gone, replaced by palpitations and terrible anxiety. Oh, to be in bed with Katrina instead, a lovely little sleepover fuelled by crisps and sandwiches, her mum outside the door telling them they had to go to sleep at some point.

Next door, the deep, jokey conversation had stopped. There was the sound of something hitting the wall—a regular thump, thump, thump. Someone groaned too, although it was impossible to work out whether it was Dod or Katrina.

Kippy cocked his head at the door. "No prizes for guessing what they're up to." His voice sounded hard, flat, even. Did he envy them having sex, or disapprove of his younger cousin's behaviour?

"Lucky them!" Daisy hazarded a reply. Would she ever

find herself in a situation where she didn't feel hopelessly naïve and unsophisticated? Or even shocked? Katrina swore blind Dod wasn't her boyfriend, but there she was in bed with him.

Kippy lay down, the length of him taking up the whole bed. He yawned widely. "How old are you?"

"Fifteen," Daisy replied.

"Under the age of consent, then."

Daisy babbled, "Doesn't matter, doesn't matter," desperate not to be middle class, posh and unsophisticated, but Kippy shushed her. He pushed himself up.

"Want to sleep with me, as in sleep?" He pulled off his tee shirt. Underneath, she could see just how thin he was. She could see all his ribs. His arms and shoulders were lovely though. He had a tattoo as well, a fire-breathing dragon that took up most of his left bicep and shoulder.

He caught her staring at it. "I designed it myself."

"Oh!" Daisy stood up beside him and touched it tentatively. Kippy looked at the hand on his arm and flexed the muscle so that the dragon moved slightly. His arms felt entirely different from hers. They were rope-like, rock hard and the flesh burning hot. Was he always this warm?

Without bothering to take off his trousers, he sat down and got himself under the covers. He lifted the duvet up. Emboldened, Daisy took her tee shirt off sucking in her stomach as much as she could as she did so. She kept her bra on, grateful that it was one she'd chosen herself. The ones her mother had bought her when she first needed them had been hideous.

She got into bed beside him. There was hardly any room in the single bed. Daisy was pushed right up against Kippy, a strange but lovely feeling. He was tall enough to put his arms around her and rest his chin lightly on top of her head. They lay there for a few minutes. Thankfully, next door's thumps and groans were no longer audible. The silence felt okay.

"Will we have sex when I'm sixteen, then?" Daisy wasn't sure if this was a question she should ask. It didn't matter anyway. There was no reply. Kippy's breathing had changed, a soft whistle in and out as he slept.

It took Daisy far longer to drop off. Sleeping with someone was uncomfortable. The sound of someone breathing so close by felt alien. She desperately wanted to change position but was too scared to move. What if she woke him up, or he took his arms away?

Nevertheless, as she lay awake, far too hot and cramped, she kept thinking of those uniform-adjusting, full made-up lower sixth girls.

"I'm one of you," she whispered to the ceiling above her. "One of you!"

They took the long way home the next morning. Katrina woke her at seven and said they should leave before nosy neighbours and cars passing the road copped two teenage girls exiting a house in the early hours.

She led them to the fields across the road and through the woods. They emerged, unseen, at the second bridge that crossed the river. Anyone who spotted them from there on would assume they were walking back from Castledykes Road, and not from somewhere in the opposite direction.

"I hope you used condoms," Katrina said, sotto voce, as they headed along the High Street towards Daisy's new home.

It didn't seem to be a question so no need, Daisy decided, to either tell her a condom hadn't been needed or lie.

MIS-STEPS

December 1990

"The Scots prefer New Year to Christmas," Tony announced, his head turning so he could direct the comment to Daisy.

He said it to console her, she supposed, make up for him dragging their family back down south for Christmas, instead of spending it in their new home. Four days too—how rotten of him. But he and her mother insisted. Yes, they needed to drop in on Debbie's parents. And no, not in a million-billion years would they allow Little Miss Daisy to stay behind on her own.

"In fact," Tony continued, "the shops used to open on Christmas day in Kirkinwall. Archie told me he remembered his father getting up at six am on the twenty-fifth December just as he did every other day of the year."

Who cared? They were still making her leave Kippy for four whole days, in which time...well, a lot of things might happen, including the Dread Other Girl. Daisy obsessed about this woman so much she now came complete with her own capital letters, a tall willowy blonde with gigantic boobs, a tiny waist and legs up to her armpits.

Barbie come to life, basically.

Unless she spent as much time as possible with Kippy, Dread Other Girl would move in, silently sliding in place beside his side so that when Daisy returned, she'd find the two of them wrapped around each other, Kippy doing all those things…

She forced her mind to still, turning to the old exam papers she'd brought with her. The prelims excuse hadn't worked, where Daisy pled four days would disrupt her studies, the work she needed to do for the mock exams she'd be sitting in January ahead of the real ones in the summer.

No, no, Daisy could bring her papers and notes with her. Perhaps the lack of boy-shaped distractions would be helpful, Debbie said, her tone arch.

Daisy had started at the town's academy in October, unbelievably nervous. A year older than Daisy, Katrina had left school in the summer, so Daisy didn't know anyone at the school. It wasn't nearly as big as St Mary's School for Girls, but the mixed classes were a new experience. The girls didn't speak out as much. They stared at Daisy when she did.

Daisy was taking 'O' Grade English, Maths, Arithmetic, French, History, Chemistry, Physics and Economics, the school's rector assuring her mum and dad that 'O' Grades were just as good as 'O' levels.

The students in Daisy's classes seemed friendly enough. She didn't like them as much as Katrina, but they were fine to hang about with at lunchtime and after school.

Her new girlfriends stared enviously when Kippy met her from school the first time. "Oh, wow. You're Kippy's girlfriend?" Linda had asked when she saw Kippy sat on the school wall, his bike beside him, waiting for her.

The next day, she noticed the way the girls treated her had changed. They appeared much more interested in her, asking questions and wanting to know what she thought about things. Later, she overheard one of them, "Daisy was on the tube in London once, and Bobby Gillespie sat opposite her!" It sounded reverential.

"I'm one of the in-crowd!" she thought, and then, "At last!"

Matthew was at the primary school next to the academy. He'd settled in no bother, spending his time after school running around with his new friends. Now, he spoke with a bit of a Scottish accent, no doubt to stop him getting teased. Whenever he said tatties for potatoes in their home, Debbie said "Potatoes, Matthew," but mildly enough. She let the didnaes, cannaes and wouldnaes slide.

Her mum was using her secretarial training, working part-time at a local haulage company, while her dad was still in London, but came up every fortnight and took days off whenever he could.

At her grandparents' house in Surrey, her grandmother talked about how no-one had manners nowadays, commenting whenever Daisy came into the room. She made sniffy comments about Kirkinwall too, remarks that made Daisy grit her teeth. How dare the old bag slag off her new home town and by association its amazing residents?

Christmas lunch was a dreary, drawn-out affair, her grandmother insistent on heaping Brussel sprouts on her and Matthew's plates. The two of them conspired to tip them surreptitiously into Daisy's bag under the table.

Daisy counted Tony's parents as her favourite grandparents, but Tony decided he'd visit them himself the day after

Christmas, driving the two hours to their Dorset village. Even Debbie seemed surprised by his insistence he went alone. Oh, they were old and confused these days, he said. No longer able to remember much, who was who in the family. His dad, apparently, couldn't tell one sibling from another anymore. He needed to see if they were okay and check out care homes in the area. Too dull for everyone.

Daisy's grandmother refused to allow any phone calls to Kirkinwall, even on Christmas day. Still, when the family took themselves out for a walk on Boxing Day, she sneaked a phone call, anyway. Kippy sounded stoned, laughing too much at Daisy's stories of her Christmas so far.

Still, when he talked about what he'd done on Christmas Day—he and Dod had hung out in the Star Tavern with Mick once he'd finished serving lunch working their way through the place's best single malts—Daisy told herself that wasn't a scenario Dread Other Girl could sneak into.

And now they were on their way back to Scotland, Daisy's heart lifting as the traffic thinned out and the mass of buildings disappeared behind them.

Her dad had been right. When she'd asked Katrina what she did for Christmas, she shrugged. "Don't really bother. The Jehovahs didnae like it, so we never got into the habit."

New Year, or Hogmanay as she'd learned to call it, was something else, though. Everyone, but everyone took themselves to the pub or a party. Then, at ten to midnight they congregated at the harbour square, waiting for the bells of the big kirk to chime in the start of another year.

If you were lucky, Katrina said, you got to snog loads of guys. Be careful where you stand, she warned, her eyes narrowing. You had to dodge the dirty old men, desperate for any excuse to press young flesh.

Part of the Christmas negotiations had involved bargaining—okay, if I come and don't moan (much!), can I go out with my friends at New Year?

The result was a compromise. Tony and Debbie would take the family to the Star Tavern, which was hosting a ceilidh. They would allow Daisy to escape at 11pm and find her friends if they weren't in the Star Tavern themselves. No amount of wheedling made her mum and dad let her off the family night out, but they gave in eventually and said ten pm.

Katrina invited herself along, telling Tony he needn't pay for her seeing as she was earning her own money these days. Tony refused anyway.

New Year promised magic, did it not? As usual, Katrina arrived early armed with her bag of hairdressing and make-up tricks, and a command that Daisy change her outfit.

"But…" Daisy said, looking down at her clothes. "I think this suits me!"

"Aye," Katrina said, rifling through the clothes hanging in Daisy's wardrobe. "It does suit you—or it would if you were ninety-five. Seein' as you're fifteen though, I'll get you something that makes you look it."

Daisy stripped off the silk blouse with its pussycat bow and the pencil skirt she'd credited with making her seem secretary-like (and sexy). The denim skirt and topaz-coloured top was much better.

"Is Mick working tonight?" She knew the answer already; Katrina's sudden wish to accompany them must be the chance of seeing Mick.

"Mmm-hmm," her friend replied. The make-up she'd put on Daisy, she promised, would be parent-friendly (i.e. not too thick) but sexy at the same time. A tall order, but her mum and dad didn't raise their eyebrows when she and Katrina made their way downstairs later.

The Star Tavern brimmed to bursting with people. It's Christmas decorations flopped, as if the celebrations that had taken place in there so far had exhausted them. A long table at the back wall overflowed with the buffet food included in the ticket price and most people took the all you can eat promise literally, their plates piled high.

Morag exchanged flustered looks with Katrina, muttering about folks' greed as she re-stocked the sausage rolls yet again. It didn't look as if anyone had given Mick free rein with the menu this evening; the food tried and tested canapes, vol-au-vents, quiche slices and sandwiches. Seafood pancakes had no place here.

To Daisy's astonishment, the ceilidh was great fun. A band played pipes and guitars, while a caller stood on the stage and shouted instructions for the dances, so everyone could join in. She'd accepted the family summons reluctantly, but once on her feet the exhortations to turn left, turn right, link arms and more became contagious.

It helped that the whole room was rubbish too, those who'd already taken in too much party spirit, mis-stepping and stumbling just like the rest. Her father faced the opposite direction from everyone else every time. Most people dissolved into giggles after a while, hysteria at each wrong-footed mistake.

On the dot of ten o'clock, she and Katrina said goodbye, rushing out of the room too quickly to hear the calls of "Be back in the house by ten past midnight!"

Katrina put her hand out to stop Daisy when they got to the door, and seconds later Mick joined them, shrugging off his chef's whites and letting them drop to the floor.

Frost had turned the ground icy beneath their feet. It made for slow going, but they finally made it to the harbour square where crowds of people had gathered already.

Daisy spotted Kippy straightaway—his bike leaning on the wall, and his arms gesticulating wildly as he spoke to someone. He still took her breath away, this young man. Her luck seemed too precious, fragile almost. What did someone so beautiful see in her, plain dumpy Daisy Walker?

Tonight, he seemed more star-like than ever—his face animated and alive lit up by the street light he stood under. It picked out the planes of his face, and moulded the hair to his head, tiny tendrils that curled at his temples and ears.

And that smile, too. Kippy didn't bother with expressions often, his thoughts impossible for Daisy to discern but tonight nothing hid what he was feeling. Pure joy, Daisy decided, which lit up the centre of her. Surely that meant he was as happy as her—the start of another year and you about to count down the end of the old one next to the person you…

Loved? Her guess, hope.

He shifted then, moving to the left and revealing his companion.

"Oh, Dod's here," Katrina said, shifting a quick glance at Mick. They hadn't been expecting him as Dod had talked about some party at a big farm nearby. He'd asked Katrina, who made rude noises about the hosts. That was why he was here, Daisy suspected. And the poor guy probably thought Mick would be safely taken care of for the night, what with him working in a hotel on Scotland's busiest night of the year.

"The inner circle!" Dod sang out as he saw Daisy, Katrina and Mick. If Mick's appearance dismayed him, he hid it well. Kippy swung round at that too, a hip flask in hand. He smiled at Daisy and slung an arm around her shoulder.

"We were just talking about last year," he said, laughter in his voice, "when this yin got us this super-strong weed and we made hash cakes. Didnae put enough sugar in them tho' and they were rank!"

"Still ate them," Dod added. "We shouldae asked Master-Chef here how to make cakes. Ah was stoned for two days!"

They dissolved into fits of giggles, too uproarious for a substandard joke. Mick rolled his eyes and took a pre-rolled joint out of his pocket. "I've a wee bit of catching up to do," he said, moving to the side so that the smell of it didn't drift too far over to the rest of the crowd.

A look flashed between him and Dod, something only Daisy saw, the effort of working it out too much for her.

"Have you had a nice night," she whispered to Kippy. A pointless question, the hilarity proof of an enjoyable night so far. The cold let her snuggle in closer, Kippy's super-hot body heat the perfect excuse to push her body in tightly to his. Next to her, Katrina had moved angling herself nearer to Mick in what was presumably the best position for a post-midnight kiss.

"The best!" Kippy said, beaming at her. "Even better now!"

Lips planted themselves on hers, hot and demanding, reminding Daisy of that time Katrina had made up them both and they'd snogged for the first time.

Did you open your eyes? Daisy's lids flickered open to find Kippy's shut. Closed so tightly he didn't know who he kissed? The thought bounced there, and she batted it back, forcing herself to concentrate on the feel of him against her. Solid, and hard…yes hard, that jutting thing that pushed against her crotch and made her mind flutter to all kinds of unknown places, hovering there and wondering what might happen.

Around them, the crowd had taken up the chant, ten

nine… Kippy broke away from her, dragging her towards Dod, Katrina and Mick. They crossed their arms in front of themselves, hands clasping those of the person on either side.

Eight, seven.

Daisy was last on the line though some old guy to the right of her grabbed her hand quickly enough.

Six, five.

Ooh, that had been a hard-on! Proof of someone's strength of desire for you, huh? Kippy's hand was loose in hers and she gripped it harder, tugging it gently hoping he might turn back to her once more. Whose face did you most want to see when the New Year dawned, only your loved—

Four, three.

A stumble, Dod, though the line of them jerked him back to his feet before he fell too far. Kippy pulled away and Daisy heard a murmured enquiry, 'are you all right' the best guess, but the tone of it—words indistinguishable and yet…

Two, one!

No matter. Daisy found herself wrapped up in a body and crushed tightly.

Happy New Year!

The words sang out around her, people nearby kissing each other. Kippy planted a splotchy kiss on her cheek and broke apart from her so he could address them all.

"Can you believe it," Dod said, "Nineteen ninety-one!"

"Last year we're teenagers," Kippy added, the animated grin back on his face as he looked at his friend. "Better make the most of it, eh? Before we're a' grown-up and wrinkly."

"Speak for yourself!" Dod said. "I'm never gonnae be old and boring, isn't that right Kit-Kat?"

But the subject of his affections wasn't looking in his direction anyway, too caught up in trying not to stare at Mick.

Dread Other Girl of Daisy's imaginings had come to life and wrapped herself around Mick, instead of Kippy.

Daisy battled pity and relief—Dread Other Girl would not bother with Kippy now, would she?

Part Two

HOLDING HANDS IN PUBLIC

You are cordially invited to the re-launch of Mackies Quality Fish and Chips!
Harbour Square, Kirkinwall
February 14, 1991. 6-9pm
Food and wine provided!

"Please come with me to the Mackies thing," Daisy begged.

The relaunch of a fish and chip shop wasn't exciting, she knew, but if Katrina didn't come it would be terrible. And if Katrina honoured them with her presence, it would be easier to persuade Kippy. Why on earth had her dad chosen Valentine's Day for the relaunch? He told his family he had to make the day extra special, extra (love)ly, explaining the parentheses when none of them got the reference first time.

The Easter holidays were in March this year, and Easter was when the tourist season started in Kirkinwall. Mackies, the new and better version, needed to be up and running well before then so it would be ready for in the influx of strangers to the town.

Daisy and Katrina were in her bedroom at Number 26. Katrina had taken up the offer to decorate the room, Kippy lending a professional hand too. The posters were also there on Katrina's say-so, and the bed linen was her choice. She'd even found Daisy an old dressing table complete with a mirror in the town's small antique shop. It was junk, rather than an antique, but they sanded it down and polished it, and it had pride of place in the room.

Sat in front of the mirror and fiddling with her hair, Katrina looked at Daisy's reflection. She screwed up her face.

"A fish and chip shop launch? That sounds a bit…shit, to be honest." She returned to backcombing her hair.

Mackies was the start of her dad's project. He told the family his savings and his generous salary had helped pay for their move to Kirkinwall. Now, he wanted to invest some money in local businesses, starting with Mackies.

The investment would bring in visitors and money to the town's economy, vital if the place was to thrive. When Debbie looked doubtful, he said the business and marketing courses he'd attended over the years would be put to beneficial use. He would make Mackies profitable in the shortest time possible.

Daisy didn't know much about what you did to make a business successful, but Mackies looked a lot better these days. The sign had been spruced up, and people now had enough room inside to sit down. Alison had taken on a couple more staff too. Whenever you walked past, customers were waiting—either for a takeaway or a seat.

It was nice that everyone in the town seemed to be so excited about it. People had been talking about Mackies a lot.

The family often got stopped on the street, locals commenting, "Aye, it's great what you're doing for Mackies." Some of them even referred to Tony as Lord Tony, something that amused Debbie and Daisy no end.

Matthew was quite happy. Anything that involved chips scored bonus points with him. Going along to a launch would mean staying up later than usual. Another plus.

How Debbie felt about Mackies and its relaunch wasn't something Daisy could work out. In front of her and Matthew, she was keen. But something was missing in her enthusiasm—the words she said delayed as if she was phoning from a foreign country. And Daisy caught her looking at her dad from time to time, her eyes fixing on him and then flashing away. There were questions in those eyes, questions she either didn't want to ask or wouldn't ask in front of Daisy and Matthew.

Tony told them he expected all the town's residents would show up for the big opening night. "I'll bet," her mum had said, "you're offering free food and drink!"

"Yes, yes," he replied. His voice held a touch of impatience. "But a lot of influential people are coming, people who will spread the word about–"

"Mackies—the best fish and chips in Scotland!" they all chorused, making Tony laugh.

"What's going to happen at this launch, then?" Katrina asked Daisy now.

Daisy tried to find ways to make the launch sound exciting.

She and Katrina saw a lot of each other. Daisy's school time and Katrina's work meant weekday meet-ups were impossible, and Katrina worked three out of four Saturdays. But come five o'clock, they met up most days.

Mostly, they spent the evenings at Katrina's house. Her mum was different from Daisy's. She didn't care what her daughter did, her only condition that whatever her daughter did, didn't bother her. Daisy and Katrina watched films, listened to music, tried out different looks with make-up and clothes, argued about what they liked and disliked, and teamed up with Kippy, Dod and Mick regularly.

"Alison hands out fish and chips and wine, and my dad makes a speech. Probably," Daisy said, aware that she wasn't making the launch sound like something that would impress your average teenager. "Lots of people will be there, though.

"Mick's going." The last killer sentence dropped in, oh so casually.

The Mick-Katrina-Dod situation was still the same. Dod adored Katrina, who slept with him occasionally but didn't call herself his girlfriend and never let him kiss or touch her in public. She looked at Mick the same way as Dod looked at her, but Mick treated her as a friend or an annoying younger sister. When the five of them were in company together, Daisy found herself goggle-eyed watching the looks that passed between the three of them. Dod stared at Katrina. Her eyes repeatedly returned to Mick, who only glimpsed at her occasionally.

Once, she caught Dod blinking, glassy-eyed. Maybe he thought that when he opened his eyes again, Katrina would be looking at him in the same way as she looked at Mick.

Katrina told Daisy plenty of things, mainly about how glad she'd been to escape the Jehovah's Witnesses and all the things she'd done since, a metaphorical flick of the vee's to organised religion in general. She never admitted, however, what she felt about Mick.

Daisy's knowledge of the subject was part of the stock of

information she'd compiled on her friend, a little jewel box that held precious things. If she asked Katrina outright, it would be like opening the box, exposing its contents to daylight glare. She suspected her friend knew she kept that box closed.

"Why is Mick going?" Katrina asked. The backcombing had stopped, and her eyes held Daisy's.

"My dad has invited this big-wig friend of his," Daisy said, suppressing a smile. "Some guy who's a food critic in London. Dad loves Mick's food too, so he told him to come along, chat this guy up and maybe persuade him to review the Star Tavern."

Daisy gave her five seconds. One, two, three, four…

"We'd better do our hair right if we're going tae go," Katrina pushed back the chair in front of the dressing table and stood up. "Can I borrow that shell necklace of yours?"

Daisy opened the drawer next to her bed, taking it out. "Here. Wear it with my turquoise camisole top if you want. They go together."

Katrina was already pulling her tee shirt over her head, exposing her thin, pale frame. You could see every bump of her backbone and the spread of her ribs. "Alright then. I'll do your hair for you. And your mum. I could do her hair too."

Katrina switched her attention from hair and necklaces to music, checking through Daisy's CD collection, which she'd policed as much as she had the room's décor. She held one up, her expression triumphant.

"Time we smelled like teen spirit, what d'ye think?"

Daisy clapped her hands together. "Too right! Let the party begin!"

"Gosh, girls. Don't you look grown-up!" Debbie stared at the two of them. Daisy frowned at her, willing her not to say what she could sense her mother was thinking: Aren't you wearing too much make-up? Or, won't you be cold?

Since moving to Kirkinwall, Daisy had lost weight. When she'd stood on the bathroom scales last week and seen the magic number, eight stone, she'd punched the air. Perhaps it was all the cycling she did now she lived here. Maybe this was what happened to you when you were in love. Whatever, her doctor was delighted with her, telling her thinner diabetics did better than fatter ones.

She and Katrina could exchange clothes these days, and they'd done so now. Daisy wore Katrina's treasured black denim jacket over a red sequinned tee shirt and black denim cut-offs. She wasn't confident enough to go bare-legged, so Katrina had persuaded her to put on a pair of fishnet tights. Katrina was in the turquoise camisole top, the shell necklace resting just below her prominent clavicle bone. She wore a pair of ripped denims and wedges that added five inches to her height.

She had used her full make-up kit on the two of them, giving Daisy smoky eyes, false eyelashes and dark red lips. Her own eyes she'd made up with blues and greens, the make-up extended to her temples.

"Mrs Double U!" Katrina stood in front of Daisy and beamed at Daisy's mum. "Would you like me to do your hair for you? I could do you a lovely wee chignon, make the most of your cheekbones, like?"

Debbie narrowed her eyes. Katrina's bossiness disguised as charm often worked better on Daisy's dad than her mum.

Debbie sighed, opened her mouth and then closed it again. "That would be sweet of you, Katrina. We'd better hurry up, though. It's six-thirty now."

They were at Mackies by seven o'clock. The place was already full; people packed into every inch of its new space. The restaurant area was done out in stripped brickwork, with huge, exposed pipes that ran around the walls, and a large window at the front that looked out onto the harbour square and the river beyond it.

"Goodness!" Debbie said, taking the place in. "Looks like no expense spared." Tony had pooh-poohed Alison's suggestion they use plastic beakers for the drinks at the launch.

"Crystal glasses only, Alison! We want to set the right tone."

Daisy saw Councillor Murdoch. He was at the launch as the official local council representative and had taken advantage of the drinks on offer, holding a glass of red wine in each hand. He spotted her and lifted one of them to toast her.

The Councillor always mentioned the Star Tavern incident, as he called it, whenever he met her. He still couldn't believe he'd let a fifteen-year-old girl persuade him into parting with so much money when Daisy had talked him into buying the Tavern's most expensive wine.

Alison told Daisy's dad the man always wangled an invite to any event where there was hospitality. When Tony explained what Daisy had done back in October, Alison burst out laughing. "I bet that shocked the auld skinflint. I'm glad Daisy fleeced him."

Behind the new counter, Alison looked flustered. She barked out orders to her staff. The place smelled strongly of frying and malt vinegar, but it was a pleasant smell—something that made people want to eat. There was a table set up in the corner. Alison and her staff kept adding small paper plates of fish and chip samples. They vanished as soon as they were put down.

Katrina had peeled off, no doubt to find Mick. Daisy spotted her on the other side of the room, leaning into Mick so she could whisper something in his ear. He pushed himself back against the wall and grinned. You could see the effect at once. Katrina glowed, an aura of twinkling light around her. Daisy thanked the stars Dod was out on the boat. She liked Dod very much—if only Katrina appreciated him as much as she did.

"Hey!" Behind her, someone pinched her bottom. Daisy whirled around, hoping her mum hadn't noticed the pinch.

"Hey, you!" The spin had placed her directly in front of him, this laughing, charming, handsome guy. "I thought you weren't going to come!"

Kippy loved innuendo. He raised his eyebrows, the gesture widening his eyes, and smirked. It was a familiar routine but comforting nonetheless.

Daisy stifled a giggle. "Maybe that's up to me!" she whispered.

He took her hand, raising it to his lips and kissing it. He'd dressed up. These days, Kippy liked to wear the clothes he thought artists did. Tonight, he'd chosen a tweed cap and a dark-blue velvet jacket over skinny jeans. She couldn't have said for sure, but Daisy thought he'd put on kohl pencil too. Those dark eyes looked bigger and whiter than usual, fringed by thick, dark lashes.

At the far side of the room, she could see Linda and her best friend, Mhari. They were staring at her and Kippy. Daisy beamed at the two of them. When Kippy tried to drop her hand, she kept hold of it.

The last four months had resulted in many incredible changes to Daisy's life. Was Kippy the best one? It felt like the most unreal change. Sometimes Daisy dreamt she was single, or that Kippy had dumped her. When she woke up after those dreams, the soar of relief when she remembered she was going out with Kippy was intense. It made her stare at the ceiling and mutter, "I have a steady boyfriend, a steady boyfriend."

There were some aspects of having a steady boyfriend that still confused her. Was this right, did boys do that? Did they all think in a certain way? But then again, what would she know? Kippy was her first boyfriend.

"Do you want some fish and chips?" Daisy asked, pointing at the sample-laid table.

Kippy screwed up his nose. "Nuh. If you grow up in this place, you eat too many fish and chips." Maybe that was another reason Daisy had lost weight. Kippy wasn't interested in food at all. She had to remind him all the time that she needed to eat regularly.

He took one of the plastic beakers of red wine from the table next to them. Daisy crossed her fingers her mum hadn't seen that either. At nineteen, Kippy was old enough to drink, but Debbie believed young men drinking were a terrible threat to teenage girls. She'd never specified what the danger was, but Daisy knew 'terrible threat' always equated to virginity and the keeping of it.

Perhaps Daisy's mum imagined Kippy drinking a glass of wine or a beer and turning into a randy little sod, unable to keep his hands from Daisy's breasts and bottom, and casually inserting wandering fingers between her legs.

The irony.

She and Kippy slipped into a pattern. Most of the time she saw him, he was with Katrina, Dod and sometimes Micky. They were seldom on their own. He always put his arm around her in public, though, or he'd hold her hand.

She asked him months ago, "Am I your girlfriend, then?" He replied, "Of course you are". Maybe she should have asked, "What does being a girlfriend mean, what does it involve?"

When he did kiss her in private, he let his hands wander. They'd drift to her bottom or slip under her tee shirt where she'd feel the fingers spread wide over her shoulder blades. He also liked to run his hands up and down her thighs, starting at the knees but stopping short of the pubis.

He'd kiss her neck too, tiny little butterfly kisses that made her moan softly. As his mouth moved downwards, she willed him to keep going. The thought of that big mouth on her nipples was unbearably exciting.

He never did.

"Not till you're sixteen," he said when she finally plucked up the courage to ask him to rid her of her virginity, hoping it might make him more adventurous in general. Boob touching or fingering would be enough. Dread Other Girl wouldn't suffer this, her tall willowy body too hard to resist.

"I don't want your dad coming after me," he added, smiling at her—the lovely Kippy broad, big-lipped smile that made you dance with joy. How could she argue?

"I wouldn't tell him!" Daisy said, trying anyway. "I wouldn't even tell Katrina!"

Katrina assumed Daisy wasn't a virgin anymore anyway. There was that condom question months ago; the one Daisy hadn't bothered to answer, murmuring an indistinct 'mmm-hmm' at the time. Luckily, Katrina then declared herself so disgusted at the thought of her cousin naked, Daisy must promise not to share any details.

Well, that was easy enough to hold your hand up and say, I will never reveal the details.

And now, now... February wasn't only about the grand

opening of Mackies, Scotland's best fish and chip shop. It was also the month Daisy had been born. In one week's time, Miss Daisy Walker would be sixteen years old.

And she and Kippy had a date.

L'AVENIR DE DAISY

"Daisy! Ça va?"

"Ça va bien, Madame de Courcy. Et vous?"

"Et tu, Daisy! Je suis heureux pour vous d'utiliser l'adresse informelle lorsque nous sommes par nous-mêmes."

Madame de Courcy pulled up a chair in front of her desk and pointed at it. Daisy sat down. She wanted to go to the library and take out some books for English, but Madame wore her usual, fevered look. Impossible to refuse.

The French teacher had been born in the UK, but her parents had emigrated to Paris when she was a child. She'd spent thirty years there, the happiest years of her life her time as a student in Paris, she told Daisy. She hadn't said why she'd left. Daisy assumed it had been a romantic attachment gone wrong. Madame never talked about Monsieur de Courcy.

Daisy was Madame's favourite pupil by far. She did her best to disguise her preference in class, but she often stopped Daisy as she left. Talking to her was such a pleasure, she said, as her French was excellent and her accent flawless. It was like speaking to a native.

All those years of holidays in France had paid off, no matter what those French waiters thought.

Madame de Courcy had made Daisy her prodigy. She sought her out, insisting they conduct their entire conversations in French. She was so keen to speak with Daisy, she insisted on l'address informelle. Daisy could say *tu* and not *vous* when addressing her teacher, so long as they were alone.

The informality and the rapid-fire conversations had been challenging at first, but after a while, Daisy adapted. Her French now excelled her mum and dad's grasp of the language.

Madame de Courcy had moved on from the generalisations—ah, the weather, so British, so shit—to the topic of conversation she always returned to, *l'avenir de* Daisy.

Daisy's future.

"Have you given it any further thought?" she asked. Madame de Courcy wanted her star pupil to take Higher French the following year.

Daisy had done well in most of her prelims. They were supposed to give you the studying practice you needed, as well as showing you what it was like to take an exam. Her best result had been her French prelim, causing Madame de Courcy all sorts of excitement. Taking Higher French was no longer enough for Madame. Daisy needed to consider the Certificate of Sixth Year Studies French qualification too and to think about studying modern languages at university. And what about a career as a translator or a teacher?

Both job prospects make Daisy shudder.

"Non, Madame. I have plenty of time," she added, still speaking in French seeing as it made the woman so happy.

Madame started on the now familiar path of pushing

Daisy to commit. "Ah, but you don't! You must make your mind up soon."

Daisy was ambivalent. No, she did not want to be a teacher or a translator and, more importantly, did she want to be too far from either Katrina or Kippy, preferably near both.

Debbie, Daisy and Matthew had been living in Kirkinwall now for four months. The suddenness of it still felt unreal to Daisy. One day, she lived in London having lived there all her life and then the next, she didn't. And now here she was six months after that fateful holiday, a teenage resident of Kirkinwall.

Madame de Courcy welcomed her with open arms, delighted to find someone who spoke French so well—a little companion she could talk to when bored of teaching life.

Back to the present day and Madame de Courcy had given up on *l'avenir de* Daisy. She steepled her hands together and asked Daisy about Katrina. Daisy couldn't fail to notice the way she said Katrina's name—as if someone who had stood on dog poo had walked into the classroom.

Daisy injected warmth and enthusiasm into her reply. "Katrina is okay! She's working so hard. I don't think she'll be here long, though."

Katrina had been working at Dulcie's for six months now. She was always looking for models she could use for practice. Thanks to this, Daisy's mum told her she'd saved a fortune in hairdressing bills.

Madame sniffed and blew out air. She made Daisy think of those French waiters again, the ones her dad always tried so hard to impress with his wine choices.

"*Et* Kippy?" She said Kippy, Keep-ie. Another French thing, Daisy assumed.

Small towns. People knew everything. Even teachers.

"He's fine. Doing lots of drawing."

Madame de Courcy was friendly with Aul' Carlton, the former art teacher who lent Kippy his studio.

"Don't let the two of them influence your decisions about the future," Madame de Courcy's voice was sharp. "I know they seem glamorous, the hairdresser and the artist, but you have to be excellent in those professions to get anywhere. I'm not sure if they are that good."

Daisy stared at her. Nowadays, she found herself looking at people's hairstyles and makeup and wondering what Katrina would have done. She wouldn't have styled Madame's hair the way it was now, for starters. It was far too long for a woman of her age, the sides of it plaited into the main tresses and hanging down almost to her waist. And her make-up was dire. Thin, pencilled in eyebrows and lip liner that went over the natural lip line, her lips red. She was like something out of the Olden Days.

As the major hairdresser in the area, Dulcie's didn't lack customers. Unfortunately, none of them was adventurous enough for Katrina. She moaned about them all the time— the women who came in and asked her to take an inch off, changing their minds seconds later and saying half an inch instead. Or the old ladies who only wanted a wash and set. She wheeled them from the sink to the stand-up hair-driers, kicking their chairs lightly.

"Alright, Winnie? That's no' too hot for you?"

She turned the settings up if they said yes. Vengeance. They hadn't let her add that gorgeous mauve colour to their wash and set.

"They will probably stay in Kirkinwall the rest of their lives," Madame sniffed.

"What, like you?" Just in time, Daisy bit back her

instinctive response. Honestly, was it such a bad idea to live here, having fun, going to wild parties and hanging out in Dod's inner circle (ken?)

"There are lots of opportunities for talented hairdressers and painters in London, aren't there?" The about-turn startled her, stopping her from getting up and leaving. They were still speaking French. Maybe Daisy hadn't heard her correctly.

"Yes, London's the place to be," Madame de Courcy gave a small smile. It was as if she'd worked out her conversation was pissing Daisy off, so she'd said something to please her.

"I think they want to go there, at some point," Daisy ventured.

Well, Katrina did.

Kippy? Daisy couldn't work out his hopes and dreams. If he only shared them, Daisy could make concrete decisions. Decisions such as when to leave school—after the fifth year or after the sixth year, perhaps even at the end of this school year—or to which colleges or universities to apply.

"London or Glasgow would be good," Madame said. "Opportunities, always."

Daisy decided she'd given Madame de Courcy enough. She scraped back her chair

"*Londres est genial.*" The brilliantness of London was prettier to say in French.

"*Rappelez-vous que,*" Madame said, reverting to the formal address.

Remember that.

SWEET SIXTEEN

"Happy Birthday to you, happy birthday to you. You look like a monkey, and you smell like one too!"

The variation of the happy birthday song was predictable. Matthew had learned it at nursery school. It had amused him then, and it still did. Because he laughed so much after he'd sung it, Daisy let him away with it.

Matthew loved birthdays in general. They didn't have to be his. He'd burst into Daisy's room that morning, not waiting for her to open her eyes and sit up before he started singing.

Daisy sat up slowly, consciousness returning slowly.

"Sweet sixteen and never been kissed!" her mum stood at the door, her arms folded. "Well, that last bit isn't true." She was grinning, though.

"Happy Birthday, love." She walked over to the bed and dropped a kiss on top of Daisy's head. "I can't tell you how quickly these sixteen years have flown by."

"Too right!" Her dad had come into the room too. "We

still think of her as our little girl, don't we Debs? The little curly-haired toddler who was always giggling. And now here she is, all grown up."

He kissed her too, holding a hand out so Daisy could take it and get out of bed. He pulled her into a hug, passing her over to her mum so that she could do the same.

"Do you think our little girl will let us spend any time with her today?" he asked Debbie, winking at Daisy as he did so.

"You can have me for the morning for lunch and the afternoon," Daisy smiled at him. "Then, can I see my friends? Katrina and Kippy have something planned, youth club disco I think?"

Daisy always paired Katrina and Kippy together when she ran anything past her mum and dad.

The town hall had recently started up weekly discos, figuring that it might be a way to bring in people and money. It wasn't youth club by any stretch of the imagination. There was a bar for a start, and people travelled in from all the surrounding towns and villages, bringing with them an exaggerated air of inter-village rivalry.

Still, the gossip about those dances confined itself to those who went. The hall was far enough away from where the Walkers lived for its noise and kerfuffle not to reach them.

Katrina had been once and labelled it totally sad. For Daisy's birthday, though, she'd decided they could all go. Dod and Mick would be joining them too, and Daisy had invited along Linda, Mhari and Kelly from school, Dod promising he'd bring some of his fishermen mates.

When Daisy told Linda what Dod had promised, her eyes lit up. Fishermen had cachet. They were young, muscular, and often cash-rich (on a temporary basis), and, apart from

Dod, they were swaggering bad boys who walked into rooms expecting a round of applause.

Daisy had no intention of staying until the end anyway. She'd come up with a plan, one that made her proud of its sheer audacity. It would mean sneaking out of the disco earlier, Kippy with her, and making their way back to Aul' Carlton's studio.

Tony widened his eyes and pursed his lips at Daisy's words. "Ooh! Aren't we honoured, Debs!" Then he winked again. "Yes, of course. If you could humour your aged parents with your company for the day, we'd be delighted."

He clapped his hands together. "Matthew, do you want to help me make the special birthday breakfast?"

Matthew nodded enthusiastically. The special birthday breakfast was a Walker tradition—pancakes with Maple syrup and bacon, a dish Tony had tried when he'd visited the States years ago and loved. They'd changed the recipe last year to make it sugar-free for Daisy. It was still delicious.

Kippy was working that day, but he was due to finish at five o'clock. Daisy took extra care to dress and get ready, staring at her reflection and wondering if she looked different now that she was sixteen.

Her mum always told her off for using too much make-up, telling her that young skin was too beautiful to cover up with foundation and powder. Daisy dusted liberal amounts on anyway. It was important that Kippy saw her as a proper grown-up. A sixteen-year-old who was mature and ready to move on to the next stage of a relationship.

The sex bit.

She opened her presents at breakfast. Her mum and dad had bought her a camera, a Nikon SLR model Tony said was easy to focus and would mean she could take non-blurry photos.

She smiled at them both gratefully, imagining the pictures she would take and stick on the wooden-framed cork boards in her room. The imaginary board began to fill with white-bordered snaps of her and Katrina, dressed up for parties, and on those nights out too. She would need to figure out how to use the camera's auto setting as quickly as possible so that she could take lots of pictures of she and Kippy, arms around each other, cuddled up together, and standing entwined.

Much to her surprise, the pile of birthday cards the postman delivered included one from Lisa and Dana. Daisy recognised the handwriting straight away, as Lisa always looped the end of her 'y's so that they curled extravagantly underneath.

Happy birthday, Daisy! How's life in Nowheresville? Write to us and tell us all about it, though we expect you won't have much to talk about.

Oh, well. At least they'd remembered Daisy's birthday.

The much-anticipated knock on the door came just after five o'clock. Daisy leapt from the sofa, but her dad got to the door first.

"Katrina! Al–, sorry Kippy! Why don't you come in for a few minutes? We've got some sugar-free birthday cake you can have."

Behind him, Daisy rolled her eyes. This scenario was what she tried to avoid all the time. It was different with Katrina who let herself in and out of the house as if she belonged there, adding Daisy's mum and dad to those people she regularly bossed around.

Kippy, though. He wasn't a 'meet my mum and dad' kind of person. They said hellos to him when he picked Daisy up, although most of the time she met him away from the house.

He never came around for dinner or to hang out with her in her room the way Katrina did.

"Er, like no, Dad?" Daisy said, sliding out behind him, so she was stood outside too. Then she softened her expression. "Thanks for all my pressies and the lovely breakfast and lunch!"

She left as he called out that she should be back no later than midnight. It wasn't ideal, but so much negotiation had gone into the agreement for her birthday celebrations she'd accepted it in the end.

Out on the street, Katrina took a small package and a card from her rucksack. "Happy birthday, Your Royal Highness! This is from Kippy and me."

Daisy stifled disappointment. She'd thought Kippy would get her his own present. Wasn't that what boyfriends were supposed to do, offering the said gift while swearing their devotion and jumping on top of you to ravish you at the same time?

Inside the parcel was a pair of earrings. They matched Daisy's necklace, small ceramic shells threaded onto silver filigree chains. The chooser of this present was probably the person who was yet to return the necklace in question she'd borrowed for the Mackies launch.

"Thank-you!"

"Open the card, then!" Kippy said.

She slid the card from the envelope. It was hand-painted, a delicate watercolour painting of Daisy. She was sitting on a wall—the Harbour car park by the looks of it—her hands either side of her. Kippy had steered away from his usual cartoon style. It was a wildly flattering picture, Daisy thought. Were her legs that thin, and her hair that smooth and shiny? Nevertheless, it had to be the best present she had ever received.

"Bloody hell. It's incredible!" she said. Kippy smiled at her, and Daisy told off the doubts in her head once more. Kippy was a boyfriend who gave you a handmade card, on it a portrait of you that he'd painted himself. If she wrote to Just Seventeen's problem page telling her that she wasn't always sure about Kippy, Fiona Gibson, the magazine's agony aunt, would give her a stern talking-to. Why are you moaning? He's a PRINCE!

[After she'd instructed all the readers on the position of the month, of course.]

Back at Katrina's house, Katrina eyed Daisy speculatively. "Will you let me do your hair, Daisy-do? You should look different for your birthday." Her voice took on a wheedling tone.

"Okay then," Daisy said, surrendering herself to Katrina's ministrations. "Anything you like, but don't cut it."

Some hours later, her hair streaked green with something Katrina assured her was temporary, Daisy stood outside the town hall with her friends. There was a continuous flow of people in and out, cars pulling up to drop off and pick up, and the thrum of music surrounding them.

Dod, flanked by two fishermen mates who were bound to fulfil all of Linda's expectations, had appeared.

As usual, Dod sported dilated pupils. Katrina had told her his fishing boat picked up more than fish on its various expeditions, which was why he managed to get high so quickly most of the time.

"Happy Birthday, Your Royal Highness!" He held his arms wide and moved forward to kiss her cheek. "I didnae get you a card, but I bought you this."

He took a half-bottle of vodka from his jacket pocket. The disco offered alcohol at the bar and pretended not to notice the suspiciously young things who asked for gin and orange juices or pints of lager. The under-eighteens smuggled in booze anyway to be on the safe side and added it surreptitiously to the soft drinks on offer.

Daisy stuck the bottle in her bag. She wasn't planning to drink anything while she was here, but when she persuaded Kippy to leave early with her, a little Dutch courage would be useful.

Inside and upstairs, people packed the main hall. Linda and her two friends spotted them as they came in and made their way over. Daisy was aware that her group was being stared at, something that made her think of those lower sixth girls and throw back her green-streaked hair in studied nonchalance.

Mick had joined them too, his appearance attracting even more attention. Linda stared at him in jaw-dropped awe.

"Happy Birthday, Daisy!" He kissed her too. Unlike Dod, his wasn't the brotherly kind. If you were the sort of disloyal girl who'd forget your boyfriend just like that and betray your best friend, the kiss would have been right up your street.

"Katrina needs to dance!" Daisy bleated, reaching behind her to grab Katrina's hand. As it happened, Katrina had just spent the last five minutes bitching about how naff the music was.

Mick grinned and took Katrina's hand. They were probably the prettiest people in the room, Daisy decided, and they were both great dancers. Mick had a hypnotic way of moving his hips, and Katrina liked to raise her hands above her head, clasping them at the top. It was a bit like watching a snake charmer draw a snake out of a basket.

Kippy hated dancing, but he seemed happy to stand at the end of the dance floor with her, Daisy pulled in close to him and his head resting on hers. He appeared as fascinated as her by Mick and Katrina's dancing. He also kept an eye on Dod, who stood beside them and kept up his usual stream of light-hearted chatter, his eyes never straying that far from Katrina and her reptilian sway.

Kippy had a word with her at one point, when she came back to top up her Sprite with Daisy's vodka, a conversation Daisy couldn't hear. From the looks they gave each other, though, she guessed Kippy was telling her off.

"Dance with me, Dod!" Katrina said, taking his hand as Grandmaster Flash and the Furious Five's the Message came on. He went willingly. They attracted an audience, space quickly enlarging around them. Dod was a fantastic break-dancer, body-popping his way along the floor. Katrina wasn't as good at the moves, but she held her own, freezing her body in complement to what her dance partner did.

"I want to go, Kippy," Daisy whispered. As the attention of the crowd was elsewhere, now was the perfect time to put her audacious plan in place.

"Aye?" Kippy didn't take his eyes off Dod and Katrina. "Are ye no having fun?"

"I am, but I think we should leave here and go back to Aul' Carlton's Studio? You know how you're always worrying about not getting enough life-drawing experience? I could–"

Whatever she'd been about to suggest was rudely interrupted. Behind them, there was shouting—loud, angry voices, swear words, and the crowd's attention moved from Dod and Katrina to the back of the hall.

"C'mon," Kippy took Daisy's hand and pulled her with him. They pushed through the people. There, just in front of the town hall stage, were two men facing each other. The guy on the right was one of the fishermen Dod had brought with him. He stood opposite the other man; his hands curled into fists.

Dod appeared at their side.

"Fuck. That's Donnie," he said, pointing at the fisherman. "He'd fight his ane shadow. We might need to gie him a hand?" He looked at Kippy, who nodded.

The burly security guards were nowhere to be seen. "Oh! You mustn't fight! You must be careful!" Daisy gripped Kippy's hand hard.

Dod turned to her, the usual slow, lazy grin starting up. "Dinnae worry, Your Royal Highness. Me and him have been fighting together for years. He's ma wingman."

And with that, they were off. The big fight had kicked off while Dod told her not to worry. Donnie's opponent had, foolishly, made the first move, swinging a wild punch at the fisherman's head. When he missed, Donnie retaliated, kicking the legs out from under him. As the man fell, he booted him in the belly and then the head. The move attracted the man's friends, who surged forward.

Katrina materialised beside her. "Where are they?"

Daisy pointed vaguely at the middle. Kippy and Dod seemed to have been sucked into a vortex of arms, legs and curses. There must be at least twenty people involved.

"Where's Mick?" she asked, and Katrina shrugged. "In there too."

The music stopped, and the lights came up, a voice booming out: 'Stop this right now! The police are on their way!'

Opposite, Daisy could see Linda, Mhari and Kelly. The three of them shrugged elaborately. Shoulders moved up and down, three people who didn't think the fight was a negative end to the night or anything to worry about. Linda's face wore a tiny smirk as she looked at Daisy. Her eyes returned to the fighting mass, centred, Daisy guessed, on the rolling body she thought was Donnie.

A whistle blew, loud and shrill.

Daisy and Katrina turned. Two policemen stood at the entrance to the hall; their truncheons held high.

"Break it up!"

The arms, legs and curses mass instantly dispersed, suddenly becoming individual bodies instead of an amorphous lump.

Three of those bodies drifted towards Daisy and Katrina. They weren't recognisable at first—the faces bright red, the clothes pulled and torn, the sense of euphoria, not one their greeters felt—but eventually Daisy realised that stood in front of her were Kippy, Dod and Mick.

Kippy put his hands on his thighs and started to laugh. "Fuck sakes, Dod! Tell Donnie to keep his mouth shut in future, aye? That was the CD Crew, and they're mental."

With that, the other two burst into laughter as well. Mick had a bust lip, while Dod's reddening right eye promised blackness in the morning.

"Too right!" Dod replied, putting an arm out and circling it around Katrina's shoulder. She shrugged it off.

In front of Daisy, the clock on the wall said eleven-thirty. Her audacious plan had depended on a timescale. The fight had hijacked that timeline completely. She couldn't decide whether she wanted to laugh or cry.

A boyfriend who dived into a fight to help a mate. Yay! But the same guy who ignored your suggestion that you leave early to…well, whatever. Not so yay.

DAISY, NAKED

Daisy's audacious plan, the one so cruelly dashed by the fight on the night of her birthday, had involved Kippy and his painting practice.

When not at work, he was often to be found in Aul' Carlton's studio painting scenes from Kirkinwall or copying some of the work of the Old Masters. Aul' Carlton cast an eye over them from time to time and made recommendations.

"You need to do more life painting, Alan," he'd told him. "It'll help with your portfolio if you ever do decide to go to art school."

Dod had compromised. He wouldn't strip off, telling Kippy only Katrina saw him starkers, but he'd go half-naked. That charcoal picture was striking nonetheless, although it made Daisy uncomfortable. If pushed, she couldn't give the reasons why other than it seemed to show that the painter and subject shared something no-one else could understand or work out.

But Daisy was going to give Kippy full nudity. He'd seen

her in her underwear. It wasn't that big a step to take everything else off. She pictured herself in a colourful silk robe, the garment beginning to slip from her shoulder. Perhaps—oh, the thrill of it—she might end up being his muse.

In later years, The Sunday Times interviews the famous painter Alan Kirkpatrick.

"Yes, my art career took off when I found my inspiration. Daisy, her name was. She was this fabulous woman I met when we were both teenagers, and she inspired me to do my best work. Daisy, Naked, is my favourite painting and one that I'd never sell, even though I've been offered millions for it.

"I always wonder what happened to her…"

In her imaginings, Kippy seemed to have lost his local accent, and she had disappeared altogether.

Two weeks after her birthday, she tried again. They were at Aul' Carlton's studio, Kippy having needed to drop off some paint he'd bought.

"You could paint me, Kippy," Daisy began. Kippy had his back to her, offloading the paints into the drawers underneath the big table in the room.

"Hmm?" He didn't turn around.

"Yes, paint me. When I'm…" Her stomach fluttered nervously, and she could feel a flush starting to spread its way across her cheeks and neck. "…not wearing anything, so you can get your life-drawing experience, build up your portfolio."

He still didn't turn around, although he'd stopped what he was doing."

"Naked?"

"Yes." Before her courage failed her, Daisy began to unbutton her cardigan and dropped it at her feet. She pulled the vest top underneath over her head and reached her arms behind her to undo her bra.

Kippy turned. "Alright then." His expression told her nothing. When the bra, jeans and pants came off, his eyes didn't leave her face.

He picked up his sketch pad and pulled out the tatty armchair Dod had sat on when Kippy had drawn him.

"Are ye warm enough?" he asked. "I can put on the gas heater if you want?"

Daisy nodded. When she'd thought up this plan in her head, it hadn't included prosaic details such as her shivering in the unheated attic. Maybe her plan hadn't meant that Kippy would agree to her offer either. Instead, in Daisy's mind, the sight of her naked had overcome every scruple Kippy had about her age, and he'd leapt on her.

"No, not like that." He shook his head as she sat down, perching on the chair with her hands resting on her knees. He stood in front of her and began to re-arrange her. He got her to bend both arms and sink into the seat, her bottom resting on the edge of the chair. Touching her knees lightly, he pushed her legs apart and stood back to look at her. He bent in his mouth inches from her.

"*This is it! This is it!*" Daisy's fluttering stomach sent tiny tremors out to the rest of her body. The shivering now had nothing to do with how cold she was.

Kippy pulled her hair forward, fanning it out around her face and onto the back of the chair.

"Perfect."

He fetched the stool from behind the easel and began to draw, the charcoal scratching noisily as it moved across the paper.

Oh well. Daisy had wanted to be a muse, had she not?

Half-an-hour later, he put his pad down. "I've done enough for now, and that cannae be comfy. I might need you to strip again. D'ye mind?"

Daisy shook her head. "Can I see it?"

He looked as if he was about to refuse, but then got up from his stool and came towards her, picking up Daisy's clothes as he did so.

"Here."

Daisy almost didn't recognise herself. She looked older, grown-up and knowing. The tip of her tongue was visible at the side of her gaping mouth, and that coupled with the way he'd drawn her eyes made her look as if she'd just…

Just, what? Sweet sixteen and never been shagged. The voice in her head sounded angry and bitter. Bet this wouldn't have happened if she'd been Dread Other Girl, huge boobs hanging out and long legs stretched out along the floor.

"Thanks, Daisy. That was good of you, and if it's okay we'll maybe do…"

Daisy cut him off. "Kippy, don't you fancy me?"

The question took the last bit of guts she had. Her mum had once told her that you should be careful asking questions sometimes because you needed to think about how it would feel if the reply was one you hated.

Kippy crouched down, so his face was level with hers. "What are you talking about, you eejit?" He leant forward and kissed her lightly. "You're ma girlfriend. Of course, I fancy you. We better get out of here in case Aul' Carlton comes back. He'd probably love it if he got to see you naked, but I wouldn't."

He smiled at her at that, his hand cupping the side of her face.

Daisy thought of how those hands had expertly re-arranged her earlier and longed for that light, gentle touch elsewhere on her body. But all her bravery had been used up. And he'd answered her, hadn't he—even showing jealousy when he said he didn't want the studio's owner to stumble upon them.

She got dressed as quickly as she could. Safely covered up once more, Kippy pulled her to him.

"Thanks, Daisy. I mean that."

The kiss this time was a proper snog. Daisy snaked her arms around his shoulders and pulled him in close.

"Anytime!"

And next time? Maybe next time, or it might be the time after that—a time when Aul' Carlton was safely packed away abroad. There was no hurry.

THE SECRETS WE KEEP

March 1991

Katrina ganged up with Debbie when the Easter holidays arrived in late March. Daisy had exams to sit and pass in the next few months. Therefore, she must study and not go out all that much. If she studied her little head off during the days, Katrina would reward her with some company early evenings.

Not for long, mind. Daisy needed plenty of sleep so's her brain could rest itself well.

It was the closest they ever came to an argument. When Daisy moaned that she was bored, bored, bored of reading and studying her textbooks, Katrina rounded on her. They were in Daisy's bedroom, papers scattered everywhere, and an ambitious study timetable pinned to the cork noticeboard.

Daisy had to study. She could either whinge like a wee bitch or just get on with it.

"For God's sake," Daisy hissed suddenly, a higher than normal blood sugar level on top of the study pressure making her super ratty. "Stop going on about my fucking exams."

It started as a hiss. It ended as a shout, and Katrina jumped back from her.

The resulting silence stretched out, neither of them willing to back down. Daisy began gathering up papers, exaggerating the movements and sighing loudly. Katrina stood still. If she watched her, Daisy had no idea as she refused to meet her eyes too.

"I wanted to go to uni. Or college, mebbe. Not just to do a stupid wee hairdressing course once a week."

Daisy sat down and patted the space on the bed beside her. Then, she changed her mind. Some conversations were better made when you were face to face. She slid herself off the bed and edged her way against the wall. Katrina sat down beside her, neatly dropping to a cross-legged position without having to use her hands.

"I didn't know that," Daisy began.

"No, you dinnae know everything about me."

Daisy thought she saw the sheen of tears in her eyes. Shit, this was heavy stuff, and way out of what she knew. Girls, in her experience, stuck themselves to each other with the glue of confessional. You said something. Your mate said something back. Maybe she'd overdone it, flinging out her likes, dislikes and feelings left, right and centre, and inviting Katrina to be part of the Walkers' lives, an arrangement so casual she even had her own key to the house. It seemed all a bit give, give, give.

Meanwhile, she went to Katrina's house and had yet to say more to her mum other than, "Hi there, how are you"; the response always, "Aye, alright." Leaving aside the whole Jehovah's Witnesses thing, and not having seen your dad since. If you left, apparently, you ceased to exist. Them was the rules, but it had to cut deep, your father not trying to see you in five years? Katrina hadn't said anything but the bare-bones about it. As an alleged best friend, wasn't Daisy's role to pry harder, deeper, longer?

Then there was the whole Dod stroke Mick thing. Shouldn't there be a cosy talk where Katrina said, "Daisy, what do you think I should do? Dod's this great guy who seems to think the sun shines out of my arse, but I'm hung up on this other bloke, someone who should be nicknamed Chocolate..."

Daisy sang out the answer to herself: "So vain, that if he were made of the stuff, he'd eat himself."

Daisy had tried all those questions once or twice and got stonewalled for them. Maybe, she should have pushed harder. Daisy had her secrets too, the reluctant virginity still in place even at the embarrassingly old age of sixteen, and her with no idea whether Kippy's reactions were normal or not.

She tried for something now, a question that would move them on. "What did you want to do at uni?"

"Business Studies," Katrina replied, and then smiled. She reached out her hand and took Daisy's. "So's I could boss people around for real and get money for it."

Daisy giggled at that, relieved the conversation had lightened once more. "Well, that's your calling, isn't it? Being bossy?"

"Aye, so you need to study. Cannae get to college or uni if you don't."

It was a deft move, Daisy realised later. She'd once more turned the conversation away from herself. But it was also a peace offering and the chance for Daisy to say, "Oh, okay Miss Bossy Boots. I'll study for my exams. Then, if I go to uni, I'll tell you all about it, and you'll realise you were right not to!"

"Whatever," Katrina leaned across her and picked up one of the bits of paper Daisy had missed. "Has your dad put money into the Star Tavern too, by the way?"

"I don't understand!"

Letting herself into the house a week later, Daisy could hear raised voices in the kitchen. There was no pause, so she shut the door quietly and stayed still. Her parents rarely argued, and she wondered if they were talking about her, maybe they'd heard about the fight at the town hall or the nude sketch…oh hell, please no.

The logical part of her brain told her the picture thing was nonsense, but the fight thing was a possibility. She felt herself go hot and cold. If they knew about the fight, they'd think Kippy was a bad influence and they might—

"I've inherited money, Debbie," her father's voice was quieter. He sounded reasonable and calm. "A lot of money, and I'd like to use that money in a way that will benefit many people."

Oh. Nothing to do with fights at discos or stripping off for boys, then.

"Who from?" Debbie didn't sound reassured, only incredulous.

"My Aunt Caroline," Tony replied. "She emigrated to Denmark years and years ago. To be honest, I haven't seen her in thirty years, and I'm as surprised as you. But her solicitor contacted me and said that I'm her nearest relative, and she's left me all her money. She was fabulously wealthy, Debbie. I met the solicitor in London and had to ask him to repeat himself several times."

"Why am I only hearing about this now?"

Daisy's mind boggled. By the sound of it, the Walkers

were now 'fabulously wealthy'. Heavens, what did that mean? More clothes, more make-up, more CDs—all the items teenagers prized highly?

"Naturally, I wanted to make sure it was real. I wanted it to be a lovely surprise. You can stop working if you like. And I've paid off the London mortgage. I want to invest in other Kirkinwall businesses."

There was a loud tutting sound.

"Look how Mackies has paid off!"

Mackies' success had been phenomenal. Every time Daisy walked past the fish and chip shop, there was a queue of people waiting, and there was a now a waiting list for BYOB Friday and Saturday nights. A picture of Tony and Alison stood outside the place on the evening it had relaunched had pride of place on their living room wall. In it, Tony's face beamed at the camera. Alison's grin wasn't quite as big, but she looked pleased anyway.

"It's all risky, though Tony? Investing money in businesses, people you've only known for such a brief time. And now you want to put money into the Star Tavern? Have you thought about this properly?"

Katrina had already told her about it, Tony's visit to the Star Tavern and his chat with Morag, Mick and Lenny, the guy who owned the place. They'd been delighted. The food had a fabulous reputation, thanks to Mick, but money could do magical things. It might cover advertising in the Sundays, for example. Or pay for more waiting stuff, so it didn't have to rely on Morag or the freelance services of Katrina and Daisy.

"As well as all this money you're proposing for that art prize and the exhibition?" Her mum said now, and Daisy wondered at that. An art prize sounded like something that would interest Kippy.

"The exhibition will bring so many people into the town. People who need to eat–"

"The best fish and chips and in Scotland?" Her mother's voice sounded sarcastic now, mocking the phrase they heard too often.

"Yes, the best fish and chips in Scotland. Alison's had to employ another three people, you know. And anyone coming to see an exhibition would need somewhere to stay. I mean, the Braemar B&B—who would want to stay there?"

There was laughter at that. Reluctant, Daisy thought, but amusement nonetheless. "Ssh," Debbie said. "I swear Mrs Burnett knows everything in this town, including when people are rude about her B&B."

Her dad said something else, words she couldn't make out. The laughter continued, though. Maybe it was an impression of Mrs Burnett, her arms folded and her face wearing that expression she favoured most of the time, the look you'd give someone who'd shat in your cornflakes.

"You won't invest in anything else, will you, Tony?" Serious now.

"No, that's my lot, Debbie. If the businesses can't thrive on what I've given them, then I can't do anymore."

The door to the kitchen opened. Daisy did her best to look as if she'd not been there all along.

"Hi!" her voice sang out. "Just going upstairs!"

She fled up the stairs to her rooms as quickly she could, her mum shouting after her to remember that she was babysitting Matthew that evening as she and Tony were going out.

The art prize was definite. She'd be able to confirm it to Kippy. Something else, admittedly, that would make him want her?

CROSS YOUR FINGERS AND HOPE

May 1991

"Ladies and gentlemen! Time up. Put your pens and pencils down."

Daisy had finished twenty minutes ago. Conscious of her schoolmates scribbling away around her, she had checked and double-checked her paper, fearful that she had missed something. Nothing obvious jumped out, and she was relieved when the invigilator stood up and shook her bell.

There was nothing more she could do. The peal of the bell signified not only the end of this exam but all of them. She had completed the last of her eight 'O' Grades, and summer could now begin in earnest. Apart from an unlucky few who still had to sit biology, most of the other people in the room were finished too. Sighs, laughter and loud conversations broke out around her.

"How did you get on?" Linda breached unspoken exam protocol. You weren't meant to ask how the exam went, and you certainly didn't talk about specific questions.

"Okay, I s'pose," Daisy answered as they let themselves out of the stifling hall. Exams shouldn't take place in the summer. Shutting up teenagers when it was warm and sunny was cruel.

Linda tipped her face up to the sun, and loosened her collar, taking off the striped red and black tie.

"You meeting Kippy to celebrate?"

"Not today. He's away," Daisy replied. Linda looked smug. Donnie had probably promised her a night out. He and Linda had been an item since Daisy's birthday. The fight on the dance floor had been the result of Linda's simultaneous flirting with Donnie and another guy, the other bloke no doubt roped in to make Donnie react.

Dod had told Daisy and Katrina that Donnie had at least two other girlfriends in the neighbouring towns and villages. He claimed to be out on the boat far more than he was.

Daisy kept schtum.

Despite Kippy's temporary absence, euphoria began to flood her body. The exams were over, and so was school. There was another month to go before the Academy officially finished for the holidays, weeks where she was meant to start on the work for her Highers, but as far as Daisy was concerned, school was over for the summer.

Katrina had promised her Morag would let her do waitressing shifts at the Star Tavern, and two months of fantastic fun beckoned for all of them—Daisy, Katrina, Kippy, Dod and Mick. They would spend free evenings at the beach and party in people's houses. They would sneak their way into the beer tents at the farm shows, and they would cycle to far-out beauty spots where they could drink, and smoke and laugh and chat.

Heaven.

"What do you think's up with them?" Linda pointed at two of their teachers. They were two of the staff smokers, rumoured to ignore any pupils smoking behind the Cochrane Hall whenever they retreated there, mooching fags off them from time to time.

The first one, Mr Murray, was saying something to the second, Mr McArthur—his face grim. They both looked in the direction of the river, just visible to the back of the school and behind the hall.

Daisy put a hand up to shade her eyes and then shrugged. "Who cares? They're probably bitching about something. Murray spends his life moaning."

But as they left the school, Linda peeling off in the opposite direction as she headed back to her own house, Daisy began to feel uneasy. She could sense something in the air; a buzz that hovered above the stillness of the late spring day.

A car flew past her, heading in the direction of the harbour.

As she walked along St Mary's Street and down to the river, she spotted people gathered around the harbour master's office. Most of them she didn't know, but as she got closer, she spotted Dod's father and mother, both pensive and anxious-looking.

The women who worked in the town's small tourist office had come outside too, one of them making her way over to the group.

Daisy saw a little exchange take place, and then the woman walked back to her colleague. Another exchange. Worried glances. Everyone looking at the river.

Alison stood outside Mackies. Not a good sign. As

Mackies was so busy these days, no-one saw Alison in the outside world.

"What's going on?" Daisy joined Alison, whose eyes were fixed on the group gathered at the harbour master's office.

"A boat's gone down," Alison muttered, her voice clipped. "The Fisher King."

"Oh!" Daisy's hand flew to her mouth. The Fisher King was the boat Dod went out on.

"Was–"

"Yes."

Alison pre-empted her question. Everyone in Kirkinwall thought of Daisy, Katrina, Kippy, Dod and sometimes Mick as a gang. Therefore, it was only natural that Daisy would ask if Dod had been on the boat that had sunk, the image unwittingly springing up in her mind now.

She saw stormy weather, clouds gathering and waves surging up. She heard shouted orders, and she saw the small boat rocking violently up and down. Men in yellow overalls furiously bailed water out, the deck filling up faster than they could empty it.

Dod could swim, though. She'd asked him once, and he'd told her he was the underwater champion of Kirkinwall. He could hold his breath for Scotland, something Katrina backed up. They both laughed at that, Daisy not sure if she understood the joke.

"But the lifeboat will get them, won't it?"

Alison turned to face her. She reached out a hand and patted Daisy clumsily on the shoulder. She wasn't usually tactile, and the gesture frightened Daisy.

"Aye. Here's hoping." She sent a last, lingering glance at the river, and went back inside the chippie.

Daisy crossed the street and headed for Dulcie's. The

salon was a hotbed of gossip and news, so Katrina probably knew already, but she wanted to be with her. Katrina would understand about boats going down, and people being rescued. They could wait for Dod's safe return together.

She didn't need to go into Dulcie's. Katrina met her at the foot of the stairs inside its front door.

"I take it you know about the Fisher King?" Daisy asked. Katrina's face was solemn, its usual sardonic expression replaced by a mouth pinched tightly together and glassy eyes.

"C'mon," she took Daisy's hand and steered the two of them back across the road and up to the Moat Brae. The grassy mound that looked out over the river already had its share of spectators, small groups of people whose eyes also searched the distant horizon for a boat.

"Not here," Katrina about-turned. "I'm no' waiting with the vultures."

Daisy didn't think they were vultures. Everyone shared the same worried expression, but she got Katrina's sudden wish to be by themselves. Dod was part of their gang, their friend, the special friend in Katrina's case. It wasn't right for them to wait in a collective of people who didn't know him that well, and their place wasn't with his parents either.

"What happened, I mean I know the boat went down, but when? And the lifeboat's gone out, hasn't it? They'll be wearing life jackets, won't they? And Dod can swim, can't he? He's an excellent swimmer. He told me he was."

Katrina didn't answer Daisy's stream-of-consciousness questions, just shaking her head slightly which could have meant she didn't know anything. She headed in the direction of Castledykes Road and her home.

Katrina's mum was in the kitchen, making cups of tea. Morag was there too. As the daughter of a one-time fisherman, Morag said she was all too familiar with waiting for news when you heard of a boat going down.

She looked at Daisy and Katrina and smiled pityingly. "Nothing you can do but cross your fingers and hope. Hope, hope, hope. Want a ciggie, girls?"

They stood in the back garden and smoked, the river visible to the left. If the lifeboat, or even better the Fisher King, returned, they would see it coming in. Morag kept up a steady stream of small talk. Maybe she sensed Katrina needed it. Had Daisy finished her exams? What stage of hairdressing was Katrina at, was she doing perms and were they allowing her to put highlights on folks?

The minutes of the afternoon stretched out, endless, and then suddenly it was seven o'clock, and Daisy knew she needed to go home. Apart from anything else, her mum would want to know how her last exam had gone.

"Come back with me?" she said to Katrina, who shook her head. Had Katrina got thinner suddenly, pounds falling off her in the time they'd been stood outside smoking and contemplating the river? She looked pale and gaunt, her body folding into itself and her hair hanging forward.

Morag put an arm around her, and Katrina pushed up against her. "You better get home, Daisy. I'll look after this yin."

Back home, her mum asked about the boat first. Her knowledge was the same as Daisy's. She couldn't add anything further, other than she knew the time the lifeboat had gone out, and she could confirm it was yet to come back in.

Daisy's dad telephoned from London. He'd heard the news on the radio and recognised the name of the boat. The sound of his voice was comforting. "I'm sure it will be fine, Daisy," he said. "It just takes a bit of time. They'll find the boys and pick them up."

If your dad said it was fine, everything would be all right. Everyone knew that.

Her mum asked about the final exam, and Daisy remembered her earlier euphoria. Debbie didn't think Daisy having finished twenty minutes before the end was a terrible thing. No, it just meant that she'd prepared and revised well. Her mum raised an eyebrow at that. She'd been worried that Daisy had seen too much of Kippy and Katrina when she should have been studying. The proof wouldn't be available until August though when the results came out.

Having spent a restless night, Daisy got up the next morning and made her way downstairs without bothering to shower or brush her teeth. Her mum was up already, sat at the kitchen table and drinking coffee. She looked up as soon as Daisy came into the room, her expression killing all final hope.

"I'm sorry, Daisy," she said. "The radio said the boat had called off the search. They haven't found any bodies yet, but it doesn't seem likely anyone has survived."

What did you do when a close friend died? Daisy's only experience of death was that of a great-uncle who'd been in his seventies. It was hardly the same thing. Dod was a smart, funny eighteen-year-old, whose mouth and eyes glowed with life. She thought of Kippy's charcoal sketch of him, that lazy grin and the mouth that looked as if it never stopped talking.

"Well, Your Royal Highness. Ah'm no' sailing tomorrow. Ah'm going out on a fishing boat where ah will work ma wee socks off. Mebbe even ma bollocks off. That's testicles to you!"

She heard the echoes of his laughter, sharp and distinctive. Mebbe even ma bollocks off.

Maybe I will work my life away. The sea will rush up on me and wipe me out.

"I better phone Katrina," she said, the words brittle and unstable. She thought the trace of Dod's laughter was still in the kitchen, but what she said seemed to quieten it. The thought paralysed her. If she crossed the room to the phone, the laughter would vanish forever.

Her mum stood up, pushing herself back from the table and moving to Daisy's side. She pulled her in for a hug.

"Leave her for a while," she whispered, her mouth close to Daisy's ear. "I think Katrina will need a little time to process what's happening. Maybe you should wait until she comes here."

The hug, the whispered words and the kindness did what the news so far had failed to do. Daisy's eyes welled up. Pushed into her mum's shoulder, wetness coated her cheeks and dripped from her nose.

The inner circle would never be the same again.

Ken?

COMFORT AND SUCCOUR

As her mum had predicted, Katrina turned up at their house that afternoon. Dulcie's had let her take the day off work, knowing how close a friend she'd been to Dod. The whole town probably knew that he'd carried a huge, flaming torch for her. They just hadn't known that somewhere deep inside Katrina, she felt more for him than she let on.

She let herself in the back door, having taken the back route to the White House so she could avoid bumping into anyone.

Daisy was upstairs, lying on her bed and listening to music mournful enough to match her mood, the same song playing over and over. Fittingly, Annie Lennox's *Why* warned of a boat sinking, as well as begging the question why. Daisy didn't know who would give her the best answer to why. Despite St Mary's School for Girls' best efforts, her belief in a deity was shaky, and her intellect wouldn't let her ask inane questions, such as why God would allow this.

The best she could come up with was Dod being in the wrong place, at the wrong time—something so random, the 'what if' outcomes kept surfacing.

What if he'd been ill, and not gone out? What if the crew had caught enough fish and come back early? What if the lifeboat had been able to get there sooner?

"Daisy! Katrina's here."

Downstairs in the kitchen, Debbie had her arms around Katrina. She exchanged a look with Daisy, a warning to let her keep hugging her friend until she was ready to let go. It seemed to go on forever.

"I never told him I loved him, Mrs Double U." The muffled admittance shocked Daisy. She'd never suspected this.

"He knew, Katrina," her mum said. The surprises were coming thick and fast this morning.

"I saw the four of you together, and it used to make me smile," Debbie continued, her soft London accent almost the opposite of Katrina's broader Scottish tones, and soothing. "'Teenagers,' I'd think to myself. 'Thank God I haven't been one for a long time', having to put up with all those hormones fizzing about your bodies and messing you up."

"I'm in charge of my hormones, Mrs Double U. They do what I tell them."

Debbie laughed at that. "That's right, Katrina. But I'm sure Dod knew you loved him in your own way. He adored you, that's for sure. And you spent time with him. I think he thought that was enough, and at some point, you'd feel the same way about him as he felt about you."

"But I slept with him and I never..."

If teenage confessions of promiscuity took Daisy's mum aback, nothing showed on her face. "Maybe he saw that as proof of your love, Katrina. Sometimes men think that about sex too."

Blimey. Debbie would be asking Daisy about just what she and Kippy got up to next, the irony being that Daisy's relationship was practically PG-rated, bound to be approved by parents everywhere.

Katrina stepped back, wiping her nose with her hand. She sniffed hard and turned her attention to Daisy.

"God, your hair looks terrible. Do you need me to tidy it up?"

Behind her, Daisy's mum nodded.

"Okay then." Daisy took a deep breath. "You can cut it if you like." So far, Daisy had agreed to dye jobs and different hairstyles but refused anything that involved locks of her hair falling to the ground, too scared that Katrina would morph into Edward Scissorhands.

Katrina's face lit up.

"Really? Magic. I promise I'm gonnae make you look like something out of the magazines."

His reaction explained everything.

Kippy was due back later that evening. He'd been out in the sticks somewhere, a phrase he used that amused Daisy. The sticks, by her London reasoning, was Kirkinwall. The locals didn't think that way. There were places far more rural and cut off than their wee town. Kippy and Lenny had been doing a tidy-up paint job for the council in the far west of the region. Kippy had told Daisy he would stay an extra night, as he wanted to paint some of the scenery while he was out there.

Cut off from civilisation—and the crappy McCallum's Painting & Decorating van did not have a radio—it was un-likely he would have heard about the Fisher King's sinking.

It was Daisy's job to tell him. She hated herself for it but being the bearer of such colossal news made her feel very important. She imagined herself telling him and Kippy's expression of shock as he registered that his best friend—the inner circle, ken? —was missing, possibly drowned. Having had time to absorb the news, Daisy would be the strong one, offering comfort and assistance.

Kippy had parked the van outside her house and knocked on the door. The plan had been to pick her up and meet up with Katrina and Mick to celebrate the end of Daisy's exams.

Daisy had been waiting for him in the living room. She rushed to the door when she heard the knock, swinging the door open.

"Oh hey. You haven't heard the news, then?" Now that the moment was here, she wasn't sure how you did this.

"Hey, yourself. What news? Have you had your hair cut? Can we go, 'cause I'm gasping for a drink."

"Ah…can you come in? I've got something to tell you. Something important. We'll go upstairs."

He looked at her warily. "Can't you tell me later?"

She took his hand. "No. C'mon."

He followed her up the stairs. Used to the different sounds of her family's footsteps on the stairs—her mother's ankle bone clicks, her father's plodding tread, her brother's scuffle as he ran as fast as he could up and down—Kippy sounded entirely different. He had a cautious and yet heavy step. Daisy felt as if she was dragging him behind her.

Inside her room, he didn't sit down, spreading his arms wide instead. "Well? What is it?"

"Kippy," she began, her tone solemn. She took hold of the hands still spread wide and pulled them in, clasping them between hers. "It's terrible news!"

The rest of the words came out as previously prepared. "Dod's boat's gone down. Yesterday morning. The lifeboat people haven't found any of the crew. They think they're all dead."

Daisy watched his face carefully. It began to crumple, the eyes blinking several times rapidly and then the forehead corrugating. He broke his hands free of hers and started to back away from her.

"No, no, noooooo."

The sound shocked Daisy. It wasn't something she'd ever heard before, a long, harsh wail that summed up pain and loss. Kippy folded forward, his hands up by his temples, and shuffled backwards towards the door. As he hit it, he slid down, head still in hands. The wailing had continued throughout.

"Is everything okay?" Her mum's inquiry, soft and gentle outside her bedroom door.

"Yes, it's okay," Daisy replied, even if it was blatantly obvious that wasn't the case. "Go away." She heard soft footsteps padding back downstairs.

Daisy joined Kippy on the floor. His face was pressed into his knees and his arms curled around them. She began to stroke his back tentatively. There was no sound, but she could feel him shuddering.

"I know, I know," she said. "Dod was your best friend."

The shuddering stopped. He shrugged off Daisy's hand, edging away from her. "You know nothing." The words came out in a hiss.

"Fucking nothing. He was…Dod was…I loved…"

He pushed himself to his feet. The eyes were bloodshot, but his face was white—the lack of colour making his freckles even more prominent than usual. A thin line of snot ran from his nose, and he wiped it off quickly with the back of one hand.

"Kippy, I…"

"Fuck off."

With that, he wrenched open the bedroom door and ran down the two flights of stairs, Debbie and Matthew watching open-mouthed and wide-eyed as he slammed his way out of the house.

HEARTBREAK AND ART

"Daisy, Daisy—can you let me in?"

The knock on the door was gentle, three soft taps. Daisy ignored it.

"Please, love. I've had this idea, and I want to talk to you about it. Get your advice."

Daisy was lying on her bed listening to music. She'd played a few different CDs now, singing along when the lyrics struck her as particularly relevant. That wasn't often. It seemed singers and musicians didn't write about what you felt like when you discovered your boyfriend of the past eight months was gay, and in love with his best friend—the best friend who was now dead.

She kept chopping and changing tracks, but no-one sang about her situation. The best she could get were lines here and there that spoke of great unhappiness.

Dread Other Girl mocked her. As well as being drop-dead gorgeous, the girl everyone stared at when she walked into a room, she was also expert at converting guys from gay, apparently.

"Please, love," her dad asked again. He'd come up from London the day before, apologising profusely. "I'm sorry, Daisy. I shouldn't have told you everything was going to be alright. I just hoped…"

By that time, though, the boat sinking's seriousness was less than what had happened subsequently. Daisy supposed it was further evidence of what a shit person she was. A major incident takes place, where people are killed, and yet her heartbreak dominated her head. There was not enough room to worry about the families of those men sent to a watery grave.

Debbie had filled him in, telling him that Kippy had stormed out of the house when Daisy told him about the accident and seemed to have finished with her. Their oldest child was so upset, she'd now shut herself up in her bedroom for the last couple of days.

Her dad was persistent. She would give him that. Her mum had insisted Daisy eat, too worried about the effect skipping meals might have on her diabetes to care that her daughter kept shooting her dirty looks and complaining that no-one understood her.

Her dad kept trying to talk to her, as he was trying now.

She got up and let him in, stalking back to the bed and pulling the duvet up so that it was right under her chin.

Her dad sat on the bed.

"I'm sorry, love," he said.

Daisy pulled the duvet over her head. Sorry? It was hardly his fault, except if she wanted to blame him for moving the family to Kirkinwall in the first place. If they'd never come to Kirkinwall, she wouldn't have met Kippy, and she wouldn't be going through this now.

Tony pulled the duvet down gently. "Okay, I'm only your

dull old dad. I get things wrong most of the time. Do you know, when your mum told me, I wanted to go to Kippy's home and smash his head in? How dare he hurt my daughter!"

The thought of her dad smashing anyone's head in was so difficult to imagine it made Daisy smile. He'd said the last sentence so vehemently too. She pulled herself up to a sitting position.

"Oh, Dad. I want to punch him too, but it won't change anything."

Tony took hold of her hand. He turned it palm-up in his own, gently stroking the palm with his thumb.

"No, it won't love."

Kippy's reaction to Dod's death had made Daisy feel many things. Firstly, she'd been shocked. *Oh! He loves—loved—Dod. He loves—loved—another man.* Then, the hurt had hit her, a massive cannonball blasted out, crashing into her full-on and slamming her against the wall. *He doesn't love me! He's never felt the same way about me as he did about Dod!* Then came shame. *What will people say, what will they think of me? Too unfanciable, too ugly, a guy would prefer his best mate?* And finally, the overwhelming feeling of stupidity.

Why didn't I realise? The charcoal drawings, the heavy petting sessions they had that seldom involved Kippy touching her, the reluctance to take her virginity. All those nagging little doubts that Daisy had suppressed, stamping down on them every time they surfaced.

When Kippy had stormed out of her house after Daisy had told him about Dod's death, her mum had bolted up the stairs, taking them two at a time. She pulled Daisy towards her, placing her hand on the back of Daisy's head. "What happened, do you want to tell me? It might help..."

Daisy was in the shock stage, the unreality of the situation so overwhelming it seemed perfectly natural to tell her mum what had happened. Kippy didn't love her after all. He never had. He was gay, really, and he'd been in love with his best friend, Dod, all along.

At least she had the sense not to tell her about the little clues. There was confiding in your parents, and then there was stupidity.

Debbie had sympathised. She tried to explain the situation from Kippy's point of view. "I think he did feel very strongly about you, Daisy darling," she said, stroking her daughter's hair as she wept, her face still pressed into her mum's shoulder.

"It must be hard for a young man growing up in a small town and knowing he's different from most people. And it must be very tough to love someone who can't love you back."

She might have been talking about Kippy and Dod. She could have meant Daisy and Kippy.

Nonetheless, feelings of hurt, stupidity and shame had kept her in her room for two days. She had even refused to see Katrina, afraid that Katrina had known all along about Kippy. He was her cousin, after all, and she'd known him for a lot longer than Daisy had.

"Can I tell you about my idea?" her dad said now. He looked at her carefully. When you were a teenager with a health condition, parents tended to disguise orders as questions. This did sound like a question. It was tentatively asked, almost nervous.

She nodded.

"I've been thinking about organising an art competition."

Daisy stiffened, remembering then that conversation she'd overheard two months ago. Art meant Kippy.

Her dad noticed. "That's why I wanted to talk to you. I won't do anything unless you are okay with it?"

Again, a question not an order. Daisy nodded and closed her eyes.

"I've always liked the idea of this place being somewhere artists came. It was once called the Artists Town as you know, so I thought one way to boost visitor numbers would be to organise a competition.

"I was going to make it straightforward—winner gets £10,000, and an exhibition takes place over the summer, one that people pay to see. Hopefully, that would bring in visitors. They could see the display and then have fish and chips in Mackies, say!"

Opening her eyes again, she smiled at that. "What, the best fish and chips in Scotland?"

He smiled back at her. Tony rarely said Mackies without saying "the best fish and chips in Scotland".

"Quite! When it was clear that all those poor young men were lost at sea, I started thinking that there should be some tribute to them. The art competition should still go ahead, but it should include another category: an artist creates a permanent tribute to those fishermen."

He took a deep breath. "Do you think Kippy would want to do something in tribute?"

Daisy thought of those charcoal sketches, the perfect recreation of Dod and his lazy, broad grin. Then she remembered the joint dangling from his right hand and that you could make out the beginnings of pubic hair as the overalls sat so low on his body.

A beautiful, beautiful picture, but not one for a tribute, she supposed. As she thought of the sketch, she began to feel better. Her mind slowed. For the last few days, thoughts had raced through her mind, flitting from one to another.

I'm very stupid. Kippy never loved me. Why couldn't I have been so wonderful, he got over his feelings for Dod—an endless loop of thoughts that kept repeating themselves

Now, they stilled, resting on the words, Poor Kippy. Poor Dod.

Daisy took her own deep breath. "Yes, I think he would. But he'd probably like to enter the competition too. Kippy could do a lot with £10,000. Go to art school, maybe."

Her dad leant forward so he could hug her. "Oh, Daisy. I'm so proud of you." He stood up, ducking, so he didn't hit his head on the eaves.

"Shall we name the competition after Dod? We could do that and make the whole thing about the tribute. I'd increase the prize money too, double it." He stopped at the bedroom door. "What was his real name anyway?"

"George McCaskill. I never heard anyone call him George, though."

Her dad opened the door. "George McCaskill? Well, I never. We're having dinner in half an hour. Will you join us?"

This time, it wasn't a question.

A SMALL, FINAL ACT OF KINDNESS

The Galloway News, June 5.

COMPETITION HONOURS LOST FISHERMEN

A new competition will honour those lost in the recent Fisher King tragedy.

The Fisher King's six-man crew are all presumed dead after the boat was lost at sea on or around May 30. Radio communication from the Fisher King on the night of May 30 indicates that she got into trouble in the Gulf of Corryvreckan, between the islands of Jura and Scarba.

Divers have found the wreckage of the boat, and the bodies of the skipper, John Iredale, 29, and deckhand, Martin McGovan, 27. The bodies of Andrew Failey, 23, James Kelly, 22, John Cathcart, 22, and George McCaskill, 19, have not been found.

Organised by businessman Tony Walker, the new art competition will be a tribute to the six-man crew. Entrants will be asked to create a work of art—a painting, sculpture or installation—that encapsulates the bravery and integrity of Kirkinwall's fishermen. The winning entry will be permanently displayed in the town.

The prize is £10,000.

Mr Walker, who commutes to London for his job, has invested considerable sums of money in Kirkinwall businesses.

He said: "Along with everyone else in Kirkinwall, the loss of the Fisher King shocked me to the core. Fishermen in this town have long faced dangers, as they battle the elements to bring us fish. It seems only fitting that we create a permanent tribute to them.

"The competition is for local artists within a twenty-mile radius of Kirkinwall, and there will be an exhibition of all entries later this year."

Councillor Murdoch, who will judge the competition along with Mr Walker and an art expert from the Glasgow School of Art, said: "Our townsfolk are still reeling from the after-effects of this terrible tragedy. A memorial cannot cure those hurts, but it can show that we will never forget the six brave young men who lost their lives on the Fisher King. Our thoughts are with their families."

Katrina put the newspaper down and looked at Daisy, wide-eyed. "Ten thousand pounds! Fuck. Where does your dad get the money?"

Daisy shrugged, spinning around in the chair. "I dunno. I think he got some money from a rich old aunt or something." That's what her dad had said when she'd overheard that row between him and her mother. She still had no recollection of the woman.

Katrina and Daisy were in Dulcie's. Dulcie's boss, the formidable Karen Grant, was out. Daisy wouldn't have been allowed to be there otherwise. It was the day after Daisy's talk with her dad. She'd made her way to Dulcie's after eleven o'clock, knowing that the little old ladies who popped in on a Wednesday for their cut-price wash and set would be gone.

Daisy sat at one of the chairs in front of a mirror. Heartbreak had taken off a few more pounds. She lifted the hair off her shoulders and sucked in her cheeks, admiring the new sharpness of her jawbone.

"What happened to you and Kippy, then?" Katrina asked, resuming her sweeping up the hair trimmings on the salon floor. "He won't tell me anything."

For a second or so, Daisy thought she would confide. "Your cousin? You were right to think he was a poof. He was gay all along. He was in love with Dod, the guy you liked to shag, but wouldn't date properly. So, there we were, the four of us. Me in love with a poof. The poof in love with his best friend. The best friend in love with you. You in love with someone who only sees you as his sister."

The viciousness of it shocked her. None of this was Katrina's fault—not Dod's death, not Kippy's real feelings. It was all so messy. Maybe love always was. So far, in Daisy's experience, l'amour hadn't been anything like what the magazines or books said. Boy meets girl, they fall in love and live happily ever after.

As if!

Daisy let her hair drop. Katrina hadn't taken that much off it the other week, but she'd done as she promised and the shoulder-length, layered bob made her look much better.

"We split up. We weren't right for each other." Daisy fiddled with the ends of her hair. Katrina had stopped sweeping up. She was leaning on the broom staring at Daisy's reflection. Daisy avoided her eyes.

"Oh? I thought you were totally in love. I got jealous sometimes. I wished someone felt like that about me."

Daisy met her eyes this time. "Dod did." Her voice sounded sharp, firm.

Katrina shrugged. "You know what I mean. I wanted…" The sentence was probably supposed to end with 'Mick to love me'.

She stood behind Daisy and rested a hand on her shoulder. "I'm sorry about Kippy. He's an arse." With that, she bent forward so that her face rested next to Daisy's. "You won't leave Kirkinwall, will you?"

Two pairs of eyes—one set brown, one blue. The brown eyes started to water. The blue eyes did too.

"He did say you'd finished with him," Katrina added. Daisy blinked; a last, small act of kindness, then. It seemed better to be thought of as the dumper, and not the dumpee.

"Yes, I'll stay. I need to finish school. I need to do my Highers, don't I?"

If only Madame de Courcy could hear her now, she'd be in heaven. Her star French pupil was now re-thinking her options, the idea of studying Modern Languages and perhaps even that career as a teacher or translator not as unattractive as it had been some months earlier.

"Do you think Kippy'll enter the competition?" Katrina asked.

Daisy nodded. "Yes. He could go to art school with that money. The portfolio's ready to go, isn't it?" She thought of the life drawing she'd posed for and crossed her fingers that no-one but Kippy and the teachers at an art school ever saw it.

She didn't know about qualifications though. Kippy had a couple of 'O' Grades, and that was it. Did you need anything else for art school, other than talent?

She'd had enough of talking about Kippy.

"When's Dod's funeral?"

A funeral wasn't straightforward when there was nothing to bury or burn. Two of the bodies had turned up, washed up on the Irish coast, but neither of them was Dod. In the beginning, his mother had insisted he might still turn up, her protests that her only son was alive gradually quietening as the days passed. She and Mr McCaskill looked terrible, the colour and vitality of them sucked out.

"Next week." Katrina grimaced. "In the big church. It'll be a memorial."

She stood directly behind Daisy once more allowing Daisy to see her face in the mirror. "We'll need to go. Will you be okay with that?"

She meant, will you be okay with Kippy being there?

Daisy swallowed and wished she could say, "I can't go. Sorry." Behind her, she thought she could hear Dod laughing, the laugh she would never hear again.

"Yes," and then to a pressing issue that shouldn't have mattered but did. "What do you wear to a funeral?"

PROPER, PROPER COOL

The art competition took place a month later

Much to Daisy's relief, Kippy hadn't gone to Dod's memorial service. He'd told Katrina that he couldn't face it. He had, however, spent quite a bit of time with Dod's parents. He and Dod had been friends since nursery school. Dod's parents were both very fond of him, and they liked to hear him talk about Dod and all the things they'd got up to over the years.

Not all of it was suitable for parents' ears. There were enough jolly japes, though, to make Mrs McCaskill laugh and cry at the same time.

Daisy had managed not to see Kippy for the last four weeks. It hadn't been easy. She stayed away from certain parts of the town, and she made Katrina tell her where he was all the time so that she could avoid those areas. The inner circle was no longer there, what with Dod being dead, and another member banished.

Mick was gone too. Tony's big-wig friend, the one who'd attended the Mackies launch in February, had visited the Star Tavern in late May. He had raved about the place. *"It is not often that you find culinary gems outside of the UK's big cities, but trust me, readers, I discovered something special, the cooking so sublime, I closed my eyes and thought myself in the finest Paris restaurant…"*

The review in one of the Sunday papers had attracted the attention of a chef in Edinburgh, who needed a sous chef. He'd phoned the Star Tavern, and within a week, Mick had found himself lodgings and a job in the capital.

He called Katrina once.

"Are you shagging your way around the city?" she asked. Sat in the room with her, Daisy recognised the sound of someone steeling themselves for a response which was not what they wanted to hear.

"Nuh. I'm knackered. I work all the hours God sends. My cock's gonnae shrivel up and drop off from lack of use. I can't even be bothered to wank."

He told Katrina to tell Daisy to thank her dad for him.

Tony had chosen the third weekend in July to launch the results of the competition and the exhibition. The timing worked as it tied in with the start of the English holidays. He'd made sure to advertise the show, sending out leaflets about it to all the tourist information offices in the area, and paying money for notices in newspapers and magazines.

All the entries were to be displayed in the town hall. The judges would choose the winner on the first day, but the exhibition would remain in place for a couple of months.

Katrina turned up at the Walkers' house after work. The launch was on a Saturday night. Tony had also arranged for

Alison to do the catering, and the two girls had been roped into helping her.

"I brought us our uniforms," Katrina said, as they retreated upstairs to Daisy's bedroom.

"Shit," Daisy said. "I didn't know we needed to wear uniforms. I'd never have agreed to this if I'd known that."

"Dinnae worry; trust your Auntie Kit-Kat!" Katrina said and opened the plastic bag she had with her. She took out two black dresses. They were sleeveless and very short. She also shook out two packets of fishnet tights and white aprons with ruffles on them.

"Waitresses wear black and white, right?"

Picking up her dress and holding it against her, Daisy thought the uniform wasn't one Morag would call by that name. Dressed in it, though, she cheered up immensely. The fishnets were incredibly flattering. They made her legs look much longer and thinner.

Katrina had also brought her full arsenal of make-up with her. She gave the two of them the same make-over: flicked black eyeliner, lots of mascara and matte red lips.

They stood side by side in front of Daisy's full-length mirror.

"We look French," Daisy said. "Proper, proper cool."

Katrina nodded, pouting to emphasise the point. "I thought you should show Kippy what's he's missing, arse that he is."

Daisy dropped her gaze briefly. It was Kippy's place to tell Katrina that nothing short of a sex change operation would make Daisy attractive to him, not hers.

"Thanks. You're a mate, you."

"You're a mate, too." She tilted her head to the side, so it rested on Daisy's shoulder briefly, and then straightened up and moved away.

The two of them had to get to the town hall early before the exhibition started. Daisy felt her footsteps drag as they walked there. In an ideal world, when boyfriends finished with you, they ought to vanish so that you never saw them again. The red lipstick helped, but dread, nerves and a masochistic need to see Kippy again battled inside her.

"You have to smile and laugh and joke," Katrina said as they made their way to the kitchen at the back of the building. "Make sure he sees you looking happy. Flirt with some of the guys too. It's always worked for me."

A reference to Mick, Daisy supposed.

Alison put them to work. Tony had also ordered a new batch of flyers and posters for Mackies too, and they started by dotting them about the venue. Anyone attending couldn't miss the references to what Tony reckoned was the town's best attraction. As people began to arrive, Alison got them to circulate with trays of small canapes—tiny portions of fish, chips and mushy peas on toasted slices of baguette.

Daisy made Katrina go first. "You need to tell me where Kippy is."

Returning five minutes later, her tray empty, Katrina picked up a bottle of Asti Spumante. "He's at the back of the hall, to the left. Next to his painting. There are loads of folk in there. If you do the front of the room, you might not see him at all."

While Alison wasn't looking, she gave the Asti to Daisy and told her to take a swig from it. The sweet fizziness didn't help. Daisy's nerves jangled. As soon as she was in the hall, people pounced on her tray and emptied in seconds. She focused on their faces, forcing her eyes to look only a few feet in front of her and keeping them determinedly away from the back of the hall.

By the time she'd dished out her third tray, her luck had run out.

"Hiya, Daisy." He stood in front of her. Daisy had dropped her gaze at once. Reluctantly, she dragged her eyes upwards, and the sight of him made her start in shock.

Oh, he'd always been pretty, but now he was beautiful. Like Daisy, he'd lost weight. He'd been lean to start with, but the weight loss gave him a chic angularity that made those big eyes and mouth stand out even more. You couldn't look at anything else. His eyes glittered, and the freckles danced across the skin.

He wore dark jeans and a velvet blazer, and his hair was longer than Daisy remembered, the waves of it touching his shoulders. He ran a hand through that hair now.

"Are you okay?"

She nodded. When his mouth moved, it looked even more inviting. There was the embodiment of loss, the knowledge that those lips would never touch hers again.

"Sorry, Daisy."

As apologies went, it wasn't great. Daisy would have liked something more, or even for him to say, *"Well, if any lassie could have turned me, it would have been you."* On the other hand, he could just have not bothered at all.

"Can I see your painting?" she asked.

His eyes lit up at that. "Aye. I'd like to know what you think of it."

She followed him through the crowds to the back of the hall. Her dad saw her go, and signalled with his eyes, 'Everything okay?'. She flashed back an 'it's fine' look.

The painting was far bigger than anything else she'd seen in Kippy's studio. It hung on the back wall and a small crowd who were studying it intensely. One or two of them broke off their staring to congratulate Kippy, telling him the painting was incredible.

It certainly was. Daisy stood in front of it. Biased or not, there was no doubt in her mind that this picture must win the competition. He had painted the Fisher King, anchored in the harbour, while six men loaded it up with supplies. All their faces were recognisable, but the one who stood out was Dod. His faced the front, almost as if he was looking at a camera, and his head was thrown back, a perfect demonstration of the expression 'laughing your head off".

While the focus of the picture was the boat and Dod, Kippy had added in his signature details. You could see Mackies in the background, with its usual queue of people, and gulls circled in the skies waiting to swoop on the unwary eating their fish and chips.

"Look," Kippy pointed at something at the back of the painting.

Daisy peered closely. There, sat on the car park wall, was a girl swinging her legs, a borrowed bicycle leant next to her.

Immortalised. In years to come, people would look at the picture. Maybe they would wonder about its subjects, seeing the fishermen first and reading about their tragic ending in the little plaque next to the painting. But if they looked long enough, maybe they would see the girl on the wall too. Who was she and what happened to her?

[She was right. Twenty-five years from now, the town hall by this time renowned for launching the career of many a young artist would host an event in honour of its favourite son: *Alan Kirkpatrick: The Home Coming*.

A thirteen-year-old girl dragged along reluctantly to the exhibition would hone in on the girl in the picture, her curiosity so piqued she couldn't resist touching the oils. "Olivia don't do that!" her mother would hiss. attracting the attention of a man stood nearby.

He wandered over and stood beside her, his head tilted to one side as he looked at the girl in the picture too.

"That was a girl I used to know," he would say. "A girl your age." Older but gay men in their forties were often rubbish at working out the age of teenage girls. "I loved her so." Yes, he would say that too, placing a hand on his chest as he did so—even though the words weren't true. In his head, Alan Kirkpatrick had recreated the memory, a sweet innocent love bound in tightly to what had enabled him to escape the small town and become an artist. *I loved her* was easy enough to say then.]

"Sorry, Daisy." There was that apology again. He had moved closer to her and without being fully conscious of what she was doing, Daisy found herself in his arms. Ah, the smell of him. It hadn't changed—Lynx, washing powder and a bit of turps.

"Good luck," she whispered.

"Thanks. You too." He kissed the top of her head. Daisy wanted to prolong the hug, but she pulled herself back, and walked away, looking over her shoulder just the once as she went.

He stared after her. She couldn't discern what she saw in his eyes. Loss, regret, relief—who knew? Daisy took a deep breath and ordered the ever-ready tears to halt in their tracks. They heard her and obeyed.

Good-bye Kippy.

NOTHING OUT OF THE ORDINARY

Some months earlier

Lucy Anderson loved a good crime story. Fact or fiction didn't bother her. If pushed she would say her favourite tales were those serial killer stories. Apparently, you could buy tonnes of those kinds of books in America, but Lucy had no idea how to go about getting them.

Did you have to phone bookshops over there and ask them to send you some in exchange for a cheque? Lucy's mind boggled at how expensive that would work out. Phoning the US, the costs of the books, sending a cheque across the Atlantic and then the postage fees for the books themselves.

She'd have to content herself with the occasional tabloid story and the crime fiction she read voraciously, PD James, Agatha Christie, and her all-time favourite book, *In Cold Blood*.

No wonder Lucy loved her crime stuff. Working in a

bank wasn't exciting, especially one as small as the Kirkinwall branch. Her mum had said it would be a steady job, evidently thinking that was its biggest plus point. Day in, day out, her forefingers flicking coppers into bags of change for shop-keepers, paying in miniscule amounts of savings to little old ladies' accounts and cashing cheques.

Nothing happened out of the ordinary. Ever.

Until now. Anti-money laundering provisions made the bank staff sit up and blow the cobwebs off their old policies and procedures. One had to check everything carefully these days. Even when you lived in tiny town, where nothing ever happened.

The account had been set up some months ago with a few thousand pounds. So far, so unsuspicious—fair do's Lucy and no-one she knew would have so many thousands spare to start a new bank account, but the gentleman was well-spoken and English. A Lord too, though he told Lucy he preferred not to use the title out with the bank.

Everyone knew posh, English people had money lying around everywhere. Or land, or second homes—they just did, especially if they had titles.

Usually, the gent dealt with Lucy. She always seemed to be free when he came in, depositing money here and there, or setting up joint accounts with his various business partners so they too could draw down money.

They all knew him in the bank. He always called out a cheery 'hello' and 'goodbye' in marked contrast to the wealthy landowner who lived nearby and was as torn-faced as they came. The sums of money, though; the cheques made out in his name?

Lucy hadn't spotted it at first, as the money came out as quickly as it went in and she wasn't the only one dealing with the account. Maybe she just didn't notice what was a deposit and what was a withdrawal, but when she looked at the paperwork one quiet morning, she had to double check the account and all the neat entries and exits a few times.

Close on one million pounds had been moved through this account in the last year. No, less than a year, the activity had been going on for only seven months.

Elliot Ness! Lucy's over-active crime detection mind started to whirl. Elliot Ness had gone after Al Capone (and The Untouchables was another Lucy late-night reading treat), eventually getting him for tax evasion. Could this be going on here? The anti-money laundering advice sheet lay in front of her. She'd read it the once, her eyes skimming the words until suddenly her brain whirled. Might be, mebbe, something like this going on here?

The man, she knew had his principal bank account in London, and that account had provided some, but not all the transactions. Most of them had been cheques made out in his name.

What should she do? The branch's manager was a stuffy wee man, who cosied up to all their customers, especially the rich ones. He wouldn't be pleased with any suggestions of derring-do. No-one likes a troublemaker, and Mr Armstrong wasn't keen on women workers in general. If she pointed at the new legislation and said, "Mr Armstrong, I thought this might be a wee money laundering thing…?", he would turn to her, incredulous.

Women, in Donald Armstrong's world, shouldn't work. And neither should they bother expressing their stupid opinions.

She talked it over with her husband that evening. Simon didn't share Lucy's love for crime stories, but he was as smart as she was, and he liked to talk over arguments, mulling over what would happen if you did this or if you did that.

What would happen if Lucy raised it with Mr Armstrong? He'd tell her not to be silly and shake his head at the fanciful notions of women. He'd insist on checking it himself, and she'd never hear about the matter ever again except when he got the credit for it.

But then, what if Lucy didn't do anything at all? Nothing much would happen. The money would continue to be put in and taken out. If Lucy were right, maybe the man would be arrested at some point. The police would come into the bank, seize all the books and interview the staff. Lucy fast-forwarded to that, seeing herself in a small, windowless room sitting opposite two fearsome, scowling men in trench coats.

"I put it to you, madam," first trench coat said, "that you knew of this crime and willfully withheld information from us."

"And I say to you, madam," number two man said, "that we should search your bank accounts. What will we find there, exactly?"

For all her love of crime stories, Lucy's sketchy knowledge of police procedure led to an automatic jump to guilty by association.

Thirdly, Simon winked at her, Lucy waited until the gent carried out his next transaction. Then, she phoned the bank in London and asked to double check if all this movement of money was right. She was just doing it to be helpful, worried about the new anti-money laundering legislation like, and didn't want to waste anyone's time.

"Imagine what will happen after that if you are right, Lucy!" Simon said, taking her hand. "It will come out in court—the bank clerk in the wee branch who spotted the crime way before the big boys in London."

Lucy stared back at him, eyes round. "Just a wee phone call and a quick, 'I just wanted to double-check, I'm probably being silly', that kind of thing? And then I could call this number here," she stabbed a finger at the anti-money laundering advice sheet she brought home with her. "The folks at the fraud squad."

"Aye. No-one will ever know if you're wrong about it."

It was the perfect solution. Lucy skipped into work the next day. Mr Armstrong had a long meeting scheduled with the torn-faced landowner, which would put him safely behind doors for most of the morning.

Plenty of time to make a call to that London bank.

A TIMELY PROMOTION

Detective Superintendent Pat McCormack read the papers in front of him once more, trying to make sense of what they said.

No, no, no this couldn't 't be true…surely the scale of this thing made it impossible? There must be a mistake. And if so, a horrifically embarrassing one. His inspector had handed over the file with a sigh of relief. If what the papers showed was correct, the level of wrong-doing was far beyond his pay grade.

The superintendent oversaw the Metropolitan Police Fraud Squad, a team of officers who found crimes against capitalism far more thrilling than those against the body, though money motivation often facilitated the latter. Fraud had many degrees, from the small business whose book-keeper kept two sets of records, to wide-scale, company-wide swindles involving millions of pounds.

Pat stood up, pushing back his chair and opened the door to his office. His team sat at desks in a large, well-lit and tastefully decorated space. The murder squads, on the other hand, worked in offices that hadn't seen a lick of paint in decades.

"Inspector Johnson?" The man appeared to have been expecting the request. He was on his feet before Pat called out his name.

Back in the superintendent's office, Pat pulled the door firmly shut and indicated that his inspector sat down. "There's no chance this is a mistake?" He waved the papers at the man opposite him.

The inspector shook his head. "No, gaffer. I got this call from a bank clerk. She works in a branch of the Northern Bank in this tiny little place in Scotland. I had to look it up, never heard of it. Anyway, she said she'd looked twice at the amounts because of the new Money Laundering Regulations."

He named the new directive that had come into force in April. The three photocopied cheques were for sums of more than £15,000, dated only weeks apart.

"But a Lord has signed these cheques," Pat said, pointing at the extravagant signature in front of him.

The inspector shrugged. "That's what he calls himself. You can buy yourself a barony in Scotland. It's quite easy if you've got the dosh. Don't think it gets you anything, though, apart from a tiny bit of land in the middle of nowhere and the right to call yourself a Lord."

Pat resisted the impulse to sink his head into his hands. The Metropolitan Police's deputy finance director. For crying out loud. The file also included a note of his record of service, the award he'd received when he'd reached twenty years' service. There was even a copy of the picture of him, shaking hands with the commissioner.

"And the money came from where?" he knew the answer anyway, but Pat wanted it repeated. The words had an air of unreality; repetition would make them absolute.

"A Scotland Yard secret fund. It was supposed to be used to pay informers and for undercover work against the IRA. When it was set up two years ago, he managed to make himself the sole signatory. That meant he could draw down the money whenever he wanted."

It was pointless to ask why something like this had been allowed to happen. That would be the role of any subsequent investigation into how senior officers ran the Met. And someone (Pat himself?) would need to stand in front of MPs at some point and explain why this would never happen again. Processes would change. They would affect not just the Met, but police forces all over the country.

"I looked at the figures myself. I thought it best that we keep the investigation to a few people."

Pat nodded. Inspector Johnson's discretion was well-placed at this stage. He could have handed that kind of grunt work over to a sergeant or even a PC, but Pat was grateful he hadn't.

"We'll need to get hold of his bank accounts. And freeze his assets."

"The scale of the thing…" Inspector Johnson shook his head. "You've got to admire it in a way."

Pat gave him a stern look, Inspector Johnson's quick reaction in response—*well, not really, but you know what I mean*—amusing him in turn.

"We need a warrant if we're to get access to his accounts."

Pat nodded once more, reaching for his phone. One quick call to a judge and the briefest of explanations later, the warrant was on its way.

"Payroll will be able to tell you who he banks with. Get along to his branch as soon as you've got the warrant," he told the inspector.

Inspector Johnson stood up.

"Do you think he's got a gambling problem?"

Pat shrugged his shoulders. "The whys aren't our concern. We just need to get the proof. And then…" He tailed off. No need to elaborate any further.

Then the process of the law will kick in.

And Tony Walker would find himself in a whole heap of trouble.

He never mentioned names.

Inspector Gregory Johnson had been a copper since he left school. He'd signed the Official Secrets Act at the age of seventeen, and the picture of that scrawled signature appeared in front of his eyes anytime family or friends tried to question him about what exactly went on in the police.

He'd also had a stint in the anti-terrorist unit, where the bosses hammered secrecy into them. And he was a freemason. Maybe he just liked the tight hugging of information to himself.

But this time, he dropped the name. Deliberately and guardedly but breaking the habit of a lifetime nonetheless. He placed his knife and fork together carefully and steepled his hands. Tina recognised the gesture—the one he always used when he had crucial information to impart and that he expected full attention.

She took the plate away from him and sat back down again facing him.

"Do you still teach that Walker kid? Daisy, isn't it?"

Tina, aka Mrs Johnson the Maths teacher at St Mary's School for Girls, shook her head. "No, not for a while. They left—the mum, daughter, and younger son. Left London, I mean. I heard they went up north to some tiny place in Scotland. It was a while ago."

He felt the hairs on the back of his neck stand up. There was a buzzing in his ears too.

"Why did they leave?"

Gregory Johnson might have thought he was being smart, but he never showed an interest in Tina's pupils. "Oh-ho!" was Tina's first thought. "What have the Walkers been doing?" She didn't let any of this show on her face, however.

"I think it was to do with Daisy's illness. Type 1 diabetes. Her mum felt she would be better off in a smaller area and school. I don't know for sure, but Mrs Allensby could tell you."

She named the French teacher. The woman had a soft spot for Daisy, thanks to the girl's excellent French picked up from many holidays in the country. Tina didn't think that made the girl skilled. If your wealthy parents could afford a month in France every summer, then it followed you could speak perfect French.

Gregory shook his head. He fully intended to talk to Mrs Allensby, but he didn't like Tina to know she had helped him.

Tony Walker, I am coming after you. I have an inkling of what you have done.

He stood up, pushing back his chair and thanking his wife belatedly for dinner. His mind was elsewhere. It was fast-forwarding, partly to what was about to happen to Tony Walker, but mainly to the aftermath: promotion.

Chief Inspector Gregory Johnson.

That would do nicely.

THE MAN
FROM LONDON

The rat-a-tat-tat on the door reverberated through the house, startling Daisy. Usually, she didn't hear anyone. Upstairs in her bedroom hidey-hole, music blaring, she missed the noise her family made downstairs.

This knocking, though. It wasn't a polite tap on the wood, more a bang, booming three times through the door, along the hallway and up the stairs. Daisy turned off her music. In the last few weeks, she'd tried to train herself out of the instinctual reaction to anything unusual. Her treacherous heart disobeyed. *Maybe it's Kippy! He's changed his mind! He's realised he loved me all along. Dod was just a…* Well, whatever.

…an overreaction to a close friend's death.

Anything might trigger those instinctual thoughts—even though she'd made her peace with the idea of Kippy as gay.

She opened the door to her bedroom cautiously. If it was Kippy at the door, she didn't want to look too keen. He should bolt up the stairs, taking them two at a time and throw himself at her door, yelling, *"Daisy, Daisy, open up!"*

The inch or so of space she'd allowed between the door and its frame didn't let her see anything, but she could hear her mum. A surprised tone.

"Oh. Officer Burnie. Er…"

Daisy sighed. No, it was not Kippy at the door, only the local police officer, the one Dod had once disrespectfully blown a smoke ring at as they drove past him.

That fat prick does nothing off duty.

Daisy heard another voice—an English accent, a Londoner. The broad London tones sounded unfamiliar, harsh almost after all this time.

Her dad had come into the hallway. Daisy pushed her door open as quietly as she could and leant over the rail. She saw the tops of four heads. The Kirkinwall officer stood next to a man wearing a dark trench coat, his hair cropped short and the hall light picking up silver bits. It was this man who was doing all the talking.

"…so, we just need to clear this up, Mr Walker. Would you mind coming down to the police station to answer a few questions?"

Daisy heard her mother's sharp intake of breath. "The police station? Can't we do it here?"

There was no answer, and Daisy saw Debbie turn her head to her dad. She couldn't see anyone's expressions, but Tony was facing the man from London. Daisy wondered if he recognised him.

"No," the man said. The 'no' was said nicely, but the word didn't allow any discussion. Daisy tip-toed to the slanted window in the upstairs hall. There was a police car outside. Ridiculous, seeing as the town's police station was less than two hundred metres away.

There was murmuring, her dad talking to her mum, and seconds later the front door banged shut.

"Mum, what's going on?" Daisy leant over the stair rail. Her mother looked up, her head tilted right back. Had Daisy ever noticed before how slim her mum's neck was? From this angle, it looked as if the head on top of it might topple off at any moment. Her mum's face was white too, apart from two small, bright spots of colour on her cheeks.

"I…I don't know, Daisy. A misunderstanding, I think." The words had the delayed feel to them as if she was speaking to Daisy from a phone in a foreign country. "Your dad's just gone to answer a few questions. Do you want to come down, watch some TV with Matthew and me?"

The last was said so plaintively, Daisy nodded and headed down the stairs.

In the family living room, done out in delicate shades of green and blue, the three of them sat on the sofa together. Debbie sank between Daisy and Matthew, clutching her hands tightly together and resting them on her thighs.

"Nothing's wrong, is there?" Daisy asked.

"No, just a misunderstanding," Debbie repeated. She sounded no more convincing second time round.

"They didn't have the sirens going," Matthew said. "In the police car, Mum. If there is anything wrong, they put the sirens on. And the flashing blue lights."

It was rubbish, but Daisy jumped on it anyway. "That's right, Mum! No sirens."

She and Matthew usually argued about what programme they watched on the rare occasion Daisy joined her family for communal viewing. Tonight, though, they both asked Debbie what she wanted to watch, putting suggestions to her.

It didn't matter. Daisy was aware of her mother staring blankly at the screen as they settled down in front of Coronation Street. She wasn't taking anything in.

Two hours later, there was still no sign of Tony.

Debbie got up from the sofa. "Matthew, you'd better go to bed. I'm sure your dad won't be far away."

Matthew didn't moan. He got up, glancing back at Daisy as he left the room following their mum. She tried to look reassuring.

Debbie returned five minutes later.

"Do you want to go to the police station, Mum? Find out what's happening?"

Her mum closed her eyes briefly. A dilemma question, then.

"Or we could call them?"

"Could you do it, Daisy?" her mum whispered. "Call them, I mean." Then, she seemed to shake herself. "No, you're right. I'll call."

She got up again and let herself out of the room, closing the door behind her. The downstairs telephone was in the kitchen. There was another phone in the hallway, but Daisy knew if she tried to listen in, they would hear her picking up the extension.

She waited as long as she could and then got up. In the kitchen, her mum had put the kettle on, and Daisy got out the tea bags and mugs.

"They didn't tell me anything," her mum said. "But they haven't finished with him. It's been more than two hours. Two hours, Daisy!" With that, her voice broke. "What are they asking him? I did always wonder..." She placed both hands on the kitchen table, letting the surface take her weight.

"Did always wonder why I had never heard anything

about this mystery aunt." It was a whisper, the words muttered to herself. Debbie looked up, her eyes meeting Daisy's, the two of them frightened by her words. If you said something, didn't that make it real?

"I mean," Debbie continued, "she's some woman we've never met who suddenly decides Tony is her favourite nephew?"

Daisy had never given Aunt Caroline much thought. She didn't even know if the woman was supposed to her grandmother or grandfather's sister. Now, it was beginning to look as if Aunt Caroline had never existed in the first place.

"Daisy, love, you look tired," Debbie took the mugs from her. "Go to bed. Your dad will be back soon."

"But I…" Then, just as Matthew had done earlier, Daisy decided it was better to obey. The world she stood in now seemed too grown-up, too frightening. In her bedroom, Daisy could put on music, stare at the posters on her wall, dream up scenarios where Kippy realised his mistake and begged for her forgiveness, perhaps even pad out the odd fantasy about Mick (don't tell Katrina).

"Goodnight, Mum." She tiptoed out of the kitchen and up the stairs.

Thankfully, the next day was not a school day. Daisy awoke early, the memory of what had happened last night slowly reforming itself in her brain. She lay still, listening out for the noises of the house.

In the morning, sounds usually drifted up from downstairs—the radio in the kitchen, exchanges between Debbie and Matthew, or Tony and Matthew.

She heard nothing.

Then, footsteps coming up the stairs to her room. A gentle rap on the door.

"Daisy?" her mum stuck her head around the door. In the darkness, Daisy couldn't see her expression. "Are you okay? Have you done a blood test?"

A good sign, surely? Her mum back to normal, worrying about Daisy's diabetes and not her husband's nighttime visit to the police station.

"Where's Dad?" she asked as she pushed off the duvet and sat up.

Her mum came into the room and sat down on the bed beside her. She smelled musty close to—of sweat and staleness. When she turned to face Daisy, she sighed out bitter coffee breath.

"They… they took him down to Carlisle. He's been arrested." The words were a whimper.

"Arrested? For what?" It was a stupid question, but 'arrest' and her dad didn't seem like words that belonged together. He worked for the police, for goodness sake. For the largest police service in the world, no less.

"For theft," Her mum's hair hung forward, hiding her eyes. "For stealing from the Met."

"Not much, though?" Daisy asked. She remembered something from school a few years ago when a secretary was found to have stolen fifty pounds from the charity fund. The head fired the woman, but she paid the money back and police charges were dropped.

Her mum stood up. She opened the curtains. Outside, it was a bright, sunny day and the streaming sunlight made her mum look old and tired. She shrugged helplessly, turning back to look at her daughter.

"One million pounds, Daisy. One million bloody pounds…"

ROBIN HOOD, ROBIN HOOD RIDING THROUGH THE GLEN…

The police arrived an hour later. They told Debbie they needed to search the house.

There were four of them, three dressed in plain clothes and Officer Burnie. The suited officers had the same broad, south London accent as the man who'd come to the door last night. He was there too. He stood in the hallway as if he belonged there, issuing instructions.

Debbie, Daisy and Matthew huddled in the kitchen, as the officers poked and prodded their way through the house. Daisy hated the thought of them in her room—Officer Burnie, in particular. She remembered the malevolent glare he'd given her and her friends that time in the car as they'd laughed back, and she imagined him fixing that image in his head.

Who's laughing now?

When they heard the officers make their way upstairs, Matthew asked if he could watch TV.

Debbie nodded. Daisy followed him through to the living room. The officers had left it tidy, but it looked different. The pile of papers that sat on top of the unit was gone. Some of the drawers weren't closed properly, the gap emphasising that someone had pulled them open, ransacked the contents and then casually pushed them shut.

Even the sofa had been subjected to the search. The cushions were piled back on it differently. Debbie liked her soft furnishings arranged just so. Whoever had rearranged the sofa should have asked her, *"Mrs Walker, how would like us to tidy up after ourselves?"*

Matthew sat as close to Daisy as he could. She put her arm around him. They found *Going Live* on the TV, Philip Schofield's voice cheery and reassuring, as he joked with Gordon the Gopher.

"Will we be arrested too, Daisy?" Matthew asked. "Will we go to jail?"

"No," Daisy said, hugging him closer. At least that was one question she could answer.

The search lasted a long time, the officers eventually leaving with cardboard boxes piled with papers, even Daisy's dad's clothes.

As they left the house, Daisy could see a small gathering of people stood on the street opposite, gawking. She recognised a few faces—Linda from school, Mrs Burnett's friend, Ida and one of the women who worked in Mackie's. She resisted the temptation to flick them the vees.

The phone in the hallway started to ring. Debbie looked at it and then back at Daisy.

"Daisy, love?"

Daisy answered the phone, saying the name of the town and rattling off the five-digit number the way her dad did when he picked up the phone.

"It's me." 'Me' was Katrina. "Are you okay?"

In the background, Daisy could hear blow-dryers and the low hum of chat. Then, the conversations stopped—the silence the sound of people desperately trying to listen in.

"Are you at work?" Daisy asked.

"Uh-huh. I'll come over later, right?"

Daisy agreed and put the phone down; grateful Katrina had worked out that she shouldn't say much on the phone.

The family spent the rest of the day in the house, Debbie told them she couldn't face going out. As Kirkinwall was so small, she was bound to bump into someone who knew them.

"Oh! Hello, Mrs Walker/Debbie"—depending on who the person was— *"Is everything okay? I heard there was a wee bit o' trouble earlier?"*

Her mum impersonated the local accent perfectly, cocking her head to one side and faking concern. It made Daisy and Matthew laugh.

Matthew had wanted to go out. His friends Ryan and Jamie often came calling on a Saturday, looking for him. They'd knocked on the door earlier, but Debbie had shaken her head. No doubt, the townsfolk would see Matthew as fair game. Up they would creep, that same question: *Is everything okay? Is your dad in trouble with the police, Matthew?*

Matthew was a rubbish liar.

Daisy was glad of the enforced lock-down. She felt tired, no exhausted. Fear and worry must be taking their toll.

Katrina arrived at 4.30pm. Dulcie's shut half an hour earlier on Saturdays. Her frequent guest status afforded her rights. Letting herself into the house by the back door was one of them.

She stood in the kitchen and gave Debbie a practised look. "Do you want me to do your hair or make-up, Mrs Double U?"

Debbie smiled at her, a weak, pathetic kind of smile. "I know. I look rubbish. Do you want to stay for dinner, Katrina or the night? We could do with the company."

"Aye. I'll stay. We could do a cinema night." She took a couple of videotapes out of her bag. "I got a couple of films here. *Robin Hood* and *Thelma and Louise*."

Matthew had started jumping up and down, the beam of joy contagious after such a shitty day. "*Robin Hood*? Ace! Can we watch that now, please Mum?"

Debbie took the tapes from Katrina, turning them over once or twice.

"I thought those films were only just out…?"

Katrina looked her square on. "Ask no questions, Mrs Double U, tell no–"

To their horror, Debbie burst into tears. She didn't move, staying where she was, leaning against the kitchen counter and crying, droplets of water dripping onto the floor.

"But that's it! I didn't ask any questions. Or if I did ask, I didn't ask enough. I should have kept saying to him, Tony, where's this money coming from, and why is there so much of it?"

Daisy and Katrina looked at each other. Katrina didn't seem surprised. Daisy guessed that meant she knew why the police had arrested Tony and what he was supposed to have done.

Matthew looked from Debbie to Daisy and back again, joy and excitement rapidly disappearing. His lip had started to wobble, and Daisy feared he was about to start full-on wailing too.

"Shall I put *Robin Hood* on, Mrs Double U? You can come through in a few minutes. We'll tell you what happens?" Katrina took Matthew's hand. "C'mon, Matthew."

Debbie nodded gratefully, and Daisy took her lead from Katrina, following her out of the room. In the living room, she stuck the video in and fast-forwarded through the dodgy foreign graphics. The film, when she eventually got to it, didn't look quite right, the picture blurring in places and the sound not as sharp as it could be.

It did the job, though. Matthew stared at the screen, transfixed, as Kevin Costner battled first infidels and then wicked knights.

Debbie came through twenty minutes later, carrying a tray. She'd made up plates of sandwiches, and there were crisps, sugar-free yoghurts and diet coke too. She placed them on the coffee table, and Katrina paused the film.

"Help yourselves," Debbie straightened up. She didn't put anything on a plate for herself, Daisy noticed.

There was a sound from the hallway, a door opening quietly and then closing again. The occupants of the living room looked at each other, their eyes wide. Nothing was said, but Katrina started the film up once more, and Debbie left the room, shutting the door firmly behind her.

"I'm starvin', Marvin!" Katrina told Matthew, stacking up sandwiches on a plate.

"I'm famished, Hamish!" he replied, pronouncing famished incorrectly, so it rhymed with the name. The exchange was one of their regular routines, the kind of set-up that happened when you had a friend who popped in regularly.

Over his head, Katrina mouthed, "What do you think

has happened?" Daisy didn't mouth anything back. A shrug was all she could manage. She listened out for screaming and shouting, but they couldn't hear anything beyond the sounds of the film.

She tried a sandwich, abandoning it after two bites and opening the bottle of diet coke instead. She was very thirsty.

Unable to stand the wait any longer, Daisy got to her feet. Katrina made a shuffling movement with her hand. Go, go…

"Matthew," she said, "let's have a crisp eating competition! Bet I can get more in my mouth at once than you can!"

Daisy left to the sounds of furious crunching.

In the kitchen, her dad sat at the table. Her mother had poured him a large glass of something. Whisky, probably. Despite his one-time experience where what he thought was whisky (and not a Temazepam-laced pudding) had knocked him out for the count, Tony had developed a taste for it, saying he should be a whisky drinker if they were going to live in Scotland.

Her mum also nursed a glass. Now that was strange. Her mum said she couldn't bear the stuff. It reminded her of old men, she said, the taste overwhelming and the drink something that knocked her for six. Again, that might have been because she'd mistaken whisky's properties for that of a drug well known for putting someone to sleep.

They raised their heads slightly as she came in. Her dad looked up and cast his eyes down. Her mum had been crying again. Her eyes were red-rimmed, her nose and cheeks flushed.

"What's going on?" Daisy asked, pulling out one of the table chairs so she could sit down. Neither of them seemed to want to meet her eye. There was no reply. From the living room, Daisy heard the film and an exclamation from

Matthew. Robin Hood must have trounced the bad guys again.

Having researched Robin Hood's story for a school project when she was ten, Daisy knew what was going to happen at the end of the film. The Sheriff of Nottingham would get his just desserts. The King would come back and reward Robin Hood. The king would agree Robin did nothing wrong by stealing. He stole from the rich to help the poor.

A good guy after all.

"I can't tell her, Tony." Debbie looked at her dad. What she said didn't sound like a nag or cross, only desperately sad. *I can't, I can't, I can't…*

Tony swirled the whisky around in his glass. The smell of it was overwhelming. No wonder her mum didn't usually like it. It reminded Daisy of hospitals, nurses swabbing her arms before stabbing needles in her veins. The liquid coated the ice cubes and a little spilt out over the top of the crystal beaker.

He raised the glass to his lips, drank half of its contents and set it down.

"Daisy, I've been accused of theft."

There was a groan. Debbie thumped the table. "Accused!"

Her dad's eyes sought hers. Did she look at him this way, usually? No. The eyes held hers, one adult, to another. There was information in those eyes, but Daisy couldn't work it out. She blinked, anxious and fearful. What was she missing here by not reading those eyes correctly?

"I did steal, Daisy."

Ah, that was it! Her dad was speaking another language. The words were unfamiliar and did not match what Daisy thought of her father. That was why it was so important to fix her eyes on his and read what was there. What was *really* there.

"I took money from the Metropolitan Police over several months, and I put it in Kirkinwall businesses—Mackies, the Star Tavern, the art competition and the exhibition.

"The Met know what I have done. There will be a court case. If I'm found guilty, I'll go to jail."

Another groan from Debbie. Tony reached out and took her hand, the fingers circling gently over Debbie's knuckles.

"I can't do anything but plead guilty. It's almost certain I will go to jail."

The whisky aroma still dominated the room, a space usually perfumed with cooking or the lavender potpourri Debbie placed on the table. Daisy wished she could smell something else. Her mouth had begun to water alarmingly, and her mind slowed. Her dad's words came from far away. They sounded like the words you hear when a robot or a Dalek speaks. I. Will. Go. To. Jail.

She closed her eyes and let her head drop. Then, remembering what she'd been thinking about earlier, she cried, "Robin Hood!"

Her mum stared at her. "Robin Hood?"

"Yes, Robin Hood!" The smell of that whisky—strong enough, it even made speaking taste disgusting, and her tongue stick to the roof of her mouth. "He…he stole from people, but he didn't really. He gave it to poor people. Poor people with no money."

Why was it so difficult to make herself understood? Her dad and mum looked at her—one in disbelief, the other, worried. Daisy couldn't work out which look belonged to what parent.

"Not wrong." The words were becoming harder to find, and hard to say.

"Robin Hood wasn't a criminal. He helped people."

Her vision had gone now. Two faces swam in front of her, two pairs of eyes blurring into one protracted line, white interspersed with brown and black. One of the faces leaked, water dripping—no, splashing onto the table below.

"I'm not Robin Hood, Daisy darling." A hand touched hers.

Once more, Daisy's mouth watered, flooding with saliva that tell-tale sign that warns you're about to—

Too late. Daisy threw up, the sandwiches and crisps, and her earlier lunch spewing out all over the table and onto the floor.

THE WITCHES OF EASTWICK

"Oh, dear God! Not again!"

The words still sounded far off. Hunched over in the chair, Daisy had thrown up again. Who would have thought she'd had that much food in her?

"Sorry, Mum, sorry, Dad." She wiped the back of her hand across her mouth, even though it disgusted her. Bits of food and viscous liquid stuck there. Her jeans were covered in the stuff too, and she could feel it on her tee shirt.

Her dad had jumped up and gone to the sink. He returned with a glass of water. "Don't be sorry, Daisy. It's not your fault. You must have eaten something dodgy."

Daisy drank the water down in record time. Even before she'd put the glass down on the table, she could feel the contents of her stomach rising once more.

"That's bile!" Debbie was behind her now, stroking her back and gathering her hair in her hands, trying to keep it away from the mess coming out of her mouth.

Her mum bent over. "Daisy, love, Daisy? Did you do your injection this morning? And what about this evening? What about last night?"

Why were they talking to her? Why were they asking questions? The effort of thinking was too much for her. Daisy shut her eyes. If thinking was impossible, a reply was never going to happen. Why were they doing this to her? She felt herself sway in the chair and put out a hand to stop herself. Mind you; it wouldn't be that bad. If she fell off, she could lie down on the ground.

She would need to find a patch that wasn't covered in vomit.

"Matthew! Katrina!"

The shout alarmed Daisy. She didn't want her friend or her brother to see her like this. Particularly not Matthew. He would tease her about it forever. Katrina would come up with a nickname for her.

Maybe she might even tell Kippy. Together, they might shudder. *Urgh, Kippy, no wonder you didn't want to...*

She puked again.

"Tony, phone an ambulance. No, phone the health centre!" Daisy's mum wrapped her arms around Daisy, puke and all. Daisy propped her head against Debbie's right side. Even with her mum's support, she felt her body slip. It did not want to stay upright.

Her mum moved the chair and, still holding onto Daisy, let her body slide slowly to the floor.

"I think this is ketoacidosis," Debbie's voice was panicky. "We need to get her on a drip."

Katrina and Matthew were in the room, Matthew's exclamations about the stink quickly hushed. Katrina had Daisy's little rucksack and was rifling through it. She found what she was looking for and handed Daisy's blood testing equipment to Debbie.

"Do you want me to prick her finger, Mrs Double U? I've done it before." She didn't wait for an answer taking hold of Daisy's hand, pulling her forefinger out, and pricking it with the Autolet. It always hurt more when someone else did it.

The results made Debbie and Katrina gasp. Daisy, distracted, begged for water. *Water, water, please, water.* If they didn't say 'yes' now, her tongue would stick to the insides of her mouth. It would swell up and choke her. Her lips would seal tight. She wouldn't be able to breathe.

Katrina got up and made her way to the sink, but Debbie stopped her. "No, she can't drink. She'll only be sick again."

Daisy moaned a 'please'. She didn't care anymore. If she threw up, so what? In her mind there was nothing else but water, cold, pure water that swirled around her mouth and coursed down her throat, the wetness of it coating the surfaces and staying there.

She had never wanted anything more than she wanted that glass of water, from the kitchen sink tap that Katrina not been allowed to turn on.

Her dad squatted down. His face looked like it always did, her sweet, dear old dad.

He held ice cubes in his hand. "Try this, Daisy. Suck them slowly."

"Katrina, do you think we can take her up to the cottage hospital?" Debbie asked. "Do you think they will have the equipment Daisy needs—a drip, maybe intravenous insulin?"

Katrina knew everything, of course. She nodded. "Aye, take her up there Mrs Double U. They'll get her fixed up to a drip. Do you want me to come?"

Debbie flashed a look at Daisy's dad, who shook his head. "I can't leave the house, Debbie, I–"

He didn't elaborate. The end of the sentence had to be—*I promised the police I wouldn't go anywhere.*

"Look after Matthew," Debbie said. Daisy's brother stood at the back of the kitchen, as far from the puddles of vomit as he could. Daisy thought he looked as if he might throw up himself. He was a sickly white colour, his eyes darting frightened glances at everyone. Ah, poor Matthew. Why didn't someone go and watch the end of *Robin Hood* with him?

Debbie moved, shifting herself from where she sat on the floor, Daisy's head on her lap. Why, why, why were these people trying to make her do things, Daisy wondered. She batted a hand weakly at her mother, remembering too late that she usually tried to disguise lethargy.

I can't be bothered pretending not to be tired. Now, there was an irony.

It made no difference anyway. Debbie was going to move her. She enlisted Katrina's help. Together, they hauled her up. She felt herself dangle between the two of them, one each side, both dragging her towards the front door.

Outside, the car was parked parallel to the house. A small group had gathered too. Daisy couldn't tell if they were the same people who'd been there earlier, the ones who'd congregated when the police had left their house, arms piled high with what they thought might be evidence of Tony's crimes.

"Fuck off, vultures!" Katrina yelled at them. Her mum didn't tell her off, Daisy noted. Did she hear right, did one of them exclaim: *Ooh, do you think she's just tried tae kill hersel'? The wee daughter, so ashamed o' her father?*

"No!" But the 'no' came out funny, a weird groan-y noise. Daisy couldn't be sure, but maybe at that moment, Debbie repeated what Katrina had said. Daisy didn't think she'd ever heard her mum use the F-word.

The cottage hospital was only a three-minute drive. The car pulled out, turned left, went straight, turned left and then right. Katrina had opened the door before the car had come to a halt in the little driveway in front of the A&E entrance. She disappeared, the doors swallowing her up.

Debbie got out of the car, hill-parked on the slope that led up to the entrance. She opened the passenger door.

"Right, Daisy. Let's get you sorted."

Daisy didn't want to be sorted. Sorting sounded like too much effort. She just wanted to stay here, collapsed against a car's front seat. It was very comfortable.

Her mum pushed her way in, undoing the seatbelt and grabbing her daughter under both arms. It made for an undignified exit.

Katrina had returned, followed by a stout nurse, her expression worried.

"Your wee lassie has type 1 diabetes, Mrs Walker?" the nurse said, her specs moving up her face as she wrinkled her nose. "We're no' used to that."

"Daisy's gone into ketoacidosis," Debbie said. "I think she forgot to take her insulin for a couple of days—what with... everything that's going on."

The nurse nodded. Yet another person who knew what was happening in the Walkers' lives.

"She needs fluids, and insulin," Debbie added. "Can you do that?"

The nurse went back inside the building and re-emerged with a wheelchair. Daisy sank into it gratefully.

Inside, they got her into a bed in a small room. A doctor, one of the town's GPs, appeared minutes later, his expression sober. Daisy heard him exchange words with her mum. The nurse had found a drip, and her arm was pulled out, a needle inserted there and into her hand.

"Water."

But no, they weren't going to let her drink water either. Pointless, they said to her, as she'd just throw it up and lose yet more precious fluids in the process.

Her mum and Katrina leant over her, their faces hanging above her. Her poor mum. First Daisy's dad and now this. When she recovered, she would say sorry, Daisy decided. And promise never to forget to take her insulin again. Hopefully, those words would bring pinkness to her mum's face. Now, she looked dreadful, shadows under her eyes, yellow-skinned.

Did Katrina wink? Daisy tried to muster up a smile in response. Tiredness hit her instead. She shut her eyes.

They kept her in overnight and the next day too waiting until her blood sugars returned to normal. As she'd been so sick—very high blood sugars did that to the body as it tried to get rid of the toxic sugar overload in any way it could—the nurses wouldn't let her eat anything, although they eventually relented and gave her water to drink.

Her mum returned in the morning. She sat beside the bed and held Daisy's hands tightly. "God, Daisy. I was so scared."

Daisy tried to say sorry, remembering that she had promised herself she would do so the night before. When she said the word, her mum cried again. Was it possible for one person to weep so much?

Katrina came in too. "It was like *The Witches of Eastwick*," she said. "You, projectile vomiting like that. Cool!"

She wasn't allowed anything to eat until breakfast the next day. It didn't matter that it was her least favourite breakfast cereal, Cornflakes and that they had given her marmalade with the thinnest, meanest slice of white bread. No tray of food had ever tasted better.

Her mum insisted on driving her home when they eventually released her.

"Where's Dad?" Daisy asked. She didn't want to push open the door to Number 26 and find the house empty.

"At home," her mum said. "He's to appear at the Magistrates' Court in Carlisle on Monday for a preliminary hearing. Nothing will happen. He will stand up. They will ask him to confirm who he is and read out the charges. He pleads guilty or not guilty. Then, they set a date for the trial."

"What will he say?" Daisy asked. The car was back outside the house. Everything looked as it usually did. Daisy had expected the little crowd that had stood outside the house to be there still, perhaps, or that someone might have spray-painted 'Thief!' on the walls.

Debbie gripped the steering wheel harder. "Guilty," she said eventually. "We think that's the best thing to say."

The door opened. Her dad stood there with Matthew, both smiling at her. Inside, Tony said knowing she was okay was the best news in the world.

No-one spoke of the other news. Maybe they were too scared. Fantastic news that a family member was home from the hospital, no permanent damage done. Why prick the good news mood balloon bubble with the horridness of the other situation?

Tony insisted on cooking Daisy a special lunch, saying she must be starving. Matthew said he wanted to help. They ate the celebratory meal—Daisy's favourite, lasagne—and talked about the cottage hospital, what a tiny little place it was when you compared it to the hospital Daisy had been taken to when the doctor first told her she had diabetes.

When Daisy announced that she wanted to go to bed early that evening, they all came upstairs to wish her good-night. The old Daisy, the Daisy who had a steady boyfriend and a dad who wasn't a thief would have objected to that. How naff. The new Daisy didn't.

Lights out and the curtains pulled firmly shut to block out the sun, Daisy lay awake for a long time anyway.

Thoughts and questions repeated themselves in her mind, but they all boiled down to one little line. What happens now?

NEW BEGINNINGS

They left Kirkinwall.

What else could the Walkers do? Apart from anything else, Tony had committed his crimes in London and while a London citizen. That meant he was likely to be imprisoned in England. His family could hardly stay in Scotland, miles from HM Wandsworth or wherever they locked him up, could they?

Daisy had the frankest conversation she'd ever had with her mother. It took place three weeks after the keto incident, as the family had taken to calling what had happened just after Daisy's dad had been arrested.

"We need to leave, Daisy. Go back to London."

The two of them were in the living room of the White House. Ever since he'd been arrested, Daisy had lost her love of her own space at the top of the house. Instead, she found herself drifting downstairs every evening, wanting to sit in company and watch TV together with her brother and her mother.

Debbie and Daisy huddled together on the sofa. Matthew was in bed. Tony was… not here. He'd been formally charged and bailed, but he had to stay at his address in London where he was registered as living.

"I want to go back, too," Daisy said. Then, brave. "Mum, will you divorce Dad?"

Her mum didn't answer at first. Her head leant against Daisy's.

"Your gran thinks I should."

Debbie's mum wasn't Daisy's favourite granny. It figured that the old cow would tell her daughter to get herself and her children as far away from her criminal husband as possible.

"I won't, though," her mum said.

Ah, the relief.

"Tony's a good man," Debbie went on, "a good man who… oh, I dunno, Daisy. Why do you think he did it?"

This was a grown-up question. Daisy heard it in her mum's voice. She asked for insight she didn't have. Maybe she hoped Daisy might tell her something that hadn't crossed her mind.

"Dad was so," Daisy stopped. Was she sure of what she was saying? "Dad was so, erm, adult. Maybe he wanted to be," she stopped again.

Her mum squeezed her hand. "No, keep going."

"Like Robin Hood?" That wasn't what Daisy meant to say, but she did anyway. It seemed the best, the nicest explanation.

Her mum smiled, the beam a welcome change from the expression she'd worn the last few weeks.

"Robin Hood? Hmm, Robin Hood! Riding through the glen. Feared by the bad, loved by the good…Did you have sex with Kippy?"

Yikes. Questions you never thought your mother would

ask or should ask. The truth, though, was a parent-friendly reply—well, one she ought to qualify as they were both in such a frank mood.

"No, but he…er…did paint me naked. Sorry, Mum."

Her mum propped herself up, so she could look at Daisy. "That picture might end up in an exhibition at some point in the future. *Alan Kirkpatrick: The Early Years*, that kind of thing."

"God."

"Oh, don't worry about it too much. I'm sure when you're an old grandmother, you can find the picture, show it to your horrified children and grandchildren, and say to them, 'look at your granny! Wasn't I hot?'"

Daisy rolled her eyes. There was something in what Debbie said though. The finished life drawing of Daisy made her look beautiful, sexy and knowing. Again, it was another of the ironies of her relationship with Kippy.

"Do you remember Uncle Malcolm?" Debbie asked, the about-turn in the conversation jolting Daisy. "Gran's brother?"

She nodded. Great Uncle Malcolm had died a few years ago, and they'd gone to his funeral. There had been a man there, who'd wept copiously. Daisy's Gran had looked at him weeping, her expression furious.

"We all knew he was gay, but he spent most of his life disguising it. Got married, even. When he and his wife divorced, he was in his mid-fifties. I think he spent the rest of his years making up for it. He wasn't quiet about it, which is why Gran was so disapproving."

She took Daisy's hand. "I had a conversation with Madeleine at his funeral." Madeleine was Malcolm's ex-wife. Unlike Malcolm's sister, she didn't seem to bear a grudge against him for his gayness. Or their divorce.

"Madeleine told me it was such a relief when Malcolm admitted he was gay. She'd spent years thinking she wasn't very attractive because when they had sex, he was so reluctant. Detached."

Daisy made to pull her hand away. Her mum's words made her squirm.

"One day, you will meet a man who will adore you. And you will feel the same. The sex will be out of this world."

Urgh. Too much.

Her mum was crying again, tears sliding down the side of her nose. Daisy stretched a leg out, pulling forward the coffee table, a box of tissues placed on top. Her mum helped herself.

"Like you and Dad, you mean? I thought you'd only done it twice—once for me and once for Matthew."

Her mum laughed, the action triggering off more tears at the same time. She blew her nose.

"Seriously, Daisy. Don't let what happened with Kippy put you off love and sex. Think of the choice you'll have back in London. I was wondering…would you like to go to a sixth form college, rather than going back to St Mary's? That is if you still want to continue your education?"

That did shock Daisy. Her mum and dad had always made it clear they expected her to continue in formal education for as long as possible. It now seemed as if her mum was dangling a Katrina-like possibility in front of her.

"I'd like to go to sixth form college," she said. She'd met girls before who were at sixth form college. They had a lick of gloss and sophistication even the lower sixth girls at St Mary's didn't manage.

It would depend on her 'O' Grade results too. Maybe she'd done enough to get her into college anyway. Taking a year out of education might be an idea. She could get a job in

London, work in a shop or a gallery, or as a tourist guide showing French visitors around the capital. Even Madame de Courcy would think that a productive use of her French.

"What about Katrina?" her mum said. She'd managed to get the tears under control. Now her eyes were just sore-looking, and her face flushed. Tony and Debbie had always welcomed Katrina into their home. Her mum saw through the bossy charm more than Tony did, but Daisy suspected her mum valued Katrina more for what she saw beyond that.

"She could come with us—that is if her mum doesn't mind her living with the family of a convicted criminal?" Debbie said.

Two thoughts crossed Daisy's mind. One, going back to London would be a thousand times better if Katrina came too, and Katrina's mum wouldn't care at all. Laissez-faire didn't begin to describe her attitude to parenting.

"Ask her," Debbie continued. The conversation had become one-sided. Most of what her mum had said seemed to have struck Daisy dumb. Perhaps she should say something now, in case her mum changed her mind.

"I will. That would be brilliant."

The conversation took place the next day. She met Katrina from work, trying to ignore the people who nudged each other and whispered as they spotted her sat on the wall that surrounded the big church.

"Feeling better then?" Katrina asked. She still thought ketoacidosis was kind of cool, seeing as it meant projectile vomiting and a drip.

Daisy nodded, though she did feel spaced out, needing that seat on the wall. With an effort, she stood up. They headed back towards the High Street.

"Shall we go and see Alison?" Katrina pointed at Mackies.

It was a Friday night, and they could see the small queue of people.

Daisy stared at her. "Are you joking? Everyone will be talking about my dad. And me as well probably. It's the most exciting thing that's ever–"

She managed to stop herself in time. The most exciting thing since what? Since a fishing boat went down, taking all the crew with her? What was Daisy's dad's nicking stuff compared to that?

Katrina's face told her she'd worked out what she was about to say too, and what she thought of it.

"Okay, then. I don't want fish and chips, though."

"You're not getting any. You're only getting a Diet Coke."

She poked her tongue out at Daisy and crossed the road. The queue at Mackies turned almost as one to look at them both. Katrina called out breezy hellos. Her gran was in the queue, reminding Daisy of that picture Kippy had painted. She'd been standing with her arms folded, a grumpy look on her face then too.

In real life, she turned to look at the two of them and smiled, the woman who had once threatened to put them both over her knee and skelp their arses. Daisy had never seen her smile before. She wasn't sure if the smile made her look less scary than she usually looked.

"It's yersels!" Mrs Burnett said. "Nice to see you, lassies. Do you want me to buy you some chips?"

"Aye, right enough, Gran. Just a drink for Daisy, though."

Mrs Burnett kept up a conversation with them both as they stood in the queue. She didn't ask about Daisy's dad, but she said several times what a busy place Mackies was these days. She didn't lower her voice either as she said it.

When they got to the front of the queue, Alison looked wary. Maybe she was worried that Daisy was here to beg for the money her dad had given Mackies. Mrs Burnett gave Alison a hard look. Her face relaxed.

"Your usual fish supper, Mrs B?" Already, Alison had moved to the fryers at the back, one hand taking papers to wrap up the order.

"Yes, and some chips and a Diet Coke for the girls," Mrs Burnett smiled and looked around her, daring anyone in the queue to whisper behind them.

As she handed over their order, Alison leant forwards. "Ah wouldnae have done this without your dad," she whispered. Daisy nodded. It was a thank you, but perhaps it was a thank you and now get lost.

Katrina ate the chips as the two of them walked back to Number 26, Mrs Burnett with them. When they said goodbye to her in front of the Braemar Quality B&B, she reached out a hand and patted Daisy's shoulder.

"You be careful. Don't be getting yourself in the hospital again."

As they walked off, she shouted after them. "Tell your dad I was asking after him."

"My mum says you could come with us," Daisy said, stealing one of Katrina's chips. They were still the best fish and chips in Scotland, after all. "To London."

There was no reply. Katrina held out another chip instead, waggling it in front of Daisy's mouth. Daisy sneered at first. She wasn't doing anything half an undignified as—ah, whoops. She took the chip from her friend's hand.

"All right then."

Very, very casual.

Daisy matched her tone. "You can live with us. It's an

okay part of London, and you can get into the city centre dead quickly."

Hang on. Could the Walkers stay there, in their Chi-Chi part of London, if Tony was in prison and not making any money? Daisy dismissed the question. The important thing was that Katrina thought there was somewhere for her to live.

"My mum knows the owner of this hair salon in the West End. She might be able to get you a job there."

That made Katrina pause. When she turned to face Daisy, her eyes gleamed. "Aye?"

"It's one of those places where famous people go. They charge, like, seventy pounds to cut your hair."

"Fuck." In Dulcie's, the town's most expensive hairdresser, a dry cut cost less than a tenner.

"Do you think I'll be good enough?"

Daisy opened the door to the White House. "Course you will. Famouses will be queuing up to get their hair cut and coloured by you. You'll be the best hairdresser in London."

The lingering smell of vinegar had attracted Matthew and Debbie, who took what was left of Katrina's chips.

"The best hairdresser in London better keep cutting my hair when she is rich and famous," Debbie said. Probably, she was taken aback when Katrina flung her arms around her.

"I'll always cut your hair, Mrs Double U! And I'll dye it too when it goes grey."

Debbie pulled a lock of her hair forward. "Oh, it's grey already. And even if it weren't, no doubt what happened here would have turned it white overnight."

Her children looked at her warily. Was that a joke?

Katrina and Debbie exchanged a smile. Debbie opened the living room door. "Come on then. We'd better plan our move. The sooner we get back to London, the better."

YOUNG, DUMB AND ABOUT TO BE…

Summer 1992

If she'd thought Katrina was cool before, now she knew she was spectacular. When she came with the Walkers to London, Katrina had looked around her and decided she needed to do more if she was to stick out.

Used to big-fish status in a small pond, she looked shell-shocked for the first few weeks. "Are you okay, Katrina?" Daisy regularly asked, concerned that her best friend hated London so much she wanted to leave as soon as possible.

"I'm all right," Katrina snapped. "I just need to…"

Daisy didn't try to fill in the blanks. 'Just need to' might cover a lot of things. *I just need to work out what London's all about.* Good luck with that one. Or maybe she was thinking about Dod. Daisy still felt the pain of that herself. How could such a young, laughing and alive guy now be dead—his promise he would never be old and boring heard by the fates and obeyed. When she looked at the Thames, she saw the same grey, squally waters that had swallowed him up. It made her turn from the river every time.

A few weeks into her stay and Katrina became herself again. It was as if she hadn't properly inhabited her body for a while and now she had stepped back into it, as cocky and confident as she'd been in Kirkinwall.

She changed her appearance, rejecting the *Desperately Seeking Susan* look she'd previously favoured. Now, she went for a grunge look—plaid shirts over white tee shirts, denim shorts and biker boots. Her hair was always fabulous. Katrina took advantage of the West End salon's constant need for models. She went through every colour of the rainbow. Currently, her hair was cropped short at the sides and dyed platinum blonde, the fringe left long, so it hung over one eye.

Even in a city as noisy and crowded as London, she attracted stares.

They'd bumped into Lisa and Dana the other day when Katrina met Daisy from school, the sixth form college she and her mum had eventually agreed on.

Daisy saw the two of them nudge each other hard, their eyes darting glances at her and then swivelling to Katrina.

Lisa walked up first. "Hi, Daisy. How are you?" She didn't wait for a reply. "How's your family?"

Everyone knew of course. The Evening Standard had been full of the story. It seemed the public loved reading about an ordinary, middle-class, middle-aged man who decided to steal so much money and take from the police of all people. Journalists had reported the court case from beginning to end, its conclusion Tony's five-year jail sentence.

Funnily enough, her mum had received a lot of letters

from people expressing admiration. A good few of those letters came from Kirkinwall people. It was Government money, one said, and why shouldn't the bloody Tories spend some cash on making a wee toon a better place to live? Tony Walker, they said, would always be welcomed in Kirkinwall.

"Fine," Daisy muttered, staring at the ground.

"She visits her dad regularly." The voice was unapologetic. "They love him inside. His accountancy skills come in useful."

Katrina pushed her fringe back. "You heard of Big Eddie?"

Lisa nodded, at the same time as Dana shook her head.

"You've no' heard of Big Eddie? Wow. He's only the biggest mafia boss in London—daein' time for fraud. He likes Daisy's dad an awfy lot."

Katrina's accent had softened since moving to London, the taes and daes changing slowly into tos and dos, the awfies vanishing altogether. Now, the full-on Scot was back. As she spoke, Lisa and Dana moved back from her.

"Mebbe Tony's making friends in a' the right places, aye? Big Eddie needs a new accountant," she continued, the tone deceptively soft. "Daisy and her mum and brother willnae need to worry about anything ever again."

Lisa and Dana had no answer to that.

As they watched them walk away, Lisa darting quick glances behind her as if to check she wasn't being followed, Katrina nudged Daisy.

Daisy touched her back. "Big Eddie?! Really?"

Katrina didn't say anything, waiting until Lisa and Dana were out of sight. "Could be true. You said he'd told your mum he was making himself useful inside."

"Teaching people to read!"

Katrina nudged her again. "Well, then. And picking up

tips too, don't you think?"

"I'd prefer my dad not to be a criminal."

"I never think of your pa as a crook," Katrina said, threading her arm through Daisy's. "I mind all the time what he did. He turned Mackies into this great wee business. He got people jobs. He introduced Mick to that food critic, and now he's working in this fancy-pants place in Edinburgh. He put money into the Star Tavern. He set up a permanent memorial to Dod and those other fishermen."

She was too tactful to mention her cousin, but thanks to Tony's money, Kippy had taken an access course to help get him into Glasgow School of Art. If he passed, he could start there in the next few months.

Daisy fast-forwarded, seeing him in years to come, the great painter she had once imagined. He was lauded in international circles, and he featured in magazines and on TV regularly. Her mind added flesh and years to the figure she'd last seen months and months ago, making Alan Kirkpatrick, older, fatter and perfectly content, another man by his side, their hands loosely joined together.

For the first time, the thought of it didn't hurt.

And the perfect thing about Tony's crime? Most of the money that he had poured into Kirkinwall—the money he'd stolen from the Met—couldn't be taken back. Mackies, the Star Tavern, the exhibition and the art prize, and the mortgage on their London home he'd paid off, all untouchable. His assets had been frozen at the time, but the Met had only been able to recover a fifth of what he'd taken.

"Do you miss it, Kirkinwall, I mean?" Daisy asked. The skies were darkening, and she was reminded of a night a long time ago when she'd left a party, full of excitement and hope. Then, she'd looked at dark velvet blue skies, very different from London's night sky, the orange neon glow of it.

"No," Katrina said. "That bit of my life is over. I didn't miss being a Jehovah. I'm no' going to miss Kirkinwall."

Daisy thought she sounded a bit too firm.

"What about you? Do you miss it?"

Yes and no. She would always associate Kirkinwall with Kippy and Dod, the loss of a good friend and that painful day when she'd found out what Kippy was. And her dad's arrest—the awful hours she and her mum and Matthew had spent waiting to find out what had happened.

But for most of her stay in the small town, it had been terrific, exhilarating, amazing and wonderful.

"That bit of my life is over." She added drama to her voice, a piss-take of Katrina.

"Get stuffed!" There was that nudge again.

"I like being in London much better now you're here," Daisy said. They had stopped at the bus stop, a double-decker making its ponderous way through traffic lights towards them.

"Fair enough," Katrina said. "What do you want to do now? Nosey at the shops on Oxford Street? Portobello Market? Cinema? A wee bit of shoplifting…?"

The last was mischievous. Katrina often gave her make-up, kohl pencils, lipsticks, single eyeshadow shades she claimed she'd nicked from Boots and Superdrug. Daisy was sure she hadn't. Well, eighty percent sure anyway. She had form for shoplifting, didn't she?

"I heard Del Amitri are going to be at the HMV on Oxford Street later," Daisy said. "What about that?"

Katrina nodded decisively. "Yeah, that'll do. I could get off with Justin Currie, and you could do Iain Harvie."

"I'll do Justin, thank you very much!" Daisy replied. The

band's lead singer reminded her of Kippy—just a tiny bit. She started singing *Always the Last to Know*, the song that was now in the charts. Katrina joined in, the two of them belting out the words, their fellow Londoners giving them a wide berth at the bus stop.

The bus had come to a stop, a noisy creaky halt. The door opened slowly, the driver glaring out at them.

Katrina jumped up to the step, looking back at Daisy as she did so. Sometimes, you'd think she was the seasoned Londoner and not Daisy.

"C'mon, Your Royal Highness. Del Amitri awaits us. We're young, we're dumb, and we're about to be full of–"

There was a hiss behind Daisy, Katrina's last word cut off in disgust by the old man stood in the queue.

Daisy burst out laughing. She leapt on the bus behind Katrina and flashed her pass at the driver.

"You bet!"

They started singing the words of *Always the Last to Know* once more as the bus pulled away from its stop, the jerky movements making them unsteady.

Two teenage girls. An exciting band. London at their feet.

THE END

PRETTINESS—A STATE OF MIND

Do you want to find out what happens next?

The Art Guy *(working title) tells the story of*
Kippy and Katrina's lives, part two.
Read on to find out more.

Glasgow, October 1992

"Oh wow. You're *so* pretty."

Kippy wasn't sure he liked a man touching his face, but Danny had reached out a hand and swept two fingers slowly from the temple to his jaw.

"I adore freckles."

There was another thing Kippy wasn't sure about: campness. Danny was as camp as a row of pink tents, as the saying went. The party hadn't been his idea, but Lillian insisted. She'd kind of taken him under her wing when he first arrived in Glasgow. She was very posh, but then he and posh girls got along if Daisy had been anything to go by.

Kippy was older than everyone else at art school, apart

from Lillian whose parents had been wealthy enough to finance her through not just one, but two gap years. She swooped on him on their first day.

"Ooh! What's your name, precious?"

He was monosyllabic, partly through nerves and because he didn't want to get into yet another Daisy situation where a woman fell for him.

She shook her head when he said 'Kippy'. "I'm not calling you that. What's your real name?"

"Alan Kirkpatrick." He was still mumbling, hoping this pushy blonde would push off.

"Hmm," she wrinkled her nose. "Terrible, too. Kippy it is, then."

She threaded an arm through his. "We need to stick together. Everyone else here is so young and so inexperienced. I hate teenagers, don't you?" Said with all the bloated confidence of one just a year out of her teens.

Kippy's worries about a repeat of the Daisy situation came to nothing. Lillian knew he was gay, she announced grandly. She had a sense for these things. As someone only just coming to terms with life beyond the closet, her revelation made him prickly.

He remembered the teasing he'd put up with while he was doing his college course some years ago. Davy, Ewan and those other apprentices, the ones skilled in wrinkling out differences in their peers, zoning in on anything they suspected wasn't just so. Had he not covered it up as well as he thought?

Kippy hadn't actually known what he was hiding for a long time. Instinct had warned him to keep quiet about how different he felt from everyone around him anyway, though. He hid behind Daisy for some months until…The Thing happened. And then his life changed, mostly for the better but the start of his new life had been unbelievably hard and painful.

Lillian was like no-one else he'd ever met. She insisted that in the 90s, it was de riguer for a la mode women such as herself to have a GBF. When he looked mystified, she sighed. "A gay best friend, precious."

She cocked her head to one side. "You're from the sticks too. I don't suppose you had much opportunity to explore your sexuality."

Honestly, sometimes it was a bit like having a conversation about sex with your mum. He squirmed.

"Auntie Lillian can help!"

She was unbelievably nosey too. She asked questions all the time, almost as if she was researching him. He half expected her to write everything down. *So, tell me about Kirkinwall? What about your mum and dad? When did you realise you were gay? Have you ever kissed a man?*

When he finally admitted that no, he'd never so much as given a guy a hug, she clapped her hands together.

"That's awful. First thing, then. I must introduce you to some friends of mine."

Hence, the party.

These being Lillian's friends, the party was taking place in a flat in the west end, just off the Great Western Road. These flats were so posh they had two floors.

Lillian had insisted on picking out his outfit for him. Kippy had been going through a phase of velvet blazers, but she turned up her nose up at them. "Too obvious!" She held up a plain white tee shirt and his old, worn Levi's.

"Be the man in the laundrette," she said, referring to the old advert where Nick Kamen stripped off, put his jeans in a washing machine and sat in his boxers waiting for them to dry.

As a fourteen-year-old, Kippy had watched the advert a lot. Even now, if Marvin Gaye's *Heard It Through the Grapevine* came on the radio, he felt his body quiver in excitement.

The outfit seemed to have done the trick. The party-goers were sixty-forty men to women. Lillian and Kippy were fashionably late arriving, and the attention that greeted them was flattering.

His eyes fixed on Kippy, the party's host made his way towards them.

"Lillian! You beautiful thing, you. Who's this?"

Danny wasn't his 'type' anyway. Until very recently, Kippy couldn't have told you what his type was. A picture swam before his eyes, a half-naked man wearing turned-down overalls and a lazy grin. He blinked several times, hoping he wouldn't cry.

Lillian leant forward and whispered something to Danny.

"I'll get you both a drink," Danny said. "And then mingle, do! We're all good friends of Dorothy here."

He winked, the eyes flashing Kippy a lustful look.

"Are you okay, Alan?" Lillian asked. She was the only person under thirty who ever called him that, but he thought he maybe liked it. She said, 'Alan', when she was being serious, or asking tough questions.

"Aye," he nodded slowly. He'd be better once he had a drink in him. Then, "Who's Dorothy?"

AUTHOR'S NOTES

You'll have heard the expression, 'the truth is stranger than fiction'? When it comes to Artists Town, that's certainly true.

The idea for the book came to me when my husband booked us a couple of nights in a B&B in Tomintoul. While he was researching places to stay, he came upon the story of Anthony Williams, a former deputy director of finance for the Metropolitan Police.

Williams sank millions into businesses in Tomintoul, money he'd stolen from the Met over a period of 12 years. He was only caught when the local bank in Tomintoul queried the deposit amounts and notified the Met's fraud squad. Williams had bought titles for his and his wife, and their bank credit cards said Lord and Lady Williams, so perhaps that muddied the waters.

In my book, I've made up Tony's family for him, shifted the location, had his family move there, downscaled his crime and played fast and loose with when anti-money laundering legislation was introduced (it didn't come into force until 1994).

As for his motives, from everything I've read about Anthony Williams I don't think I'm that far from the truth. He appears to be essentially a decent man. When asked about his crimes, he later said there were no excuses and it could only be described as greed. If you look up what he did do with his money in Tomintoul, it doesn't look that much like greed; more misguided philanthropy. He paid well over the odds for everything he bought up in the town, and many of them didn't go on to make any profit.

Anthony Williams pled guilty to 19 counts of theft and asked for 535 others to be taken into consideration. He was sentenced to seven and a half years. Of the close to £5 million he took from the Met, only about £1 million was able to be recovered.

The Police Commissioner at the time apologised to Londoners for the breach of trust. It triggered several internal investigations.

If you'd like to read more about the real story, here are the links:

http://www.nytimes.com/1995/05/30/world/tomintoul-journal-good-lord-scotland-yard-has-its-pockets-picked.html

http://www.independent.co.uk/news/uk/double-life-of-laird-at-centre-of-pounds-4m-inquiry-accountant-with-metropolitan-police-adopted-1377515.html

Sadly, the beer referred to in those articles, the Laird of Tomintoul, is no longer produced.

ACKNOWLEDGEMENTS

Many thanks to all the people who worked with me on this book. Gordon Lawrie and Erl Wilkie gave suggestions for developing the plot from a rough synopsis, and Erl helped shape and improve the first part of the story to make it more interesting.

Thanks to my mum for her encouragement and comments. I'm a type 1 diabetic who was a teenager in the late 80s. Debbie's sort of my mum; mostly not. Mine is three hundred times better, of course.

Caron Allan provided useful feedback which helped me make the text consistent, and lots of advice about indie publishing in general, and thanks to Stephen J Carter whose Storyworks method is hugely helpful when it comes to devising and refining plots.

Sharon Bannister proofread the text for me—any remaining bloopers my own! Fiona Buchanan, Pilates teacher extraordinaire, said lots of lovely things about the book in draft form and helps me iron out my hunched-up writers' shoulders.

Kirsten and Chris McLatchie advised on police procedure when someone commits a crime in England and is arrested in Scotland. All subsequent errors are my own.

Enormous thanks to Sandy, who keeps saying "when you're a world-famous author…" in exchange for letting me continue to do this. I'm so grateful.

OTHER BOOKS BY THIS AUTHOR

I have other books—

Katie and the Deelans and *The Girl Who Swapped*, and both are available on Amazon, as is the non-fiction book, *The Diabetes Diet*, which outlines how to use a low-carb diet to best effect.

I hang out on Twitter and Instagram @pinkglitterpubs, and my website is *https://emmabaird.com* If you sign up to follow my blog at the above address, I can keep you up to date with how I'm getting on with my other books and I'll attempt to make you smile as often as I can. My cat features frequently (cats rule the internet, right?) so at the very least you'll see your fair share of cute cat pics.

Finally, if you liked this book please review it. Reviews help authors like me get found, sell more books and encourage us to keep writing. Writing's a lonely, vulnerable experience. We cherish the flattering reviews and store them up to keep us going. Many thanks!

©Emma Baird 2018

www.ingramcontent.com/pod-product-compliance
Lightning Source LLC
Chambersburg PA
CBHW031630200726
48288CB00019B/522